Mary Hocking's many novels include *March House*, *He Who Plays the King*, *Look Stranger!* and *The Mind Has Mountains*. Her most recent work, 'The Good Daughters Trilogy', comprises *Good Daughters*, *Indifferent Heroes* and *Welcome Strangers*, all available in Abacus.

Mary Hocking lives in Lewes, Sussex.

Also by Mary Hocking in Abacus:

GOOD DAUGHTERS
INDIFFERENT HEROES
WELCOME STRANGERS

Mary Hocking

AN IRRELEVANT WOMAN

AN ABACUS BOOK

First published in Great Britain in hardback by Chatto & Windus Ltd, 1987
Published in Abacus by Sphere Books Ltd, 1988
Reprinted 1989

Printed and bound in Great Britain by
Richard Clay Ltd, Bungay, Suffolk

ISBN 0 349 10040 3

Sphere Books Ltd
A Division of
Macdonald & Co. (Publishers) Ltd
27 Wrights Lane, London W8 5TZ
A member of Maxwell Pergamon Publishing Corporation plc

To J. Neville Ward

[1]

The house stood high above the village and at a sufficient distance to discourage those whose pleasure it is to drop in on neighbours. An untidy hedge overhung the narrow lane so that passage was not easy and the chance passer-by was afforded only a limited view of ancient chimneys and mossy, tiled roof. To anyone sufficiently determined – and prepared to brazen disapproval – to push hard at the dilapidated wooden gate, a curve in the rough drive would still deprive him of a full view of the house. If such an intruder were to venture on, he would soon come upon a rambling sixteenth-century house which, though plainly habitable, did not appear to have suffered much in the way of modernisation.

On this particular day the intruder was not of a kind to concern himself with the upkeep of property. As he looked across the wide green lawn his eyes did not dwell on clumps of clover or unkempt bushes, but focused on the bird table which was well-provided with nuts and strips of fat. The intruder continued up the path.

It was April and the day, although early, was already warm. Crocuses were unfolding in flower borders and beneath the trees on the lawn. A few elderly garden-chairs had been left out all night, collapsed against the wall by the french windows. From the far corner of the house came the clatter of pots and pans. He walked in that direction.

Through the kitchen window he could see a woman standing in front of an oven. As he watched, keeping well to one side, she pulled on a pair of oven gloves and stood poised. A look of uncertainty came over her face which, for no apparent reason, changed rapidly to one of dismay. And worse. In this unguarded moment the woman's face betrayed the naked terror which might be occasioned by coming without warning, in a nameless place, to the edge of a precipice; or by being confronted in one's own household with a forgotten, long-locked door behind which may lie ultimate chaos, a rotting human corpse, or an equally defunct mouse. The woman opened the oven door and peered inside. Whatever she saw did little to reassure her and after a moment, during which she made no attempt to touch, or indeed to examine, anything, she closed the door and remained crouched forward, dark head bent.

She appeared to recover after a few seconds and straightened up. Now that the terror had left her, the face composed itself to present a woman in middle life in whom the perceptive observer might still discern the child lingering behind the adult façade. A kind of deliberate absentness in the large grey eyes verged on the fey – one might imagine her to be willing either her own disappearance or that of the oven and its contents; but the firmly rounded chin gave notice that she was accustomed to command whatever forces troubled her, while the wry lines about the mouth were evidence of a humour which should surely have enabled her to answer what challenges life, let alone her kitchen, presented to her.

She looked down at the oven gloves, as though surprised to find them on her hands. The oven door was opened again and this time the meat dish was pulled forward and the sizzling joint expertly scrutinised before being returned and the heat adjusted.

The kitchen window was open and for a moment the room was full of bird song. Then the shadow of the tramp fell across the open doorway.

'Could you cut my bread for me, missus? My knife ain't sharp enough.' He stood quietly, patient rather than deferential, as if he had been waiting all night unwilling to risk disturbing anyone until he saw that the door was open.

'What a start you gave me!' The response was made in the manner of one who says, 'You frightened me' in the hope of thereby disarming any intention to frighten. She took the bread from him. It was dry enough to break, no need to cut it. But if she was suspicious, she did not show it and as she walked to the table she turned her back on him, preferring risk to rejection. After she had cut the bread she buttered it and put thick wads of ham between the slices.

'You can stay in the outhouse if you like,' she said.

'No. I'll be on my way, missus, thank 'ee.' He had been looking round the room, not angry or wistful, just curious. Perhaps he had wanted to see what it was like inside a house on Easter morning.

The woman watched him walk away. She had offered him the outhouse as if he was a stray cat. 'I should have asked him to eat with us,' she said aloud. 'But he would have been even more embarrassed than us . . . Or would he?'

From the interior of the house came the sound of raised voices discussing acid rain.

The kitchen door opened and an elderly woman floated in, an illusion much aided by a flimsy, flouncy elegance of dress reminiscent of the early Thirties, a period in which the wearer would have been at her most attractive. She stood by the kitchen table, fanning herself with a lace handkerchief, blue eyes blinking from a crumpled face.

'Janet, how do you put up with Patsy?' The handkerchief waved aside any answer. 'I know you think I am intolerant, but you don't *live* among them. Believe me, it's like being surrounded by the Pilgrim Fathers and not being one of them. I am an outcast, my dear. I slink into my house with my white bread hidden at the bottom of my shopping basket. And worse than that, I'm a carnivore among the herbivores. I tell you, this new secular puritanism invades every part of life. If we have a rainy day they are all out the next day, not weeding, but looking for the effects of acid rain. That's what she is on about now. A few moments ago it was Barclay's Bank. "You don't bank at Barclay's," she informed me. "Barclay's is for daubing red paint on." They will be having their own version of those awful Puritan names soon – Green Peace Jones, I-went-to-Greenham-Common Smith, Organic Potato Browne – with an 'e' because they're very middle class, just like the rest of us.'

Janet had by this time moved to the sink and was wringing

out a cloth as though determined that not one drop of moisture should be retained by it. She said, 'I think Patsy is a good woman.'

'Haven't you been *listening* to me? Of course she's a good woman. That's what is so intolerable. It makes me understand why the Christians got fed to the lions.'

'Patsy's house is terribly untidy.' Janet made a small, deprecating gesture as though offering a modest gift. 'And she makes an awful mess of her relationships.'

'Yes, that *is* a comfort. But not to you, I suppose.'

'I was very upset when Hugh had to leave her, naturally.'

'Then why do you put up with her?'

'I like to see my grandchildren. Surely you can understand that, Deutzia!'

The sharpness of her tone surprised Deutzia who backed away to the kitchen door. 'Where are they, by the way?' She peered into the garden. 'She is talking of going soon.'

'Hugh has taken them for a walk.' Janet let go of the cloth which fell into the murky waters of the washing-up bowl. 'They won't be staying for lunch, I'm afraid. Poor Hugh!'

'So I shan't be seeing Hugh if he doesn't come back soon.' Deutzia examined her wristwatch, holding it up ostentatiously to the light. 'I was so hoping for a glimpse of him. As you know, he is really my favourite.'

Janet retrieved the cloth and dealt with it briskly. 'We aren't often together as a family now, Deutzia – otherwise I would ask you to stay to lunch.'

'How ruthless you are, Janet. I can't think of anyone else who would so speed a departing guest.'

'I didn't ask the tramp to stay.' She hung the cloth over the cold tap. Her mind wandered into the garden. 'If I could turn *him* away I suppose I must be ruthless.'

'I hardly see a connection between myself and a tramp!' Deutzia looked more attentively at her companion, disconcerted by this strange intervention.

'I run away from people like him; but this is my house so I couldn't run away.'

'Are you feeling well? Even from you this is rather odd.'

'Did you know that Patsy goes into town twice a week to work in a canteen for the homeless?'

'I knew she did something or other.' Deutzia was irritated by the reintroduction of Patsy, a subject which she had now exhausted. 'You must find it very tiresome – her doing voluntary work, I mean, when she could be helping to support herself and the children.'

'I went with her once or twice. You wouldn't recognise her there. She is so much more effective than in her own home.'

'No doubt she is well supervised.'

'And she is so good with even the strangest people. She never gets her reactions wrong – it's as though she breathed with them. But I couldn't cope with it.'

'They are hardly your sort of people, are they, my dear?'

'I don't know what is my sort of person. And anyway, it wasn't that. It was the end of the afternoon, when we were clearing up – we had to leave the hall as we found it . . . Some of them would help us to fold up the trestle tables. And then, when we had it all straight, they would just go away, very quietly. By the time Patsy and I left it would be dark and bitterly cold. I thought: where have they gone? Patsy didn't seem to ask herself that. But I couldn't think of anything else. I used to lie in bed, listening to the wind, wondering. I only went twice.'

'That nice man who manages the County Hotel told me it is quite impossible to get staff these days because people won't work unsocial hours. I'm sorry for anyone who is homeless, of course, but if they won't work . . .'

Janet was staring into the garden; her face had the drawn, puckered look of a short-sighted person straining their eyes. Deutzia thought perhaps it was a little vain of her not to wear glasses. Janet said, 'What goes on out there, beyond that hedge? I have no idea.'

Deutzia said kindly, 'I think you are a little run down. And, of course, it must be so quiet here now, with Katrina at college and Malcolm having left home at last. I thought you were going to have trouble there, although I didn't say anything because I know you think I like to interfere. But I was very relieved when this repertory thing cropped up. Not that it is what one would have wished for him, of course . . .'

'He was such fun to have about the house, dear Malcolm!' Janet seemed lost in contemplation of the garden. 'So many different roles in one day. I do miss him.'

'Darling, you mustn't let yourself repine. The important thing is to keep doing things. I have had years to find that out since Herbert died. It is so important to be active.'

'My husband hasn't died, Deutzia.'

'Murdoch does die to the world in some strange way during the greater part of the day, doesn't he? So you must make your own life. And that doesn't mean going to dreary canteens with Patsy and morbid things like that. Now, did you look at that programme of art lectures that I dropped in on you? I know several people who go. It's not too intensive and afterwards they have a nice tea. The meetings are held in different members' houses, some of which are quite delightful. One or two I have always wanted to see.'

Janet, who was still looking out of the window, spoke loudly as though she was addressing not so much an unseen audience as a court which might be judging her. 'I am not artistic.'

'You know, my dear, age gives one certain rights. And I think I can take it upon myself to tell you that you have rather got into a habit of sacrificing yourself. Now that all the children have gone, you must get away from here more often. It's not as though Murdoch needs you – shut away all the time writing.'

'I am the keeper of his peace,' Janet responded as if she was quoting.

'And you have done it so well all these years that you don't really need to spend any time on it now. People *know* that they must never telephone him during the morning, that they shouldn't call on him in the evening, and that if they call in the afternoon he will be out on his walk. Even I, who have known you all these years, hardly dare to call. I was not at all certain of my reception this morning even. Easter morning . . .'

Janet said, 'Yes, Easter morning, even then . . .'

'It isn't always easy for me. I am not unaware that Murdoch finds me tiresome.'

'That isn't true.' Janet responded with a flash of real concern, though on whose behalf was not clear. 'I can't think of anyone whom Murdoch finds tiresome.'

'Because you take the burden from him as soon as you think he is threatened. Only last week, when I was trying to show an interest in his writing . . .'

'Reading his books is the only way to show an interest.'

'You know that I never read anything but biographies.'

'Murdoch doesn't mind your not reading his books, Deutzia. But he doesn't know how to answer when people ask him if he writes in his dressing gown and that sort of thing.'

'Then you should try to bring him out more. He might get on television if he was prepared to talk about *how* he writes rather than *what* he writes. It does seem extraordinary that he is so famous and people hardly know what he looks like. I pointed him out to Althea when she was staying with me and she said, "*The* Murdoch Saunders!" quite reverently. One interview with Melvyn Bragg would probably be worth more than all those literary prizes.'

'I'm sure it would! Murdoch never wins the prizes which bring in much money.'

'Money is not to be sneered at, Janet. I often wish I had a little more. I should so love to go on that Greek cruise Mona went on. Not that I should have wanted all those lectures. She came back more exhausted than when she went. But even if I can't afford a cruise, I expect I could manage a week abroad if you fancied that, now that you will have more free time. Anyway, think about it, my dear . . . Although I get the feeling you haven't paid enough attention to know what it is that I am suggesting. Is there someone *out* there?'

She came to the window but saw only the hawthorn hedge, its intricate pinkish-grey mesh of branches studded with little green rosettes and, beyond, spring wheat sprouting on balding fields. 'It's a bit late, this year,' she said sadly. She was old and a tardy spring mattered.

The kitchen door opened to admit a woman who wore clothes which proclaimed that she would not wish to be seen dead in anything which fitted her. The purple skirt was too wide across the hips and the uneven hem trailed about her ankles, as muddied as her boots. The pink shirt sloped, shoulder seams just above the elbow, cuffs at finger-tip level. Both shirt and skirt were generously creased. Cleanliness, however, seemed to be important and had obviously preceded the creasing process. She ran a hand through tangled dark hair and said, ignoring Deutzia, 'I'll be going now, Janet. I expect I shall meet Hugh on the way. I'll bring the children round on Friday if you don't mind having them while I'm at Greenham.'

'Yes, all right, Patsy. I'm sorry you're not staying now.'

'Hugh has had them all the morning. I am sorry you are cross.'

'I didn't say I was cross.'

'I can feel that you are. But it's much better for them to see us separately.'

'Did you bring your car?' Deutzia asked hopefully.

'That old banger?' Patsy appeared to resent the suggestion that she might own anything which answered the description of car. 'I only use it because there are so few buses into town.'

'What about Greenham?'

'We are going by coach. You could come, too, if you liked, Deutzia.' She made the suggestion without a hint of provocation.

'I'm afraid I'm too old for that sort of caper, my dear. Not that I mean to criticise. I did some funny things when I was young.' Something ingratiating had crept into her manner. 'At least we can walk back to the village together. I like a little company – particularly on Easter Day.'

'I shall be going over the hill. I expect that is where Hugh has taken the children.'

They walked into the hall together, interrupting a scene between two small children and a tall, flaxen-haired woman with the implacably patient air of an oracle waiting the moment of pronouncement.

The younger child was howling, 'You promised we would see Sam.'

Patsy said, 'I'll go and head them off, Steffie. If they actually see one another we shall never prise them apart.'

'You could stay to lunch.'

'It's far too much for Janet.'

Stephanie regarded her with raised eyebrows. 'Really, Patsy! If it suited your purpose you would stay. After all, you don't think it is too much for Mother to have them while you are at Greenham.'

Patsy looked genuinely surprised. 'I hope I haven't upset anyone?'

'Only Hugh and your children and my children ...' Her youngest child slapped her leg and howled, 'I hate you!'

'You are overtired, Marcus. You weren't in the least interested this morning when I told you you were going to see Francesca and Sam.'

'You were cross with us because we weren't interested,' the older boy pointed out.

His mother turned on her sister-in-law, imperiousness getting the upper hand of patience. 'Patsy, if you *are* going ...'

'Well, *I* am certainly going.' Deutzia was fretted by this scene. 'I'm at the age where I find raised voices very upsetting. Now, where is my coat?'

When this was produced for her, she draped it round her shoulders and stood testing the air on the front doorstep. 'Your mother has thrown me out,' she said, laughing lightly.

Stephanie, who had now picked up Marcus and slung him over one shoulder, said, 'Well, don't take it to heart, Deutzia. You have known us a long time.'

'I have known your mother ever since I married. Your grandfather and my dear husband were cousins.' They already knew this but it gave her the opportunity to talk about her husband. 'Do you know, Herbert used to take me out to lunch *every* Sunday. I was never allowed to cook lunch on Sunday. We used to go to the Country Club for a drink. It was so pleasant, so many nice people there – people who knew how to enjoy themselves. And then we would go to Paul's Restaurant in Ealing. In the Broadway. All gone now, of course. But what can you expect with people like Mr Kinnock living there?' She put a dainty foot on the path. 'Well, goodbye, Steffie. Goodbye, my treasures. Say goodbye to Hugh for me. It's so long since I saw him.'

'Perhaps he will walk down to see you this afternoon,' Stephanie said.

'Oh, I shouldn't expect him to do that. I know that your mother wants you to be together today.'

'Together in our family doesn't mean you can't spend five minutes apart.' Stephanie watched as Deutzia walked stiffly down the path. 'We can't let her walk home, can we? I'd better get the car out.'

'She walked here,' Patsy pointed out. 'Uphill all the way.'

'That was because she came uninvited. If we had asked her for a drink she would have expected to be picked up. Deutzia! Wait a minute ...' She off-loaded Marcus on to his brother and strode down the drive where she exchanged remonstrances with Deutzia. When Patsy passed them Deutzia was saying, 'I wouldn't dream of it!' A few minutes later, as Patsy walked up the hill she heard the sound of a car turning out of the drive. In the distance Hugh came into sight, a small child in his arms, another trudging beside him.

Patsy walked to meet them and she and Hugh greeted each other briefly. As they talked the wind blew their hair about. Windblown hair became Hugh who was a diffident, rather solemn man. Patsy remembered that when he was a youth the solemnity had been rather touching. Now it had developed into a tetchy anxiety. She resented the anxiety which she saw as a reflection on herself. She gathered the children to her and they went on over the brow of the hill, while Hugh walked back to the house.

In the garden he found his father and his younger sister, Katrina, who had just returned from church. He and Murdoch began to pace the lawn while Katrina went into the house. She stood in the hall, eyes closed, fists clenched, breathing heavily, not entirely because she had catarrh. She seemed concerned to breathe disquiet into the very atmosphere of the house. After a few moments, she toted her burden of anguish into the sitting room and flung it on the hearth rug. As she lay, head pillowed in her arms, small distressful noises escaped her.

Eventually Stephanie returned from doing her duty to Deutzia. She stood in the doorway and considered her sister. 'Did you go to church looking like that?' She might have been a school matron good-humouredly chiding a naughty but lovable child.

Katrina sat up, clasping her knees. 'I'm not sure how I look. Tell me about it.'

'Dressed for the circus.' As Katrina wore striped pink and white baggy trousers and a pink shirt beneath a black embroidered waistcoat this was not entirely unfair. Her hair was dyed a dark, metallic red and stood up spikily around her head. Stephanie said, 'Poor Daddy!'

'I don't supposed *he* noticed. The vicar looked a bit surprised and the woman next to me hung on to her wafer and dipped it in the chalice in case of Aids.'

'Well, I hope you are going to change for lunch.'

Katrina shambled out of the room. She joined her mother in the kitchen. 'Steffie is being stuffy.' She nibbled a piece of raw carrot. 'I hope I won't be like her when I'm her age.' She wore no make-up and beneath the garish red hair her face had a lost, unfinished look. 'I want to talk to you,' she said portentously to her mother. 'I've been waiting for the opportunity.'

Her younger brother, Malcolm, appeared at the window, beckoning. When Janet inclined her head towards him, he said, 'I am your son. But don't let it get about. There are spies everywhere.' He withdrew and Katrina said, 'I wonder if I count for anything in this household?'

While Hugh folded his troubles and uncertainties within himself, Malcolm had always made a package of his feelings — whether of joy or sorrow — which he presented, gift-wrapped, for others to share. He had the ability to make a pleasure of the transaction. Even Stephanie acknowledged that 'Suffering with

17

Malcolm is more rewarding than celebrating with Hugh.' Today, in good spirits, he sidled in at the back door, exaggerating each movement for the sheer joy of demonstrating yet again that he had a lithe, supple body.

'Not Ariel again!' Katrina said.

'No, Puck. Much more interesting.' He straightened up. 'Has D gone?'

'Our big sister took her home.'

'Let it not be forgotten that I bore the burden of the day.'

'That's your reward for being ungodly and not going to church.'

'I went to the First Mass of Easter last night with Mother. It was really quite splendid. That moment when the candle is brought into the darkened church . . .'

'Did D ask you why you only wore one earring?'

'No, I think we've got that straightened out now. She had a long confidential talk with me about some poor woman she once knew who was in rep. *and* never got a decent part, *and* passed all her days in cheap lodging houses, AND never learnt how to live in the Real World.'

'*And* you said . . .' Malcolm dodged behind Katrina, looking over her shoulder, and they chanted together, 'But which is The Real World.' They did a few shuffling steps around the kitchen, singing "Underneath the arches I dreamed my dreams away . . ." until Katrina, pointing a shaking finger at a baking tray, shouted, 'What is this I see before me?'

Malcolm said, 'You mustn't misquote the Scottish play.'

'Mum, you haven't put the potatoes in!'

'Oh dear, neither I have.'

They looked at her in dismay.

Katrina said, 'They won't do now, will they? We shall have to have them *boiled*.'

'I expect Patsy would say they are better for us this way.' Janet took a knife and began to scrape off the fat.

'We're too young to bother about healthy living,' Malcolm objected. He took a piece of kitchen paper and moodily helped to rub the remaining fat from the potatoes. 'You have ruined my

18

lunch, but I shall always love you.'

Katrina said, 'I'm not sure I shall. I hope you haven't forgotten anything else.'

'I don't think I laid the table. You can do that.'

'You *don't think*? What is this all about?'

Katrina went out of the room. She stood in the doorway to the dining room, frowning. 'No, you haven't.'

Stephanie joined her. 'What's wrong?'

'Our mother has had a brainstorm.'

'Perhaps you would like me to lay the table while you get dressed?'

'It's not funny any more, Steffie. *And* she forgot to put the potatoes in to roast.'

'She *is* slipping. I've noticed one or two signs myself.' They began to lay out the cutlery. 'We must make sure she does something that will stimulate her now that we have all left home.'

'Like what?'

'Well, certainly not dwindling away doing housework and little jobs with the WI. Open University might be the answer.'

'I've never thought of Mum as being at all academic. Suppose she didn't pass?'

'She doesn't need to be academic, only intelligent.'

'But how intelligent is she, would you think? I mean, you should know.'

'Psychology isn't just a matter of administering intelligence tests!' Stephanie said rather sharply. While she was talking Janet came into the hall and stood listening. 'And anyway, it's difficult to tell when it's a member of one's own family. But I have a feeling she might do well enough if she came out from under father's shadow.'

'But what would he think about it?'

'It wouldn't interfere with him provided she studied while he was writing. So long as he was fed he wouldn't really notice any more than Matilda and Humphrey. In fact, Humphrey would be the more put out, since he might not get his early morning walk. After all, Daddy is not a man who makes small demands. He doesn't want Mother to go rushing in to admire every paragraph he writes. Not like Piers who expects me to stand by with a hammer every time he bangs in a nail.'

'She couldn't do English, could she? That would be ...' Katrina bit a thumbnail. 'Sacrilege.'

'Katrina!'

'That's how I felt. I imagined being asked to analyse one of his books and I knew I just couldn't do it. It would be a sort of invasion – not just of the book but of us as a family.'

'Is *that* why you chose Management Studies, of all things? I always wondered.'

'Yes, as unlike as possible.' Katrina sounded glum. 'Malcolm wanted to do English. He chose History instead and came unstuck.'

'I should have had something to say had I known all this nonsense was going on!'

'That's why we didn't tell you.'

'To allow one's parents to exert such an influence!'

'Why do you think Hugh chose law?'

'Because he's a dull old stick who needs to have everything cut and dried. Patsy was the one unconformist impulse of his life.'

'And you? Why did you choose psychology?'

'Clairvoyance, I should think. To help me deal with Piers when he came into my life. It had nothing whatsoever to do with my family.' Perhaps aware that she was speaking a shade too vehemently, she qualified this, 'At least, no more than all our choices can be said to grow out of our childhood.'

'Oh, quite, quite! So, we've established that Mum can't do English, so what are we to do with her?'

'She ought really to do something which would enable her to take a part-time job. Social studies would probably be the answer. Her trouble is that she is so used to seeing other people in relation to Daddy. But if she could learn to adapt the skills she has employed on him I see no reason why she shouldn't become a good auxiliary social worker – so long as she was well supervised.'

'What was that?' Katrina said sharply.

'Only a door banging.'

'You've been away from home too long! Doors in this house can't usually be made to close, let alone bang.' Katrina went into the hall. 'Oh hullo, Hugh. Did you slam a door?'

'No.' He was on the threshold of the front door. He looked quiet and perplexed, older than his twenty-seven years and the last person to close a door in anger. He followed Katrina into the dining room and busied himself at the sideboard uncorking a bottle of wine. 'You'd think we might rise to two bottles for six people!'

'Not till Daddy's on the bestseller list!'

They were soon joined by Malcolm, who exclaimed, 'A quarter to two! There is nothing for it. The woman will have to go.'

Murdoch Saunders appeared in the doorway. He had come in from the garden where he had received his wife's instructions and had not yet removed his cap. He was a short, rather stockily built man and the cap, so often accessory to the aplomb of the country gentleman, in his case accentuated a pawkiness reminiscent of a Scots comedian. He stood, moving his head from side to side – calculating the number present to see how many times he must make his announcement. His features were knobbly without being bony and would lend themselves to a variety of parts. It would not have been surprising to discover that he was come here to preface a tragedy or to tell a lewd story. In fact, what he said was, 'Mummy would have you know that lunch is ready.'

As they prepared for their respective duties, he said to Stephanie, 'Where is Piers?'

'Daddy, I told you last night. He is taking some quite impossible children from his school on a camping weekend. I suppose he chose Easter as a way of reminding God that He isn't there any more.'

'That means I shall have to carve. Heigh ho!'

[2]

'She talked about Herbert all the way home,' Stephanie said. 'Of course, I don't remember him very well, but I did get the impression when he was alive that she wasn't all that satisfied with him. George, you can either go into the garden and play with Humphrey, or you can eat your dinner. I leave it to you to decide.'

Hugh said, 'Well, he's dead now.'

'I am aware of that.'

Malcolm said, 'Hugh meant that we should let Herbert rest in peace.'

'Letting him rest in peace is one thing, consenting to his canonisation is another.'

Katrina said, 'Oh, stuff it, Steffie.'

Stephanie said to Murdoch, 'Would you be willing to take Mother out for Sunday lunch each week?'

'I like your mother's cooking too much.'

'But *would* you, if she wanted it?'

He looked down the length of the table, his eyes screwed up as though viewing a figure at the wrong end of a telescope. '*Do* you want to go out to Sunday lunch?'

'I don't want you to become like Herbert Stapleton.'

'Mummy!' Stephanie exclaimed. 'What is the use of trying to help you?'

'Help me?' The words were flung back at Stephanie like a deflected knife.

'All right, all right!'

There was an uncomfortable silence during which Stephanie helped Marcus to cauliflower which he did not want.

Malcolm said, 'In the pause which followed Hugh began to speak about his children.'

Hugh looked bewildered and Marcus began to cry. Malcolm said, 'How were Sam and Francesca?'

'At first they were shy and by the time I had overcome that, they were tired.'

'Succinct. Not very informative, but succinct.' Malcolm turned to Katrina. 'What news from you, my sister Northumberland?'

'A bleak and barren place we will not speak of.'

'You have only been there for two terms,' Stephanie said.

George said, 'Our cat eats wool. And when she does her business it's all pink . . . or blue . . .'

Murdoch took no part in the conversation, but it would have been a mistake to assume that he was in no way involved in what happened around him. The truth was that he had difficulty in making much sense of what was said. His critics frequently noted that he was not good at dialogue. But, more than anyone else in the room, Murdoch *felt* what was going on around him. As he looked from one to the other his nerves quivered, exposed to so much pain – Stephanie's insecurity, the frustrated desire of Katrina, Hugh's sense of rejection and Malcolm's loneliness, all this he felt. They surrounded him, busy hands and busier tongues, clothed in the garments best suited to protect them, but to him, all peeled.

How can he write so powerfully when he never seems to notice people? they often asked themselves. But it was not his gift to see people – other than his wife – as sharply differentiated individuals, but rather to experience them as raw material. And so the members of his family talked without taking him into account, maintaining a precarious order in their lives, passing mint-sauce and pouring wine, and all innocent of their unpeeled state.

Today, however, there was something new. A different element was loosed somewhere, deeper, deeper than he could reach; something he might not be able to use and therefore very disturbing since it would not go away, but remain there beyond his power to transform its substance. Until now, for him the process of writing had been a feast at which the water was

23

constantly turned to wine. He had always accepted that one day there might be an end to this.

They were leaving him now, carrying plates, the children banished to the garden. Katrina was saying, 'You *did* put the apple tart in?'

In the kitchen, Janet said, 'Go away and don't fuss me.'

'Surely there is something we can do?'

'Please!'

'The cream, at least.' Katrina picked up the jug and they went out.

In the hall, pausing before going into the dining room, Stephanie said, 'It is rather overpowering in there. She needs an extractor fan. To say nothing of a modernised kitchen with a dishwasher.'

Katrina said, 'I expect they could do with central heating, while you're about it, Stephanie. That would stir up a few spirits who haven't been disturbed much over the centuries!'

'I don't know about spirits, but I doubt whether their bank balance or the structure of the house could afford central heating!'

Janet stood looking round the kitchen. It had happened again. The colour had gone and the kitchen was black and white, save for the eerie blue flame above which the kettle was boiling. She turned off the gas and stood bracing herself to open the oven door. When she did so, it was as she had feared. The pastry was pallid, sepia, just as the meat had been. Ever since she was a child the world had presented itself to her eyes with a jewelled brilliance, its outlines crystal clear. It had taken her a long time to understand that others did not see it in this way, that this acute awareness of light – sheen on fruit, bloom on a child's skin, transparent delicacy of an old face, gossamer spider's web, intricate pattern of leaf or fretwork of frost – all this was her special gift. Endless joy, it had seemed, no single effect of light ever repeated. Now gone. She turned away from the oven and opened the garden door.

In the dining room, Katrina said in a low voice, as if speaking during the action of a play, 'She *can't* have forgotten to put it in because I can smell it.'

Hugh got up and Stephanie said, 'Don't hustle her.'

He looked at her in surprise. 'I was going to pour more wine.'
He held the bottle up to the light. 'Only enough for half a glass.
Should we open another bottle?'

Murdoch, to whom wine was a luxury, put a hand over his
glass.

Hugh looked at the others, none of whom was prepared to
make the decision for him. He poured the remaining wine into
his own glass and sat down again.

Malcolm exclaimed, 'She's out there!'

They all turned to the window. The children were playing
hide-and-seek in the shrubbery. Janet was sitting on the bench
beneath the apple tree, the golden retriever leaning against her
leg. Both appeared to be asleep.

Stephanie scraped back her chair. 'I *said* it was too hot in that
kitchen!'

In the garden, Katrina said shrilly, 'She's not like my mother.
Don't touch her.'

'Who do you think she is?' Malcolm joked. 'Queen Mab and
our father Old Hob o' the Muirs? I always knew there was
something strange going on in this house.' He laughed but stood
back.

Stephanie said, also standing back, 'We must be very careful
about this.'

Murdoch squatted beside the retriever who opened bloodshot
eyes and gazed at him in bleary sadness.

'Of course we must touch her,' Hugh said and laid a hand on
her shoulder.

At once, she woke and looked from one face to the other,
smiling and benevolent as she had always been.

'I can't think what came over me,' she said, restored to the
dining room, the apple tart distributed and pronounced a
success.

Stephanie said, 'It's much too hot in that kitchen.'

Katrina and Malcolm looked at each other and looked away.

Hugh brought his mind to bear on this and said, 'But the

kitchen is no different from what it has always been.'

Stephanie said, 'But Mother is older,' and Katrina mouthed at Hugh, 'The time of life.'

Murdoch asked Stephanie, 'What can be done about the kitchen?'

'You should get an extractor fan.'

'I will get one on Tuesday.'

'You will need to get someone to install it for you.'

'I have no doubt I could do that myself. I expect they come with instructions.'

Hugh said, 'I don't think the kitchen needs an extractor fan, Stephanie. It has windows on two walls, one of which is usually open for Matilda, and a garden door, which is usually open for Humphrey. There is a more than adequate through draught.'

Janet said loudly, 'I think I shall go to Greenham Common with Patsy. Does anyone see any reason why I shouldn't?'

She sat crouched forward as if about to spring. Instinctively her children averted their gaze, each hoping not to be the object of her attention. 'Well?' she said. 'Has anyone got a better offer? Deutzia has suggested art lectures or a continental holiday. And I believe Open University has been advocated.' Stephanie flushed scarlet. 'I think I might learn more at Greenham Common.'

Malcolm sat with his body hunched, hands gripping his knees. Katrina pressed knuckles against her teeth. Hugh said objectively, studying the stem of his wineglass, 'Who will look after Sam and Francesca?'

Janet leaned forward, staring fiercely down the length of the table. 'You could look after them for one day,' she said to Murdoch who alone was prepared to meet her gaze. 'You would like to look after your grandchildren, wouldn't you? They could watch you putting in the extractor fan. *That* would be fun for them.'

Murdoch said, 'I thought it was Friday that Patsy wanted us to have the children. You put a ring round the day on the calendar.'

'And . . .?'

'I was proposing to put the extractor fan in on Tuesday. But it can wait until Friday if you would prefer that.'

Janet sat back. 'So that is settled.'

Stephanie said, with an attempt at good-humour which was a little too highly-pitched, 'You are not going to cut wires, or worse, I hope. I wouldn't put it past Patsy.'

Janet collected the dishes within easy reach. 'What a silly phrase that is, isn't it? "Put it past Patsy".' She went out of the room.

Stephanie said, 'Phew!'

Katrina said, 'Oh well, it *is* hot in the kitchen.'

'Don't be so snide, Katrina.'

'If *that's* the best psychology you can come up with!'

'I don't want to analyse my own mother.'

Murdoch said, 'I should hope not.' He and Malcolm gathered the remaining dishes and went out.

'Perhaps Mother needs a holiday,' Hugh said. 'We are all a bit difficult to deal with, when you come to think about it.'

'But she loves dealing with us,' Stephanie protested. 'She is a born enabler. That has been her fulfilment. She enables father to write and, I suppose, she enables each of us, in a way, though to do what, I'm not sure . . .' They pondered this, none of them having a satisfactory answer.

'The thing that troubled me,' Katrina said, 'was the way she looked at Daddy, so angrily. But *he* didn't seem surprised. It makes me wonder how long this has been going on.'

Stephanie shrugged. 'He probably didn't notice.'

Hugh said slowly, 'That's one thing you can't say about him. They have always had a way of looking at each other as though . . .' He got up and went to the window, seeming to have difficulty in speaking of this. 'As though they had a loss of memory overnight and discovered each other again every morning.'

Katrina looked at him in surprise.

'I don't know about that,' Stephanie said. 'But there was certainly something rather naive about them.'

'So what made her turn on him like that?' Katrina asked. 'You don't think that Daddy – he couldn't, surely?'

'I rather think he could, if he had a mind to it.' Stephanie considered her father thoughtfully. 'But who with? That's the question. Opportunity would be a fine thing in the village!'

'He does take long walks every afternoon. And he never asks her to go with him. What do you think?'

They both turned to Hugh.

'I don't think he has ever looked at another woman. It wouldn't surprise me if it hadn't even occurred to him how many other people – men and women – there are around.'

His bitterness surprised his sisters and Stephanie tried to rephrase his statement in more acceptable terms. 'Of course, he is rather exceptional. His writing undoubtedly stimulates him and gives him a kind of fulfilment. An alternative pleasure, almost a licensed infidelity, one might say . . .'

Malcolm returned, his face grey as lard. 'I think you had better come.'

Janet was lying on the kitchen floor weeping, attended by Murdoch and Humphrey, each ineffectual after his own fashion.

Hugh said, 'She had better lie down in the sitting room' and Stephanie said, 'Get her out into the garden. She needs fresh air.'

This being what most of them needed, they moved Janet into the fresh air. They propped her once more on the bench beneath the apple tree where she slumped, looking uncomfortably like a straw figure.

'She looks so *pale*,' Katrina said. 'Not a bit like my little nut-brown Mum.'

[3]

The doctor was a young man, very concerned to live up to every word of the Hippocratic oath. Were the village to be smitten by plague, he would stay to the last. In a believing age he might have been a priest. It was unfortunate for him that his first big test should be a woman in late middle life, a period about which he had had no personal experience and had received no adequate instruction. In fact, the only comment which came to his mind at the moment was that of a testy old man – 'In my day the answer was delicately tinctured water – violet was particularly effective, I recall. God knows what they do with them nowadays!' He sat gazing levelly at Janet, striving to present himself as a man who was sympathetic, soothing, shrewd, wise and, above all, in control, these being the attributes which he imagined she most needed in her doctor at this moment.

Janet saw a man in his late twenties with an eager, sensitive face beneath a neat pudding-basin haircut. 'Don't let me down,' the eyes pleaded as he talked to her. 'I can't afford a failure at this stage. I have such dreams and so little self-confidence.' She recognised him as a kindred spirit. He would never make his mark in the world. She felt that she was the physician faced with the decision whether to tell the patient he is doomed, or to allow him the few unclouded years which may lie ahead before the disease tightens its grip on him.

How could she say to him, 'My children have all gone. But they return from time to time to talk about what I should do and to disparage what I have done. My husband behaves as though nothing has changed; now that I have more time – a fact he does not seem to realise – he does not ask me to share his long afternoon walks. Deutzia tells me what I should do which means that half the village is thinking about what is to be done with me. But there isn't any solution.' Oh, how *could* she say that to him when he was so desperately anxious to find one for her? It would be cruel to tell him the truth, to say to him, 'I am not a modern woman. I am a series of "nots" – not typical, topical, current, competitive, controversial, contentious, protesting. I am not given to confrontation, nor am I concerned with success as most people understand it today. I am passive, accepting, quiescent, unmotivated, uncommitted, and therefore uncaring and irrelevant. My trouble, doctor, is that I am an irrelevant woman.'

But he would have no cure for that, so she accepted what he had to offer because it would do her little harm and might be of some help to him.

When Stephanie telephoned the following day, Murdoch sounded quite cheerful. The doctor did not seem to suspect anything sinister, but he had given Janet a thorough examination and taken a number of tests, the results of which would be available next week. It was obvious that both Murdoch and the doctor gained confidence from the fact that Janet's problems were now contained in specimen bottles.

The following week Murdoch telephoned Stephanie to tell her that the tests were negative. 'So,' he explained, 'there isn't anything really wrong.'

'So what is this all about?' Stephanie demanded.

'The doctor thinks that your mother has been pushing herself a bit hard for a number of years and needs a rest.' Murdoch spoke quietly as though anxious not to wake a sleeping child.

'He may be satisfied,' Stephanie said to Piers. 'But *I* should like to see for myself. I think we'll go down for the day next weekend. The children can stay with your sister. We have hers often enough, goodness knows!'

Piers noted three assumptions in one short speech: that he would accompany her, that his sister would have the children, that his sister would resent having to have the children. He set his mind to the business of finding valid objections.

'I have a lot of marking to do. And we can't just assume that Angela and Bill have no plans for the weekend. You were furious when they accepted that invitation to Ascot on the assumption that we would have their kids.'

'Then I'll go down on my own.' Her eyes filled with tears. Piers was so astonished that he surrendered unconditionally.

'There is nothing you haven't told me?' he asked, and hastily narrowed the issue before she could reply. 'About your mother, I mean.'

'I just want to make sure that doctor knows what he is about.'

'He's quite young, isn't he? He's bound to be up-to-the-minute in treatment.'

'I don't want my mother to have up-to-the-minute treatment. I want her to have the right treatment.'

Piers studied her gloomily. As she stood by the window in the early morning sunlight she had the ripe perfection of a corn goddess; one could imagine pygmy mortals trying to climb the thumping great pigtail which hung down her back. A benign goddess, she wore an air of being tolerant, though still surprised by the fact that other people had ideas different from her own; and, while she meant to be kind, her big, candid eyes could not conceal the fact that she could do most things better than the person actually struggling with the task. He was sorry for the doctor.

'What are you staring at?' she asked.

'I was wondering which of your parents you take after.'

'I take after my maternal grandmother, as you well know.'

Piers' eyes rested on a photograph of a truculent old woman sitting, arms folded, on a bench outside a cottage door. She did not look as though tears had come into her eyes at any time during her adult life and it was hard to imagine her as having had a childhood.

'Are you planning to stay the night?' he asked.

Stephanie wavered. 'What do you think?'

'We could ask Angela to take them for the night, just in case.'

They contemplated the picture of their return to a house emptied of children.

'Yes,' Stephanie said. 'Let's do that — just in case.'

They set out early on the Saturday. Neither of them questioned whether their arrival would be welcomed by Murdoch and Janet.

'It will do you good to get right away from school. There is nothing like an exchange of problems for refreshing the spirit,' Stephanie said as they travelled out of Surrey. She spoke consolingly, making amends for what he might consider a certain highhandedness in her behaviour.

'I like school.'

'You need to get away from it sometimes, nevertheless.' After they had negotiated Farnham, she said, 'And, anyway, you can't possibly like it. You just feel you *have* to like it because you left the church.'

A few miles ahead Piers turned the car into a lay-by. His thin face was white, the eyes like glass. Stephanie looked at him in alarm. He expressed her fears. 'One day you will go too far.'

'It's only because I want to help you, Piers.' The practised reasonableness of her tone was undermined by an unprofessional note of appeal. 'You're not cut out for this.'

'On the contrary, I feel this is my real vocation.' His voice was cold, his mouth unforgiving.

She reacted sharply. 'Then why do you insist on being "Edward" to your colleagues at school?'

'How could I teach in a comprehensive with a name like Piers?'

'It's very confusing for George and Marcus.'

'*They* don't notice. How often do we have anyone from the school into our home? I should think most of them have no idea where I live!'

'I am not going to entertain people with whom I must constantly remind myself not to mention my husband's name.'

'You could call me Edward.'

'Certainly not! It was as Piers that I took you for better or for worse, in sickness and in health. I went through all that trauma of your withdrawal from the church. I even *sat* there while you preached that incredible last sermon.'

'The Christian faith *is* incredible.'

'Well, we won't go into that now. But I am not going to call you Edward – ever!'

He remembered how she had stood between him and his parishioners, refusing entry to his study, arguing with them in the sitting room. She had even argued with the bishop. 'You were very good about all that, Steffie. And you're right. I do find it hard at school. But then so do all the others. I'm no different from them.' His hands tightened on the steering wheel. *This is not going to fold up on me.*

'So long as you don't drive yourself over the edge. Now that Mother has been taken ill I feel anything could happen.'

'Your mother needs a rest. Why can't you accept that, Steffie, instead of rushing in and interfering? Antagonising the doctor won't help.' He started the car again.

'But why should she need a rest? She hasn't *done* anything, Piers! Only looked after all of us. And *I* helped with that. I was the eldest. I was always the one who was put in charge. Just think what you and I do in a week in comparison. Me at the clinic, you at school, taking incest and grievous bodily harm as part of our daily diet!'

'I don't know about incest.'

'Then you are falling down on your pastoral care.'

He winced and she said, 'I can't help it if the terminology is the same.'

By lunchtime they were at Shaftesbury where they stopped for a meal because Stephanie said that Piers needed a break.

'Why don't you take over?' he asked.

'I can't drive with you sitting beside me, behaving like the examiner who failed me for the third time – the one who said I was too impetuous.'

In the hotel she telephoned Murdoch to inform him 'We shall be with you soon after three.'

After lunch Piers drove slowly and Stephanie looked out of the window at scenes which, however often she viewed them, she could never reconcile with her present way of life. She had lived in Dorset all her childhood and to her the village had been the normality of life, what lay beyond it a kind of failed chaos which was not to be taken seriously. Now she saw this part of Dorset as the one isolated area of deep country in the South of England. It wasn't simply that the villages were far apart, leaving a lot of uninhabited space in between, but the villages themselves were still rural with leftover rainwater lying in the ruts of unmade-up roads and big stone houses owned by people who were too busy farming to prettify their dwellings. And then there were the valleys which lay like deep pockets of the past. She found herself thinking it was rather sinister. No wonder Hardy's books were so full of foreboding.

'Man is still at the mercy of Nature here,' she said.

'Don't you believe it,' Piers answered. 'Nature is on the retreat here as elsewhere.' He sounded displeased about this.

'You wouldn't have been any happier had you lived a hundred years ago,' she said, reading his mind. 'Think of *Jude the Obscure.*'

'There was a certain form to life then, a shape.'

'Hardy gave it form and shape. If it is form and shape you are after, you should have stayed in the church and worked through your problems.'

'I shall never lack problems to work through.'

'But you no longer have anyone to blame for the world being the way it is – apart from President Reagan, and he isn't much of a substitute for God.'

'Steffie, I know that you feel secure once you have got some sort of order into a situation by analysing it, but I wish you could understand that even the soundest case loses something by constant repetition.'

'I would have thought that was a statement which most educationists would want to challenge. It seems to me that nowadays teachers proceed on the same assumption as TV pundits – that no one takes anything in until it has been repeated at least six times.'

Piers drove on for some minutes in silence while Stephanie talked, then he intervened, 'You are scared silly, aren't you?'

She turned her head away. 'I shall be all right once we are there and I have seen her. I shall know what to do then.

It's the uncertainty I can't stand.'

'Mightn't it be wise, just this once, not to *do* anything?'

'And who would take charge if I did that? My father? And even if he was different, and capable, that would still be unthinkable. He has just begun his revise.'

'That could wait.'

'Think what the world would have lost if Hardy had put his books to one side to comfort Mrs Hardy.'

'Mrs Hardy would have gained.'

'My father is a genius. You don't understand about genius.'

The road had been climbing and now they came to heathland. Ahead a signpost standing at an angle where only one crossbar was visible, looked like a gibbet. A big black bird was perched on it. Beyond lay miles of sour grass rising to distant indigo crags. Purple clouds massed overhead.

Piers said, 'It is so beautiful in autumn when all the heather is out.'

'I've never liked moors.'

'This is only heathland.'

She closed her eyes. 'That, too. It makes me think of the Brontës, coughing themselves to death.'

'The price of genius, no doubt.'

'I don't think I am going to be able to cope with this weekend if you are going to get at me all the time.' She counted slowly up to three hundred, telling herself that by this time they should have turned off the heath road, but when she opened her eyes it was still all around her, this seemingly limitless space. 'I think perhaps I am mildly agoraphobic,' she said.

'A little while ago you were uneasy about the enclosed valleys.'

'And mildly claustrophobic, too.'

He said, to distract her, 'Did Murdoch understand about being a father?'

It was not a question which Stephanie found disturbing so she considered before answering. 'He was always there, by which I mean there was no gap in our lives. I remember very clearly one thing which happened when I was quite small. There was a big do at the church – I've forgotten what it was all about, if I ever knew. For the early part of the service we children were hived off into the church hall so that we wouldn't get fidgety. Then, at a certain stage in the proceedings, we were returned to our parents. Only I couldn't find mine. I was terribly frightened. The church was full and all the people seemed tall as trees. It was like one of the nastier fairy stories and I was the child lost in the wood. I set up a terrible howling. When we were talking about it years afterwards, Mother told me that my cries seemed to echo round the church and she could not tell where the noise was coming from; but Daddy was like a bird with an in-built radar system. Quite suddenly he was there, in the aisle, with his arms outstretched to me. He behaved as though there were only the two of us and the rest *were* just trees.'

Piers said, 'Hmm.'

'So if I ever got lost in a wilderness like this, it is to him that I would call out, not Mummy.'

'Or your husband.'

'One tends to regress at such times.'

'I sometimes get the feeling you don't really like your mother.'

'Piers, I shan't tell you these things if you make such a non-sense of them.'

Later, when the heathland lay behind them, they turned off the main road on to a sunken lane which twisted down, wooded hills rising steeply to one side. Below, in shadow at this time of the afternoon, lay the village, not much more than a hamlet with a few houses unevenly distributed along a winding street. The gardens sloped down to a small stream, placid between green banks. At the far end of the village they came to a bridge beyond which the narrow lane climbed to a grassy plateau. Stephanie said, looking back at a dour little house now softened by massed daffodils, 'I wonder what made Deutzia to come to live here.'

'I suppose she wanted to be near her children and this was the only place she could afford.'

'The children are some distance away and she doesn't see much of them. She should have stayed in Kew and kept the family home going.'

'Even after the family had gone?'

'Children need somewhere to return to. And, anyway, Kew would have been so useful for them, easily accessible to London.'

'I don't think Deutzia sees her role in life as being useful.'

By the time they arrived at the house the sun had come out and it was fine and warm, but Stephanie felt a familiar tension stretching her forehead which warned her that the day was not to be trusted. Janet was in the garden wearing an Indian cotton dress and a large hat which she might have borrowed from Deutzia. The dress smelled of moth balls. She was quiet and shy when she greeted them, like a child who knows it has been naughty. Yet there was a gleam in the demurely glancing eyes which made Stephanie feel that she was obscurely pleased with herself.

Murdoch said, 'She spends a lot of time in the garden now,' and pointed to a trug. They all looked at the trug as if it was a toy. Stephanie saw a few clippings in it – rather half-hearted a collection for a morning's gardening. Murdoch looked at them as though anticipating words of encouragement. It was almost, Stephanie thought, as though he was colluding with her mother.

'Have I seen that dress before?' she asked.

'I wore it to your wedding.'

Stephanie said, 'I will make tea for us,' and ran into the house. After a few minutes Piers followed her. He found her standing in the kitchen, hands clasped across her breasts.

'Whatever is wrong?'

'That was cruel, cruel!' He stared at her blankly and she stamped her foot. 'Can't you see? She put that dress on on purpose.'

'What purpose? To remind us of our wedding day? Is that cruel?'

'To go back nine years without warning . . . like plummeting down in a lift.'

He turned his head away, pulling at his ear lobe. 'I was intensely proud and happy on my wedding day. I could scarcely believe it – this radiant girl was marrying me!'

Stephanie said unsteadily, 'And now?'

He put a hand on her shoulder. 'I didn't know the half of it then! But I wouldn't change you.'

Murdoch came to the window and said, 'Janet would like to have tea in the garden. She seems to like being out-of-doors. We had breakfast in the garden. And lunch.'

They had tea in the garden and later they had supper in the garden. By this time the light was not good, large bruised clouds crouched above the valley and it was becoming very chilly. Stephanie, controlling an impulse to run out into the lane and run and run and run, said quietly, but firmly, 'Should we go indoors now, do you think, Mother? You will get cold out here.'

Janet smiled down at her hands and, noticing that they were blue, rubbed them together, pausing every now and again to examine the palms. Murdoch went into the house and came out with a travelling rug which he laid gently around her shoulders. He performed this act in a manner which was at once comic and intensely sad and, perhaps because of the outdoor setting and the impending storm, Stephanie was reminded of Lear's fool. Unthinking, she slipped into the role of poor Tom.

'Won't you please come in, Mummy,' she pleaded, sitting at Janet's feet, 'because *I* am getting cold.'

Janet darted her a look of malicious glee as though seeing through this inept performance to something hidden behind it. Stephanie was left sitting on the ground feeling rather idiotic. Piers, looking at his wife, recognised his own rising panic when confronted with a youth whom he could neither persuade nor control.

'She is just being mischievous,' Stephanie said, righting herself, taut with anger.

For half an hour they took it in turns to plead, cajole, reason, browbeat, all to no avail. Thunder rolled in the distance. 'If it pelts, what are we to do?' Stephanie quailed at the thought of manhandling her mother into the house and doubted whether either of the men would prove very effective in such an emergency. But as the first heavy spots of rain began to patter on the leaves of the apple tree, Humphrey appeared. He was obviously deeply distressed. He walked ponderously across the lawn, sat down in front of Janet and placed a rough paw on her knee, snagging the fine cotton of the dress. She looked into his eyes and said, 'Haven't they fed you?' Then she got up and accompanied him into the kitchen where a tigerish tabby was pacing to and fro, little pink mouth opening and shutting in silent complaint. 'Oh, my darlings!' Janet crooned. 'My poor darlings!'

After she had fed the animals Janet became commendably submissive and suffered Stephanie to put her to bed. As she lay back against the pillows, she said, not quite ingenuously, 'I am your little girl now, aren't I?'

Stephanie went down the stairs and interrupted the two men, who were talking about Murdoch's book. 'You had better go to bed soon, Daddy, We don't want her to get disturbed again.'

'Yes, of course.'

She turned to Piers. 'We shall have to stay the night now. So could you get the case from the car.'

When they had gone, she regretted having despatched them so summarily. The washing-up had been done, by whom she could not imagine, and she herself had made up the bed in the room which had been hers ever since, at the age of twelve, she had rebelled against 'always being in charge and not having anything to show for it'. Alone in the pretty room under the eaves, Katrina had cried for a week. But Stephanie had been resolute, convinced that she had mastered the process of growing up. Now, standing alone in the hall, she said aloud, 'I tried to separate too soon.'

She went into the dining room and crossed to the window. Lightning ripped across the sky and all the house lights went out. Thunder fulminated around the house and then went grumbling away over the fields. The rain poured through the leads in the windows, but by the time Stephanie had felt her way into the kitchen and returned with towels, it had eased. She laid the towels along the window sill and made her way to the front door. As she looked out Piers came round the side of the house, carrying a case. She could hear but not see him and for a moment an absurd fear seized her – suppose this was not her husband but the tramp of whom her mother had spoken on Easter Day?

'Where have you been all this time?' she asked crossly when she had established that it was indeed Piers.

'In the car. I didn't see any point in getting drowned. Have the lights gone?'

'Yes. I expect a cable has come down.'

They stood in the porch, smelling the wet earth and listening to the constant patter as raindrops fell from the eaves. At first there was utter darkness and then the clouds parted and they saw the outline of trees and hedge. Stephanie said, 'Well, that's over.'

Piers said, 'A spring shower.'

Janet appeared better in the morning. She was up early and seemed to have prepared breakfast much as usual. Before she left Stephanie made her father promise to see the doctor again. 'Tell him he must give her something to help her to relax. Not that I approve of drugs as a rule; but it is no use telling someone to take things easily if they are wound up like an alarm clock.'

As they drove away she said to Piers, 'I hope he *will* go to the doctor. If he doesn't I shall have to take a few days off and sort things out.'

'I expect he will. All this must be interfering with his work. He has written a book about the Falklands War. Did you know?'

'We shall have been overtaken by more recent escapades by the time *that* comes out.'

They were nearing the village now. 'We had better not call on Deutzia,' Stephanie said. 'We don't want to be inveigled into taking her out to lunch because of the electricity failure.' They came to the bridge. The stream rushed beneath, almost level with its banks.

'I wonder if we should have stayed a bit longer,' Stephanie said. 'I could have seen the doctor. He lives in the village although his surgery is in town.'

'Perhaps we are making a bit too much of all this? After all, what does it amount to? Janet is a bit weepy.'

'A little more than that! Refusing to come indoors last night!'

'You said you suffered from claustrophobia.'

'That's true. But she isn't *herself*. At least ...' Stephanie frowned, displeased at making such a naive statement. 'She isn't the self we all know and love.'

'She is overtired and weepy and claustrophobic. So she wouldn't seem like Janet to us, would she?' He elaborated this particular consolation before it could get away from him. 'People *aren't* themselves when they fail to be what we expect them to be. And we expect Janet to be – well, not easily tired or given to weeping.'

'Yes,' Stephanie said. 'Yes ... I daresay ...'

When they reached the heath, she said, 'I wonder if that tramp had anything to do with it – or gypsy or whatever he was. *If* he was.'

'Translation please.'

'On Easter Day. Do you remember my telling you? She seemed troubled about it. I think I shall tell the doctor. Or I could tell Daddy. He has quite a rapport with the gypsies. *Romanies*, he calls them.' She shivered. 'A breeze is getting up.' She wound up the window. Piers laughed, and they said in unison, ' "There's likewise a wind on the heath".'

[4]

Murdoch sat at his desk. It was the first of May and a bright, sunny day which anticipated the summer. Matilda sat by the open window keeping watch for the house martins which were nesting in the eaves. Humphrey stretched out on the rug, nose twitching as in his dreams he chased through corn fields. It was peaceful. Katrina had come for the weekend and she had taken Janet on a shopping expedition because 'stocks have got a bit low'. Before she left she had put a packet of cheese sandwiches and a vacuum flask of coffee on Murdoch's desk. 'You won't need to move out of the room all day now!'

'I always walk in the afternoon.' He had been surprised. 'Had you forgotten?'

She had not forgotten, she had been making a protest. He had not understood, but after she had gone her anger stayed on in the room and he was unable to concentrate his mind on the Falklands ar and its aftermath. Stephanie's comment that 'We shall have been overtaken by more recent escapades by the time *that* comes out!' would have had little meaning for Murdoch. He did not choose a subject because it was topical. He did not, in fact, have much say in the choice of subject – it was presented to him. Nothing, however, was being presented to him this morning.

Perhaps coffee would provide the necessary stimulus. He put out a hand for the vacuum flask. The hand remained poised above it. His lips moved, releasing the stream of obscenities which had sometimes surprised, and endeared him to, his agent while leading others to account him coarse.

Patsy came to the window and pushed her head past Matilda's. 'I know you are working,' she said, as though the acknowledgement cancelled out the interruption. 'But I've brought your supper.'

He came to the window and saw that a large iron casserole rested on one hip. The children stood beside her, gazing up.

'Is Humpy there?' Francesca asked.

Murdoch took the casserole from Patsy. It was heavy, but not, he suspected, by virtue of its contents. Humphrey was now demanding to be let out. Murdoch opened the door and Humphrey preceded him to the kitchen where Patsy and the children awaited them.

'And what is it this time?' Murdoch asked, putting the casserole down on top of the gas stove. 'Stewed thorn leaves?'

'You went off for days with the gypsies. That should have taught you something.' Patsy was not in the least resentful of this lack of gratitude. The broad planes of her face were made for impervious magnanimity.

'Romanies are good poachers. There was more than the fruits of the hedgerow in *their* billycans!'

'It will be good for you. You are beginning to get paunchy, Murdoch.'

'That's beer, girl! Not good, red meat.'

'Lay off the beer, then. I'll bring you a herbal brew.'

'I couldn't let you do that, Patsy.'

'It's no trouble. I like to share.'

'Then share this lovely morning with my dog. He needs a walk.'

'Janet not here?'

'She is shopping with Katrina.'

'Perhaps they took Deutzia with them? I called on her but she was out.'

'Do you feed Deutzia as well, you noble girl?'

'Oh dear no! Deutzia is quite capable of feeding herself. And, anyway, she wouldn't appreciate it.'

'And I do?'

'No, but you are disadvantaged, Murdoch. So I do it for you just the same.'

There was a wail from the garden and Patsy went out. Soon Murdoch heard her say, 'Samsara, don't make such a fuss.'

'Samsara' was for Murdoch's benefit, to remind him of the perfidy about which Patsy had been so forgiving. Patsy and Hugh had had considerable difficulty in choosing a name for their son. Patsy maintained that she had accepted Sam on the understanding that the full name should be not Samuel but Samsara which, she said, was a Buddhist term for "the flow of the stream of being". Hugh said he had simply given up arguing with her. Patsy insisted that it was not until the baby was being sprinkled with water that she had realised what was intended. Only her love for the child had prevented her from tugging it out of the arms of the vicar as he pronounced the name Samuel. Hugh said they had both been present when the vicar was given his instructions with the utmost clarity. This had been, if not the first, then the most significant instance of the imbalance in the marriage which was subsequently to cause so much unhappiness. Hugh was intelligent, wary, given to analysing any situation in which he found himself before taking even the smallest step. Patsy was impulsive, emotional and prone to react with hostility to any form of abstract reasoning. Moreover, she assumed that her dear ones thought as she did on all issues which were important to her and she was capable of putting the wrong construction on discussions which to most people would have seemed capable of only one meaning.

A lovable creature, Murdoch thought as Patsy walked slowly back to the kitchen having restored peace of a kind, slapdash but lovable. Hugh should have made something of that marriage.

'So what is the book about?' she asked as she joined him.

It was a question most people had learned not to ask, but Patsy was uninhibited, or insensitive, or both.

'The Falklands War.' He was surprised by his own indulgence.

'It takes you a long time to hear what people are saying. But it hasn't taken so long for you to catch up on the Falklands as it did on Vietnam. You're making progress, Murdoch!'

'What people are saying seldom makes sense to me, Patsy. During the Vietnam War – while you, no doubt, were doing your homework – Janet and I used to watch television.' Matilda's great grandmother would have been performing her ablutions on the hearthrug, and the children playing their last game of the day in the garden. He remembered that more vividly than the newsreels. 'The Vietnam War was about as real to me as the Crimean War – they had both taken place. I wasn't any more involved in the one than the other.'

'But you saw those ghastly scenes on television.'

'Burning villages, refugees dressed in the sort of clothes which turn a person into a bundle, napalm flame throwers, together with bits and pieces of human bodies which the networks had decided were compulsory viewing – is that what you have in mind?'

'It didn't move you?'

'It's a sort of black miracle that the small screen performs for me – containing within its frame grief, horror, terror, violence, defusing it and making it safe. The passion to inform debased into a mission to accommodate.'

'Yes,' Patsy conceded. 'It it is very difficult to educate the masses in these matters.' She looked solemn and he had a picture of her stirring the witch's brew she had prepared for his supper and reflecting on the difficulty of distilling wisdom for the masses.

'So why did you write it?' she asked. 'I thought it was a bit limited, mind you. But passionate. Really surprisingly passionate. Where did you get the passion from, Murdoch, you sly old fox?'

'I was sitting in my study, reading a Sunday paper.' Why am I telling her this? he wondered. They had always talked easily but not about things like this. He did not usually analyse the way ideas came to him – that would be questioning a gift, inviting who knew what retribution. Yet a kind of recklessness drove him on. 'I came across an article written by a foreign correspondent. In this article he referred to a Vietnamese family with whom he had stayed in peacetime. To supplement the war pictures, there was a photograph of the family. And there, Patsy, among the obligatory pictures of Vietnam represented as one

45

great devastation area, was a group of people picnicking on the banks of a river. They were as formally dressed and disposed as subjects in a painting by Watteau. The woman who was the centrepiece wore a white, high-necked dress. The picnic hamper rested on a large, white cloth. Can you imagine that? Not your kind of picnic, with the tin-opener and teapot left behind at home.'

'That only happened once.'

'This was a scene so peaceful that, in England, one must have gone back to Edwardian times for its like.'

'And this really got to you?'

He had sat staring from one picture to the other, trying not so much to reconcile, which was not his business, as to relate them in time and place. And the background? Was it possible that the river should still flow so quietly, the trees bend so gently towards it, the grass yet grow in that meadow? And *they*, anonymous, archetypal refugees, had once known *that*?

So it happens, he had thought, looking out of the window at his children playing on the swing with Janet standing watchfully by. It happens not only to other people, it happens to us. It happens to the woman of whatever culture who has prided herself on her clean home, the hospitality of her board, the woman who in her own small sphere has established and maintained a necessary order; a person not like Mother Courage, born and bred to the battlefield, but having the pride and dignity due to one who has achieved what is expected of her in the society in which she lives.

Gradually as he studied the pictures day by day, they began to merge, he saw what journey it was these people had had to make, he felt the wounds of people and place.

'Yes,' he said. 'That really got to me.'

'I liked the way you did the woman. But I was surprised that you concentrated so much on her. What about the massacre?'

'Every war has its massacre. The journalists can deal with massacres better than I can.'

She let this pass, although plainly dissatisfied. 'And the Falklands?'

'The same sort of thing.' But it *wasn't* the same – he was still revising the book, yet he was talking to her about it and seemed unable to stop. He, who had always said scornfully, 'When you have to explain your books you are finished,' was now worrying away at it like a terrier digging for a buried bone.

Patsy said, 'But you didn't seem very stirred at the time.'

'I wasn't. But then, when it was over, one paper sent a reporter to cover the return of the ship which had brought back the coffins of the dead. A grey, wet day, and only a handful of relatives come to see their soldier home. Pictures again – a glimpse of bemused faces beneath umbrellas.'

'And *that* stirred something?'

'I thought, looking at them, these are the people for whom no one speaks, certainly not the politicians, blaring away about patriotism or warmongering, according to their persuasion.'

'You saw those ships blazing, all those men in the oily water, still on fire, and that did nothing to you!' Her face had gone quite flinty, the whole texture of her body seemed to have changed; if that sacklike garment were to burst apart a load of gravel would spill out!

He said, 'I can't respond to the media coverage. The media is concerned with the numbers game, casualty figures are more important than casualties.'

'And that means?' He had lost her sympathy.

'It is the one death which matters; death is no more grievous if it is multiplied by a hundred or a thousand, only more newsworthy.'

'Thanks for the sermon.'

'I've listened to plenty of yours.' He shrugged his shoulders. 'But call it my failure, if you like.'

'Humility is not your thing, Murdoch.'

'It is in the small and the intimate that the likes of us can best hope to come to some kind of understanding of the forces which move in the world today.'

'I'm glad to have your word for it. I just hope for your sake that all your Right Wing friends . . .'

'I have few friends and none of them Right Wing.'

47

'... won't find it offensive. Giving the Argentinians their comeuppance is the only thing they have had to shout about in years, poor things.'

His agent had expressed similar fears.

'It isn't about us and the Argentinians,' Murdoch had protested. 'It is about one family whose son was killed in the Falklands; a family who must remake their inner world while going about the routine of their lives in an outside world which has lost its points of reference, where there are no longer any signposts. A world in process of returning to chaos.' The agent had not been impressed. He tried something more direct on Patsy. 'It is about people who have been so badly shocked that some kind of *dis*location has taken place. You might say, I have tried to see a small area of London through the eyes of someone who has never been exposed to civilisation before.' A countryman himself, he had this feeling whenever he stood in Piccadilly Circus.

Patsy said, 'London isn't civilisation.'

She is so thick! he thought. Why should it seem important to try to get ideas to penetrate that dark tangle? He tried again. 'We have lost our identity.'

'I could have told you *that*,' she said scornfully. 'Ever since we lost our Empire.'

'But think what it *means*! Without a corporate identity we find ourselves trying to do what society once did for us. We try to find our own way. It's not possible, of course. But there is some sort of inner effort which we have to make which once wasn't required of us, which perhaps shouldn't be required of us. Don't you feel that, Patsy? When you wrestle with these enormous issues – which I see reduced to single statements on your car windscreen – doesn't it all seem too much for you on your own?'

'I don't mind being on my own,' she said defensively.

'Of course you mind!' He was becoming passionate about it and he could not understand why. 'Man does nothing on his own. The solitary individual does not reach the Antarctic; he may be the person who actually stands there and plants the flag, but there are people behind him who have brought him thus far.

48

One scientist may take the leap that results in a great discovery, but he will not have pioneered the whole territory on his own. When we go right out on our own, we lose our way and our minds.'

'I don't think I've deserved that, Murdoch. It was Hugh who left me, remember.'

'What *are* you talking about?'

But she had gone. He watched her marshalling children and dog for a walk; and then, when the garden was empty, he remained staring across the lawn to the hedge which so badly needed clipping. He heard Janet saying, 'What goes on out there? Now that I have more time to give to the outside world, I find I am unable to make sense of it. Can't you help? Can't anyone help?' That had been several months ago and he had not taken her seriously. But now it struck him like a blow in the stomach that the woman in his book, and in the book before that, the woman without identity, for whom there were no signposts, for whom a kind of *dis*location had taken place, was Janet.

All the way in to town Deutzia exclaimed, 'Primroses! See! See the primroses! How very fortunate we are to live in such a beautiful place. And celandine! Just the colour I used to love, though I couldn't wear it now, not with this old white head of mine! And *what* is that little pink flower?'

'I didn't think you liked the country,' Katrina said.

'I haven't liked it so much since they cut down the bus service.' Deutzia was in high spirits now that she was on her way to town. 'I should never have moved here had I known how isolated I was going to be. But on a morning like this I don't regret it one bit.'

'So the dismembering of the bus service was withheld from you in mercy?' Janet said. 'Otherwise we shouldn't have you among us.'

Katrina turned her head to stare at her mother.

Deutzia said, 'I don't know what you mean by that.' But she understood the caustic tone. She fanned herself with one glove.

'I talk too much, I know that. Wait until *you* live alone.'

'I practically do,' Janet said indifferently.

'Mum!' Katrina protested. 'What's got into you? Look! Look at the pretty lambs!' She thought: for goodness sake, Mum, look at them before D tells you to!

Katrina could see that it had been a bad idea to bring Deutzia. 'I suppose it would be mean to leave her behind,' she had said, imagining she was echoing her mother's thoughts – her mother, after all, was the one who usually suffered Deutzia with good grace. But there was nothing gracious about Janet today.

Katrina had never thought of her mother in moral terms. In her mind she had given her the attributes of a friendly wood sprite – a soft, brown, gentle creature, but rather unpredictable. She had relished the unpredictability, as had Malcolm. Its form was innocent enough – a tendency to provocative teasing and a certain contrariness which meant it would not be wise to take reactions for granted. What one could rely on was acceptance. She accepted other people and because of this never seemed to find any occasion for being really hurtful. There was a shyness appropriate to a woodland creature, a reserve which distanced her from those outside her immediate circle, but although she always viewed the world from a field's length away, she had given the impression of enjoying what she saw.

Yet here she was this morning, looking almost sullen and being so stingingly nasty to poor old Deutzia.

'All so green after the snow!' Deutzia said.

Charcoal, Janet thought. What would they say if I told them it was only a charcoal sketch?

They came to the outskirts of the small town and Deutzia applied her mind to the essentials of the day. 'Now, I know you want to go to the supermarket, Janet. But if we *did* have time, I would like to look in Lucinda's and perhaps just glance round the Gallery. Lovely animal paintings! Do you know his work? He has done the Queen's corgies. Ah! Now *I* am going to pay for the parking, Katrina!'

It was still early in the morning and the car park was almost empty save for three cars which had disgorged families crawling with recalcitrant children and dogs. At the moment a baby was evincing a marked lack of interest in its potty while a greyhound was disdaining to drink from its bowl. The parents were young, cheerful and patient.

'Ah, how that takes one back,' Deutzia said vaguely. 'Now, when we have been to the supermarket, you must both have coffee with me. I insist!'

It was inevitable that she would ask them to have coffee with her, but somehow Katrina had not foreseen it. She had forgotten Deutzia's craving for company and had imagined her selfishly insisting on going her own way once she got into town. It would be the same at lunch, unless by that time Deutzia had met one of her cronies. Katrina had banked on having either coffee or lunch alone with her mother. This was the one time when you had another person at your mercy; once seated and served you could rely on at least twenty minutes – half an hour if it was lunch – when they could not decently get away from you. Katrina had a lot to say to her mother.

'Now, what is it that you want?' Deutzia asked when they had tugged baskets free of their entanglement in surrounding trolleys. 'I expect you have made a list. I have to list everything now. And I leave messages to myself all over the house. It must look like a treasure hunt sometimes.' She was overcome with sadness at her plight. 'Except that there isn't any treasure.'

Not only had Janet not made a list, she had not even considered the matter of purchases. The supermarket was small but its shelves had recently been restocked and the variety of choice was overwhelming. Janet recalled how Katrina had protested when she was studying the courses available at universities. 'There is *too much*! I wish I had been born years ago and Daddy had had to save every penny for me to have this wonderful opportunity never hitherto enjoyed by a member of our family. And it was all desperately important and only the one chance. It would have meant something then. And I would have written a book about it in later years – *my* brilliant career!'

Janet stopped so abruptly that a woman pushing a trolley bumped into her thus causing a series of small collisions more appropriate to a shunting yard than a food store. 'Katrina, my little one! Are you happy doing Management Studies?'

Katrina said, 'However did you . . .?'

'Tell me, *tell* me!'

'Yes, I will! I want to. But later . . .'

Janet looked at the shelves laden with dun-coloured tins bearing indecipherable legends. 'I must make a joke of this,' she thought as her heart began to pound. Aloud, she said, 'I wish I lived in a mud hut and your father went out and hunted for food and all I had to do was cook it. Once man stopped hunting he should at least have undertaken the shopping.'

'Hadn't we better move along?' Katrina was now more impatient than ever to get the shopping over and done with. 'You don't want anything here, do you?'

'Don't I?'

'Well, you have never yet fed us out of tins!'

They moved away. But where should I go? Janet wondered, fighting to master panic.

'What do you *want*?' Katrina demanded.

Janet tried to think in terms of a menu, but her head was stuffed with cotton wool. She reached out a hand and Katrina said, 'Mum, you'll get fresh fish at The Ark, surely?'

Janet closed her eyes. 'Katrina, will you please go away and wait outside. I can't think with you pouncing on me all the time.'

Katrina turned on her heel and strode away. Janet waited until Deutzia caught up with her, then she said, 'I have a headache, Deutzia. Could you possibly take me in hand?'

'Yes, of course, my dear. What do you want?'

'Whatever you think I want.'

'But what are you short of?' Deutzia looked around her vaguely. 'After all, your deep freeze is so much bigger than mine.'

Janet felt a slithering and sliding somewhere deep beneath the hatches. She made a great effort to keep herself in ballast. 'A bit of everything, I should think.' Even that involved endless choice: white bread, wholemeal bread, whole grain bread, granary bread (very indigestible according to Deutzia). She bought wholemeal bread because this was what Deutzia seemed to expect of her. The same performance followed with flour. She chose stoneground flour. She chose cereal with honey and raisins. The choice of fruit juice was overwhelming and she ended up with a concoction containing cocoanut and passion fruit. 'I don't believe a word of it!' Deutzia said. She turned the carton over and read details of additives.

'I thought you had bought the shop!' Katrina said crossly when they eventually joined her.

The sun was bright now and light sparked from the pavement as they walked. Janet put on sun glasses. Ahead was the town square. Deutzia pointed to the restaurant on the far side. Janet was finding it difficult to keep her balance and she had stopped several times on one pretext or another – pointing irrelevantly in shop windows, stopping to admire undistinguished flowers in a window-box – to disguise a tendency to lurch. She looked at the cobbled square in dismay, wondering how she could possibly venture out into the large open space. But she knew that whatever happened she must not take Katrina's arm because once she did that it would all be over with her and she would not dare to walk unaided again. Slowly, step by step, she advanced. 'How difficult cobblestones are!' she exclaimed. 'I'm glad I didn't live when all the streets were like this.'

Katrina walked ahead, fists bunched in the pockets of her anorak. It was acceptable for Deutzia, who was over eighty, to make such a fuss, but she was ashamed of her mother.

In the little restaurant, Deutzia said, as though picking up the threads of an interrupted conversation, 'Of course, I never cook out of tins, either. I make a point of that. But some people make such a performance of cooking nowadays. I had the Percivals and Patsy to dinner last week. Not quite my sort of people, but one must try. After all, a village only offers limited scope for hospitality. Well, of course, they all talked about this nuclear business. And I know we are all going to die in the nuclear winter, but it still doesn't seem real to me. So I just let it go over my head. But what really upset me was that I had spent *days* preparing the meal and that tiresome woman Mrs Percival walked round the kitchen exclaiming about my still using aluminium saucepans until I felt I was poisoning them.'

Katrina turned her head away and stared accusingly round the room which had a bay window which bellied out like a small prow overlooking the square. The walls were panelled in a light, pinkish pine which Katrina thought repulsive and the tables were covered with pale lime cloths which were undoubtedly tasteful and, therefore, in Katrina's view, worse than repulsive. A little bowl of violets had been placed on each table, a felicity which had led Deutzia to exclaim, 'They *never* have plastic flowers here!' There was a large 'no smoking' notice. The proprietors owned both the restaurant and the boutique beneath and crocheted skirts and dresses, pastel sweaters and a variety of expensive scarves were displayed on the wall of the stairway. Deutzia pointed to a ribbed tomato oblong which Katrina thought resembled an overgrown tabard.

'Now, I can just see Katrina in that, can't you?' She addressed Janet as if Katrina were still so young she could best be communicated with through her mother.

Katrina said, 'You never will see me in it.'

'It would need dressing up, of course. A little scarf and a belt, perhaps.' She fanned herself. 'Summer is coming, after all, and you won't be very comfortable in trousers and boots when it gets warmer, will you? I find it quite warm enough now. I wonder whether we could have the window open . . .' She looked round for someone to pester and gave a little cry of delight.

'Excuse me, I must just . . .'

An elderly man at the window table was struggling to his feet. His female companion's amused expression suggested that in her opinion such gallantries should be dispensed with once they can no longer be performed with ease. Deutzia rewarded his efforts with a kiss. The other woman extended a thin, elegant claw and they talked while the old man laboriously resumed his seat.

After a few minutes Deutzia rejoined Janet and Katrina. 'Oh dear, how embarrassing! They insist that I have lunch with them. I couldn't refuse. We haven't seen each other for months and we are all getting older so these opportunities *are* precious . . .'

'When shall we pick you up?' Katrina was eager to settle matters. 'And where?'

'Oh, I rather think Roddie will run me home.'

'It's not just round the corner.'

'Even so, you don't ask someone to lunch and then leave them to make their own arrangements. Roddie would certainly expect to run me home.'

'I expect she is now telling them how badly she feels because she couldn't possibly have asked us to wait around for her, particularly as you haven't been well and I am so impatient,' Katrina said when she and her mother eventually sat down to eat in a dimly-lit, smoke-filled cavern.

Janet had not objected to Katrina's choice. She had welcomed the haziness of the atmosphere as if it were her own natural habitat. When Katrina lit her second cigarette she made no protest.

Katrina said, 'Sorry about this. But I have to talk.'

Janet wondered whether it was because they had been drained of colour that the jacket potato and its accompanying froth of cheese and butter had lost their goodness, or whether her sense of taste was now affected. It was very difficult to digest food which looked so unappetising and tasted like cotton wool. Cotton wool in my head, cotton wool in my stomach! Pills would be better – at least I would only have to swallow once.

Katrina had not started to eat. She was finishing her cigarette while she talked. '. . . and his *wife* came to see me and made a scene! It was like something out of George Eliot! I didn't know people still thought they had these proprietary rights!' In the dim light she looked like a very sad Harlequin. The fingers which stubbed out the cigarette shook. She said hoarsely, 'It was all so hideous. She was crying. I didn't know anyone could *feel* like that . . . still . . .'

A married man, Janet thought. But who? Why wasn't I listening?

Katrina said, 'I don't know what to do.'

'Don't see him for a while.' After all, time heals – and if it doesn't, God help us all!

'He's my *tutor*, Mum!'

This kind of situation would always have been beyond me, Janet thought. I am not an advice giver. I have given what I have to give and now that my children have left home they should manage, or mismanage, their own affairs.

'It hurts,' Katrina said bleakly. 'It hurts so much.' Just as if it was her first aching tooth and Mother must kiss the pain away. As Janet said nothing, she asked, 'Did it ever happen to you?'

'No. There was only your father. There weren't a lot of young men on Mull. I grew up on one island and married another. I am fifty and I have spent all my life on one island or another.'

'Don't bother to go on. I don't think John Donne is the answer to my problem.'

For a moment the haze seemed to clear and Janet pounced through the gap. 'Do you have a problem? If there are no proprietary rights then it's the open season for predators.'

She watched as Katrina seemed to fold herself in half. 'Did you expect me to sympathise? I'm a clanswoman. Married women with children are my clan.'

Katrina's voice came muffled from the region of her stomach. 'I shall never tell you anything again as long as I live.'

They only spoke once on the way home. Katrina had been forced to stop while a herd of cows made its leisurely way across the road. She sat tapping her fingers on the steering wheel, maddened by the ponderous beasts with their milky breath and laden udders. Janet said, with the new sharpness which characterised much of her speech, 'The vicar called last week. Did one of you put him up to it?'

'Not I.'

'Someone did. He would never think of it himself. He's too busy girding himself for the battle against women priests.'

'Well, it wasn't me.'

'He asked if anything was troubling me, so I told him I worried about the Eucharist prayer ". . . send us out in the power of

Thy spirit to live and work to Thy praise and glory . . ." I told him I hadn't been "out" for years.'

'What did he say to that?'

'He muttered something about going to Matins instead. His only practical suggestion was that it might do me good to become a chauffeur for the halt and maimed among his flock.'

'The way you drive the number would soon be doubled.'

This observation appeared to please Janet who gave an appreciative bark of laughter. It must also have satisfied her that Katrina was not the culprit and no more was said of the vicar's call.

Over supper, however, she suddenly announced, 'I feel like a car which has some mechanical failure. There is a queue of people eager to peer about in my bonnet.'

Katrina said, 'You can count me out.'

Murdoch said, 'Anyone found contemplating obscenity on my wife will be thrashed within an inch of his life.'

'Including the vicar?'

'I don't think he would know how to set about it. I doubt if he has ever lifted a bonnet to any purpose.'

After supper Murdoch went to his study while Katrina did the washing-up. Janet collected flowers from the garden and arranged them in a bowl in the sitting room. She howled as she did this and then, holding the discarded stems to her breast, she went out of the front door, making little mewling noises which she switched off as she passed the kitchen window.

'Where are you going?' Katrina demanded.

'To the dustbin.'

'Why are you doing that?'

'Mayn't I do anything without being questioned?'

Katrina slammed the window shut.

Janet mewled over the dustbin and then turned and walked towards the house, moving slowly and carefully, her grief like a bowl full to the brim which must be contained without spilling a drop.

Katrina met her in the hall. 'We'll watch television. There's bound to be something on the news to cheer us up.'

'There won't be any news yet.'

There was a discussion programme on the role of television. A BBC pundit talked earnestly about urban deprivation and race riots, rape and child molestation and the importance of bringing reality into the sitting room.

Janet said, 'Is he suggesting that reality is race riots, murder, rape and sex-on-demand?'

'Sshh . . .'

'And that the sooner this becomes reality for everyone the better? That there is something unfulfilled about people who have been deprived of these attentions?'

'Sshhhhhhh . . .'

Janet, however, was now addressing the BBC pundit. She stood, arms akimbo, one hip thrust forward, as though confronting a live person. Katrina was reminded that her mother was no mean actress. 'And what about my kind of reality – the lives where nothing much changes from hour to hour, from day to day, from year to year? When are you going to bring *that* into the bar parlour?' Her face was flushed, her voice getting louder. 'God knows how you would make it compete with all the bashing and the slashing and the blasphemy. But you must have some little genius tucked away in a corner just waiting for a challenge like that. It's the only challenge left – you've exploited all the others!'

'Mum!'

'I'm not ashamed. I am not *ashamed* and you are not going to make me ashamed!' Janet turned and ran out of the room, holding her hands cupped over her mouth. Katrina remained sitting staring woodenly at the television screen.

Half an hour later Katrina opened the study door. 'I'm going to bed,' she said to Murdoch. 'Sorry to interrupt you, but I think Mum has gone off her head.' She slammed the door and thudded up the stairs.

Janet was in the sitting room when Murdoch came in. There was only a light from a small table-lamp and she was by the window, staring out into the darkness. She looked quite peaceful. He held out a tray on which there was a cup of hot milk and two biscuits. She regarded the offering in surprise and then said, 'That was very kind of you, Murdoch. I'll have the biscuits; you drink the hot milk, it makes me sick.'

He sat down beside her.

'Katrina is unhappy,' she said.

'Yes, I know.'

'A married man.' She laughed wryly. 'I thought they had it all sorted out, but it still happens.'

'It still hurts, too.'

'Should I have done something?'

'There is nothing one can do, is there?'

'That's a comfort. The only real comfort is being helpless.'

But she did not sleep that night. The house was dying, bleeding to death. She saw the flaked skin on the walls, the deep scores in the fabric. All the things they had neglected over the years reproached her at every turn – the terrible wheezing of the hot-water system, the groaning of the lavatory cistern as it roused itself for another effort for which it no longer had the necessary force, the complaint of stair treads, the agony of floorboards, the wind howling through broken tiles, all cried out that it was enough. This had gone on far too long, the house could endure no more. And she had not the resources to pour into it to restore it to order, nor even to alleviate its lesser ailments.

5

The following weekend Stephanie went to see the doctor. He had been thinking about Janet and hesitatingly volunteered the idea that 'perhaps your mother needs her breakdown.'

Stephanie put this idea down with a withering reference to Erich Fromm. The doctor, daunted, was willing for Erich Fromm to take the blame.

'And anyway,' Stephanie said, 'it is not a breakdown.'

In which case, the doctor could see that he was quite incapable of diagnosing whatever mysterious ailment it was from which Janet Saunders was suffering. He therefore consented to Stephanie's suggestion that Janet should see a psychiatrist, inconsistent though this might be with the insistence that a breakdown be ruled out of court.

When a few days later he telephoned to tell her that he had arranged for Janet to see Dr Georgina Potter, Stephanie almost shrieked down the telephone, "*That* woman!'

Dr Potter had a reputation for indiscretion, bad temper, and making impulsive and capricious judgements which her many detractors felt were in no way justified by her occasional flashes of insight and an enormous capacity for work. On the day on which she saw Janet she had been up all night dealing with a crisis at a women's prison. Included among the papers on her desk was a letter from Stephanie telling her all the things which were *not* wrong with her mother and going on to say that while she appreciated that Dr Potter was a disciple of Melanie Klein, she herself had considerable reservations about this lady's work – which she elaborated in some detail – and considered that many of her theories were based on false premises – of which she did not give a single example. She concluded by saying that in her view Janet would have been more receptive to a male psychiatrist. 'One would like to know more about this young woman's infancy,' Dr Potter had commented, putting the letter to one side but not out of her mind.

So she and Janet faced each other, neither with high hopes of this encounter.

Janet saw hair in which the birds of the air might nest in summer, bushed about a face in which every feature had suffered a misfortune – an eyelid drooped permanently over one of the beady eyes, a monstrously flanged nose overhung the crooked mouth. Perhaps with a face so grotesque, eccentricity was the only answer; if so, Dr Potter might have been said to have embraced this solution rather than being driven to it. She wore a long black robe with batwing sleeves enlivened by a heavy rope of glittering emerald green beads which served as an erratic pendulum. The awareness that the beads were emerald green gave Janet an irrational feeling of having made some kind of connection.

Dr Potter saw one of those quiet, anonymous women she occasionally noticed in supermarkets. Calm, unsurprised, never guilty of embarrassing their friends and family with wild outbursts of enthusiasm or anger – women who seemed to be in a perpetual state of balance. And yet, because of that very quietness – and the shyness which is almost always associated with it – giving an impression of having kept something to themselves, something which most people have had to hand over as the price of adulthood. She had felt she wanted to turn them upside down and shake them until their secret dropped out. But, of course, you would not be allowed to continue in practice if you resorted to such tactics. You could get up to most things in psychiatry so long as you did not physically abuse the client – *that* was the surgeon's prerogative.

Dr Potter said, giving a particularly vicious swing to the emerald rope, 'Tell me something about your childhood.'

'Is that necessary?'

'Probably not. But we have to do it for the form book.'

Janet, rather amused at the idea of her placid father as stallion and her doughty mother as mare, drew a picture of a home

61

where there was constant bickering but a great deal of love.

'An island and all that love must have been rather stifling.'

'We weren't stifled by it.'

They had had no need to foregather in the same room (this, in fact, had seldom proved a success) and had been content to be busy in different parts of the house, garden or island, aware of one another's presence without the aggravation of the actuality. She had been so secure in her parents' love that separating had not initially presented problems.

Dr Potter noted, 'This family has long tentacles.' Later, she wrote, 'Love at home — yes. I don't hear a child crying in this woman. So why this lack of self-confidence? Vicar has told her to forget herself. Silly old fool! People who are uneasy with themselves find it very difficult to think about anything else.'

'But your schooling? That must have taken you away from the island — at the secondary stage, in any case.'

'I went to a school on the mainland for one term,' Janet said indifferently. 'But I didn't like it. They tried to teach things that were none of their business — how to dress and speak and "comport oneself". So I ran away. I just ran away all the time. In the end I had my lessons at home from a peripatetic teacher.' She smiled reminiscently, 'Janet's peri, we used to call her.'

Not such an anonymous woman, after all, Dr Potter revised her opinion. 'This woman will find means of getting her own way when it is important to her.'

'And your own family?' she said.

She wrote down details of the children, taking particular interest in Stephanie. Oldest child, pushed off its mother's knee to make way for the newcomer, always put in charge, domineering and *very* insecure. So what does she do? She studies psychology! Dr Potter gave a gleeful hoot of laughter.

'And your husband?'

Ah, of course, Murdoch Saunders, author of those extraordinary books!

'He didn't come with you this morning?'

'My son brought me here.'

'Why not your husband?' If you ask this woman for the salt

she will explain why the porridge is cold!

'My son wanted to come.'

'So by inference your husband didn't. A pity. I should like to have met him. His is a most unusual gift.'

'He is not very good at talking about it.'

'I am quite capable of doing the talking.'

The same could not be said for her client. Janet provided facts about her children but gave little indication of her feelings for them. 'They are not troublesome – they don't even protest!'

'By which you mean they present no problem to society?'

'I doubt if they think much in terms of society.'

'Another island?'

'Stephanie *talks* about social problems but I don't think she does much more than put a toe in the water.'

Dr Potter knew when to keep silent. After a moment, Janet said, 'Do *you* go to Greenham Common?'

'I have been, yes.'

'I wanted to. But I wasn't well enough to travel on the day.'

'Only the one day?' This hardly had the ring of social involvement. 'Why did you want to go?'

'I felt I should like to understand about Patsy. Patsy is my daughter-in-law.'

'Tell me about Patsy.'

'She isn't like us. She wears what I think of as cottage industry clothes – the draggly, droopy variety, not the expensive wool ones. And she has causes stuck all over her like leeches. But she wasn't always like that. It has come about gradually since she married Hugh – the ill-fitting clothes and the causes. I sometimes feel it is us as a family that she is demonstrating about.'

'And you? Do you support any of her causes?'

'Me?' Oh, we're not going to talk about me! 'I don't have the time.'

Towards the end of the session, Dr Potter said, 'What do you think is wrong with you?'

'The doctor says I am over-tired. My children all have different ideas ...' Dr Potter noted 'unprepared to discuss her illness at this stage'.

63

'Would you like to come to see me again?' she asked.

'Would you like me to come?' Janet was polite as if it was a social invitation.

Dr Potter reflected for a few moments and then said, 'I think perhaps we should leave it that you will get in touch with me should you feel it would be helpful to see me again.'

After Janet had gone, her secretary said that the son wished to see her. 'He says he won't go until he has seen you.'

'The son?' Dr Potter paused on the verge of outrage and glanced down at her notes. 'Which son is this?'

'The married one.'

'Ah yes. Married to the Patsy. All right. I'll see him.'

Hugh had been instructed by Stephanie to insist on being given some information about Dr Potter's findings. Dr Potter proved more than willing to oblige.

'Each of us has a model of life,' she told him, sitting at her desk looking uncomfortably like a tipsy judge, wig slightly awry. 'And we observe what our model leads us to expect.'

'Yes,' he said. 'I can see that.'

'I'm sure you can. But we shall perhaps conclude this more expeditiously if you refrain from giving each of my statements your vote.'

It was all Hugh could do to refrain from saying, 'Yes, m'Lud.'

'As I was saying, we all have a model of life. Sometimes, for a few people, the model is broken. This seems to be the case with your mother, but why this has happened, I don't yet know.'

'I suppose scientists have a series of models,' Hugh said, rather at a loss. 'When one fails, they make another . . .'

'We are not talking about scientists, though, are we? We are talking about your mother, who does not strike me as being in the least scientific. And when we make another model, we have to do it with the materials at our disposal. So it is a matter of collecting a lot of shattered fragments, and that is not easy.'

'I don't think anything has happened to shatter my mother,' Hugh said uneasily.

'Life is a series of shattering experiences, Mr Saunders.'

A look of pain darkened Hugh's eyes but he made no reply. It was apparent that if there were members of this family who were prepared to snap up challenges, Dr Potter was not seeing them this morning. She went on, 'An alternative explanation is that a breakdown is sometimes a protection. In your mother's case, I don't yet know what she might be protecting. Have you any idea?'

He looked baffled, a reaction which she guessed was *his* form of protection.

'Come, come! You are her son. You must have some ideas. Your sister, Stephanie, who has been in touch with me, doesn't seem short of theories, albeit negative ones.'

'Stephanie is very clever but she does tend to trip over her own brains from time to time.'

Dr Potter looked at him with increased interest. 'Why did you leave your wife?' she asked abruptly.

The baffled look intensified.

'Come! You insisted on seeing me. Now you must answer a few questions.'

He accepted this illogical statement without protest. He must have been pathetically easy to discipline as a child. He said, 'Each morning I tried to put my house in order and Patsy spent the day taking it apart again.'

'One can have too much order.'

'And too little. For example, I am one of those people who actually likes to have breakfast before I leave home for work.' He was quite animated about this.

'*No* regular meals?'

'The only thing Patsy ever did on time was to catch the coach to Greenham Common.'

'There was only the one coach?'

'Yes.'

'That would seem to argue a certain ability to organise herself.'

'Precisely! She can do it when she wants to. But order is a necessity to me and a threat to Patsy.'

'How much did this upset your mother?'

'I think she was very upset for the children. I have a feeling she blamed me for leaving home. She is very fond of Patsy. Patsy *is* very easy to love.'

'Nothing that has so far been said would seem to support that.'

'Oh, but she is.' He applied himself to the righting of a wrong impression much as he might have corrected a legal document. 'She is affectionate, generous, very loyal ...' He ticked the attributes off on his fingers.

'Is she as intelligent as you?'

He went bright red to the tips of his ears.

'And when you had arguments, I suppose you drove her into a corner?'

He had assumed his baffled expression. Dr Potter said, 'Has it ever occurred to you to look upon your wife as a princess locked in a pattern of behaviour from which she is unable to escape?'

He reflected on this. 'That may well be so. But it makes it more hopeless, doesn't it?' He was no knight errant, but a country solicitor unqualified to deal with dragons.

When he left he said with unexpected intensity, 'What my mother needs, Doctor, is not analysing, but healing.'

'You can't have the one without the other from a poor mortal! And as all that the Holy Spirit has moved your vicar to say is that she should "forget herself" I think you might be wiser to stick with me!'

'I don't think you should see her again,' Hugh said as he drove his mother home.

'Why not? I liked her emerald beads.'

'You haven't lost your ability to concentrate on the inessential. That's a good thing.' He sounded as though he might find genuinely affectionate comfort in this.

'How did you get on with her?' Janet demanded.

'I thought she was impertinent.'

'Stephanie may feel *you* concentrated on inessentials.'

Hugh made no comment and Janet went on, 'Stephanie thought that being a solicitor you would elicit significant information from Dr Potter simply by asking for it.'

'How ridiculous!' Hugh said uncomfortably, recalling how few questions he had, in fact, asked.

'Stephanie has a respect for the law which far exceeds her respect for psychology.' Janet reflected on this for a few minutes and then said, 'We are a very law-abiding family, aren't we? Do you think that is because we believe that it is the cornerstone of civilisation, or simply that it has never inconvenienced us very much?'

'Mother, how long have you been doing all this thinking?'

'Didn't you think I was capable of thought?'

'Well, not of putting it all together like that.'

'Don't worry. It's all very random, really.' She sat back, suddenly tired. They travelled in silence until Hugh turned the car on to the lane leading down to the village, then she said, 'And when is Malcolm coming?'

'Malcolm?'

'Yes, your brother. He must be included, surely? You are all taking it in turns. Katrina was here last weekend. Who drew up the rota? Stephanie, I suppose.'

'It is only natural that we should be concerned, Mother.'

'You don't think your father is capable of looking after me? Capable – or willing?'

'Father is doing his revise.'

Janet looked down at the water in the stream, black now save where needles of light penetrated the trees' dark mass. 'Have you ever thought what a relief it would be to be ill – really ill, for weeks and weeks and weeks? So ill that you drifted out of range of concern of any kind?'

'I think perhaps your GP has the answer to all this. You are overtired and you need a long rest. We are becoming too sophisticated and we have lost sight of simple solutions.'

He turned the car towards the village street where he was immediately confronted with a number of simple solutions. Patsy's car stood on a grass verge near her cottage, festooned with stickers advocating nuclear-free zones, noninterference in Nicaragua, troop withdrawal from Northern Ireland and sanctions against South Africa. Her near neighbour was obviously

67

not of her political persuasion. Since no one had thought it worthwhile to produce a sticker saying "Soviets out of Afghanistan" he had remedied this omission with one of his own devising. The two cars stood bonnet to bonnet. The neighbour's car was large and muscular with teeth – one snap and it could swallow Patsy's Mini.

They drove through the village and were on the narrow uphill lane when Hugh said, 'Those stickers are all black and white, like their literature. That is how they see issues.'

Janet said, 'No colour. All dark, so dark. Hugh, can you stop the car please!'

The request was made with such urgency that he jammed his foot hard on the brake and the car shuddered to a halt. 'What was it?' he asked, peering through the windscreen.

'I'll walk from here.'

'Good God! I thought I'd run over a cat or a dog.'

'I need fresh air. Please, Hugh.'

He looked at her, anxiety rendering his usually bland face as wrinkled as wash-leather. 'Mother, what is it?'

'It's the darkness. It starts on top of my head and works its way right down through me. It's worst of all when it gets to my stomach.'

'You wouldn't like me to leave the car here and walk with you? I can come back for it later.'

Janet said wearily, 'If it will help you. I can see that you have to deliver me in one piece.'

He left the car near the entrance to a field and they walked slowly uphill towards the house. Hugh looked about him as he walked, making mental notes of his surroundings which would be recorded later in his diary. Since he left Patsy and the children he had made a daily record of sensual experiences – an under- taking few, even among his intimate relations, would have asso- ciated with him. Quietly, meticulously, he noted the small things which might otherwise be overlooked and so not pass into memory's safe-keeping. Already, he realised that even at a time when one might be tempted to see life as a long stretch of unadulterated misery, a surprising amount of pleasure is incorporated into everyday experience. One wet January day, travelling by train from Sussex into London, he had noted umbrellas folded like wet cabbages, umbrellas large as café sunshades, black, striped; white and blue, and fun umbrellas – one with a Donald Duck handle – carried by people not amused by another day's rain. Rain soaking into the little leftover commons of Clapham, Balham and Streatham. When he reread this entry, he smelled the rain and found himself refreshed as he had probably not been at the time. So now, in the hope of future refreshment, he noted hawthorn white and dusty pink; hedgerows feathered with Queen Anne's lace; a rusty farm gate open and – beyond an apple orchard dotted with buttercups – a dappled cow rubbing its head against a wooden paling . . . One day he would completely rewrite his life, imposing order on it, extracting joy from pain, redeeming loss.

Beside him, Janet walked head down, darkness crushing her chest, weighing heavy as a dead child in her womb. She tried desperately not to snatch for breath, which might alarm Hugh.

Hugh wrote in his mind's diary – "spring's climax, summer's threshold . . ."

6

'People are so difficult nowadays,' Mrs Beaney, the vicar's wife, said to Deutzia. 'They want an open-air service, if you please. Because it's Pentecost. And we shall have all the other denominations there, to say nothing of the Evangelicals. Most of them don't understand what it's about – only that "something" took place in the open air.'

Deutzia, interested in more recent events, exclaimed, 'There goes Janet!'

Mrs Beaney frowned out of the window, short-sightedness augmenting a perpetual air of having come down in the world. She had been a beauty, but the high temper which had once been splendidly matched by auburn hair had gradually been damped down, leaving the faded face more irritable than mettlesome.

'She is probably driving into town,' Deutzia said. 'All on her own, too. If I had known I would have kept her company.'

The doctor's young wife, who had called at the vicarage to sell flags for cancer relief and found herself taking coffee, wondered if she might leave now that they were all standing up. She fluttered ineffectually between the two old women like a pretty little moth.

'Do you think she is well enough to be out on her own?' Deutzia said to her.

'Well, I suppose she must be.' Ann Bellamy tried to look as if she had no idea that there was anything wrong with Janet Saunders.

Mrs Beaney had long since decided that discretion is the last resort of those who want a quiet life. A quiet life in a village being a kind of death, she had adopted as her maxim "the truth never hurt anyone" and now enjoyed a reputation for forthrightness to which she was pleased to conform. She said, 'If she is on her own, she has no one to blame but herself. She has never tried to make a friend of anyone in the village.'

'She has spent herself looking after Murdoch,' Deutzia said in mitigation.

'I know that everything in that house centres round him. But who planned it that way? It is women who really control what goes on in a house. For me, of course, it is different.' Her eyes rested on the shabby sofa and worn carpet. 'Our house is subject to constant invasion . . .' She lost the thread of her argument. Deutzia obligingly picked it up for her.

'I have to admit that outside her own home Janet is not as selfless as one might imagine. She can be quite ruthless if she doesn't want to be involved with people.'

'She takes part in the dramatic society's productions,' Ann Bellamy pointed out.

'She takes a *leading* part,' Mrs Beaney corrected. 'But she never lifts a finger to clear up afterwards.'

'She is a very good actress, though.'

'*Very*.' The bitterness of this response was as impressive a tribute as any amount of praise. 'She makes the others look painfully amateur.'

Ann Bellamy flushed. As Mrs Beaney was aware, Ann was invariably cast in any part demanding a presentable young female whether fifteen or thirty.

Deutzia said, 'She has persuaded one or two very good instrumentalists to come to the music society.'

'Oh yes. And she does do quite a lot at the pageant, helping with the costumes. But there it ends. We are lucky if we get so much as a jar of marmalade for the bring and buy stall and she can't even be relied on to do the church flowers. I know these are small things, but they have to be done.' Who should know this better than the daughter of a bishop who should have had other things to do than concern herself with the small change of village life?

Ann Bellamy said firmly, 'I must be on my way.'

'Where?' Deutzia demanded. 'Where are you going?'

'Well, I . . .' Ann muttered something about early lunch and Deutzia turned away.

'I thought perhaps you were going in to town.'

Mrs Beaney said, 'Is there something you particularly want to get?'

Deutzia said she needed to restock her freezer.

Mrs Beaney said, 'What a pity Hector has the car. Otherwise I would have taken you.'

Ann Bellamy saw Deutzia's distress as the dazzling prospect of a trip to town was withdrawn before she had had time to contemplate it and good-nature triumphed over the desire to put her feet up on a garden chair. 'I could take you this afternoon,' she offered. 'If you don't mind risking yourself in my ancient Beetle.'

Deutzia expressed willingness to risk herself and they left the vicarage together. 'It is so embarrassing to have to depend on the kindness of neighbours when one's own relatives live nearby. I can't think why Janet didn't ask me to join her.'

'Perhaps she wasn't going to town? And anyway, I shall enjoy the outing. I find life rather dull here,' Ann Bellamy confided. 'But it is difficult to get a part-time job. I had wondered whether I dared offer to do Mr Saunders' typing.'

'It would probably give you melancholia, my dear. I did try to suggest to him once that there is a need for books which people can enjoy.'

'What did he say?'

'He said he didn't "sit down each day resolved to give people a pain in the arse". He can be rather crude sometimes, I'm afraid.'

'He probably doesn't mean his books to be depressing. I always find he leaves me with a feeling of hope that man won't pull out the plug.'

'Oh dear! I'm afraid I need rather more than that!' Deutzia came to her garden gate and rested a hand on it. 'Now, what time will you come for me?'

'Would two o'clock be too early?'

'I'll be waiting at the door.'

After Ann had walked away, Deutzia remained by the gate,

looking across the road to the banks of the stream, the water now hidden by the bright green branches of sallows. 'Pull out the plug!' she said. 'Oh dear, oh dear, oh dear!'

Janet was driving in the direction of the town. She was not quite sure why, but perhaps by the time she arrived it would all fall into place, just as on stage, when the next bit of the action has gone completely from one's mind, the cue is given and the lines are ready to be spoken. That was what happened on stage. The dreams were different – standing in the wings, not having learned the lines; or worse, on stage, realising that other people were enacting an unfamiliar play. Very soon, with no hope of escape, one was going to let everyone down. What would they say? How could one ever live with them again?

But this was not a dream, only the usual stage lapse of concentration – it would all come right the moment she got into the supermarket car park. The supermarket was very important. It was a symbol of modern living and she must learn to find her way about it. Once she had done that, she would be well again.

The road stretched over the heath like a giant toll-bridge with wilderness on either side. The wind buffeted the car and she had to grip the steering wheel tighter and tighter, fighting to keep the car on its course while waves of nausea assailed her.

And suddenly, there it was – a rough stake driven into the grass at the side of the road, bearing a board with the invitation "Come to the Fayre". The cue given in the nick of time. She accepted it gratefully. An arrow pointed westwards down a narrow track. On either side the heath bore the scars of clay workings and fine white sand was blown on to the windscreen. Its glitter hurt her eyes. She remembered running down a sandy track, her eyes stinging, crying out joyfully, 'The sea! The sea!' For a moment it ceased to be a memory and she *was* that enraptured child plunging towards the ever-miraculous blue. The child was always there, but only very occasionally, when its guardians relaxed their hold, could it be free again to run, arms outstretched. 'No one knows we are here,' she said to the child. 'We have the whole day.'

The track did not bear marks of recent passage. Possibly she was the only person to turn off the main road. She thought how some fifty years ago people would have walked miles on foot to sample the fun of the fair. Perhaps a few still did? Gypsies, a tramp . . .

The track ran downhill and soon she saw the roofs of houses and the field on the outskirts of the village where the fair had been set up. She bumped the car onto the grass at the side of the track. 'I might come back,' she said as she got out. 'On the other hand, I might not.' She could hear music and she walked towards it.

The front of the fairground organ was decorated with brightly painted flowers and a variety of precocious animals. 'Did you paint it yourself?' she asked the man who seemed to be in charge of it. She spoke in a tone appropriate to a work of art.

'I do the painting.' He was flattered. 'My mate does the mechanics. Most people don't notice the painting.'

'The colours are so wonderful.'

'I reckon I've a bit of an eye for colour,' he conceded modestly.

His mate was at the back of the organ divulging the secrets of the mechanics to an audience of small boys who received his words with the solemnity appropriate to revelation. For them, the miracle was not in the music, much less the painting, but in the all-important matter of how the machine worked. Janet could imagine Hugh among them, but not Malcolm.

She walked on, past a stall where a man in a striped apron was grilling hamburgers, to a tent in which a dog show was being held. A voice over a loudhailer repeated, 'Ringer. Have we got Ringer?' Then, in an aside, 'Oh, the plum duff? All right. Which one is it we *haven't* got? Pickles?' His voice blared into the loudhailer. 'Can we have Pickles, please. Pickles to the dog tent.' Pickles was a Jack Russell who had been entered in the contest for the Dog with the Waggiest Tail. Janet watched as the entrants received encouragement of the kind judged by their owners to produce the maximum agitation. Rope-tailed German Shepherd dogs, feathery-tailed retrievers, wagged accommodatingly; but the very weight and majesty of their appendages imposed a certain gravity of pace which prevented their indulgence in the uncontrolled ecstasies of Pickles' little travesty, which responded so furiously one might have expected him to become airborne at any moment. After he had been rewarded for this vulgar display, there followed a contest for the Dog with the Best Party Trick. None of the contestants was on form and the award went to a ragged black mongrel who loped by and paused to pee against the judge's leg. To the relief of the shambling youth who came in some trepidation to claim him, he was presented with a bag of Winalot.

'What is his name?' Janet asked the boy.

'Beresford.' He noted her surprise with satisfaction. 'One of my stepfather's jokes.'

He was a tall lad who did not seem easy within his own skin. He had big shoulders and a small, round head and his limbs moved awkwardly as though he had not yet claimed these bones for his own and imposed his personality upon them. Or perhaps it was the awkwardness of the personality which had imposed itself on the bones? Certainly he paraded his anger – not a man's anger, but the anger which some teenagers use as a protective shield with which to batter their way through situations which they have no other means of handling. There had been a difficult spell when Malcolm was like that, before he became so involved in the theatre. Janet had seemed to dig so deep into her resources of love and understanding that she had feared a time would come when she had nothing left to give. Was it the memory of this which made her feel suddenly threatened?

'Does your stepfather know you are here?' she asked the boy.

He was old enough to resent that question, but had a bigger resentment to air. 'He wouldn't care where I was so long as I was out of his sight.'

They walked out of the tent together. It seemed to Janet that there were three of them now. The third person walked close as a shadow to her, whispering, 'Don't waste sympathy on this load of trouble. You will only come to grief if you do.'

The boy broke open the bag of Winalot and threw pieces to

the dog who cavorted around him barking hysterically.

Janet said, 'You don't live at home?'

'That'll be the day!'

'Where, then?'

'There's an old place out on the heath.' He was nonchalant, but hoped she would not be. 'It's for sale but no one wants it. I doss down there.' It's an everyday occurrence, his manner implied while inviting her to be shocked so that he could become even more indifferent. 'Manipulative,' the shadowy companion warned.

'Your family must be worried.'

'My stepfather won't have me in the house. Mum gives me meals when he's not around, but I'm not allowed to sleep there.' He noted that this disturbed her and said, 'It happens all the time, you know,' wanting her to be angry.

'Where is your real father?'

'He went off to Canada with this bird from his office, didn't he.'

'You are an only child?'

'I've got a sister. She's like our cat. So long as she's fed regularly she's no trouble to anyone.'

'Break this up now,' the shadow advised, urgent, agitated. Janet dug her fists into her jacket pockets and asked, 'Did you try to get on with your stepfather?'

'You can't *get on* with him.' He spoke as though her obtuseness had been maddening him for a considerable time – perhaps she reminded him of his mother. 'You just have to do everything the way he thinks it should be done and like the things he likes. He's got a sailing boat – so you've got to like sailing or there's something wrong with you. Same with rugger.'

The shadow was at her elbow whispering, 'Kids are spoiled nowadays. They are brought up to think the world revolves around them and the first time they encounter any real opposition they turn nasty.' Janet forced herself to study the boy carefully. She saw a big, sensitive, truculent, vulnerable, clumsy, opinionated teenager who must have tried his stepfather hard; but she saw nothing spiteful in his face, detected no real viciousness in his anger.

'Are there many of you out there?' she asked. 'In this place that no one wants.'

'A few. They come and go.'

'Tramps, some of them?'

'Some.'

They walked past a group of punks sitting on the grass drinking beer. All in black, Janet noted; shiny black blouses, tight black trousers, black boots, only a spume of pink at the ends of the silver-feathered hair. The day seemed to be getting darker and yet she could feel the sun on the top of her head.

'Are you still at school?' she asked. 'Or do you have a job?'

'A job! You're joking!' He looked around him, baffled, seeking someone to blame. 'I've been for a few interviews, but they're so *stupid*, the people who interview you. I don't bother with them any any more. They don't know what they're talking about most of the time. All they want to know is what exams you've got. Provided you had exams they'd give you a job in a workshop if you didn't know the difference between a meat cleaver and a hack saw.'

'Do you *want* to work in a factory?'

'I thought of management at one time. But those clowns are the worst of all. They can't do their own jobs so they don't want anyone around who knows better.'

'You see!' said the shadow. 'Wilful, spoiled . . .' Janet shook her head vehemently. 'Knowing better than other people is another defence. It may lose him the chance of work and in a few years' time he may be unemployable; but what if he were to humble himself, try to present the required image, promise to take exams? The chances are he still would not get a job and he would have lost his dignity.' The shadow warned, '*You* are losing your balance.'

'There's a lot of things I might do,' the boy was saying. 'Journalism, publishing, something in that line. Or I might start up on my own. I've got ideas.' The statement carried no conviction. The world was too stupid a place for him to have any confidence in the future. *This* is Patsy's nuclear winter, Janet

77

thought, beginning to shiver. The shadow said, '*That's* going it a bit!'

Nearby on the boundary hedge a man dressed as a friar was standing guard over a straw figure with an enormous trunk and disproportionately short limbs. 'They've done that all wrong,' the boy said.

The friar was being interrogated by two children. 'When you going to burn it, then?' the little girl asked.

'Not for hours and hours and hours, so it's no use your hanging around.'

The little boy said, 'My teacher says they used to burn a real person in it – a sacrifice, like . . .' He eyed the figure dubiously.

'Are *you* going to burn a real person in it?' The little girl appeared to have no misgivings.

'One of you two, if you don't buzz off.'

'How'd they pick on him?' The little boy was clearly anxious – anxious and fascinated, just as Malcolm would have been at his age. 'The one they burned, I mean. How'd they decide?'

'I expect it was the one that talked the most,' the friar said.

'They drew cards,' the little girl said in a superior tone. 'The one that got the Ace of Spades got burnt.'

'They didn't *have* cards then, did they, mister?' The boy appealed to the friar who ignored him. The little girl said, 'Yes they did. Cards are ever so old.'

'But they didn't have *paper*.'

'There's always been paper,' she said resentfully. 'Look at the Bible. How'd we know all about the Ark and that if there wasn't paper?'

'How *did* they decide who to burn?' Janet wondered as she and her companion walked away.

'At random,' he replied with relish. 'They just pointed a finger and said "you for the bonfire".'

All random, she thought – my children loved and cared for and wanted however badly they behave and this lad turned out with nowhere to stay and no one to care. The shadow said, 'He will set up in a flat somewhere with a couple of friends and social services will foot the bill.'

They stopped to watch a thin girl edging forward like a caterpillar across a slippery pole. 'Why don't you have a go?' Janet said to the boy.

'It's only for kids,' he said scornfully. 'It's the weight that counts. Don't you understand *anything*?' He was disgusted by her stupidity.

'Very little, I'm afraid,' she said wryly.

'Oh, well . . .' He seemed dismayed rather than mollified. After a few moments, during which the thin girl fell off the slippery pole, he said, 'I'd like to buy you something. Will you have an ice cream?'

'That's very kind of you.' She wondered if he could afford it, but knew he could not afford to be asked.

'Wait there!' he said sternly to the dog who squatted obediently at Janet's feet, peering anxiously between the forest of legs and occasionally snapping at an ankle, his temper obviously as unpredictable as his master's.

When the boy returned it was apparent that his goodwill gesture had unsettled him. He pushed an ice-cream cone at Janet and said, 'Well, I'm off now.' Before she could thank him he had whistled the dog and was elbowing his way into the crowd.

'I don't know your name,' she called. She tried to follow him but soon lost him. 'And if you had caught up with him – what then?' her shadowy companion asked. 'He's none of your business.'

People moved from stall to stall. Janet watched them as she stood licking the ice cream. None was known to her. As she studied them, she noticed that several of the children had clowns' faces, bright red noses, red weals on the cheeks, brilliant slashed mouths. The bizarre faces seemed more appropriate than those of the blue-rinsed matrons presiding over the cake stall. 'We keep some back, you see,' one of the inappropriate ladies said kindly, leaning across to speak to Janet. 'Otherwise they all go in the first five minutes.'

Janet bought a cake because this seemed to be expected of her. She walked on and came eventually to the booth where the faces were painted. The woman in charge looked surprised when

Janet presented herself, but all she said was, 'What do you want? Clown, witch . . .?'

'The one with the brightest colours, please. Nothing black.'

'Clown, then.'

The making of the new face excited her. She felt the stirring of an unknown spirit and dared to ask, 'Where am I?'

The woman regarded her creation uncertainly.

'I mean, what is this place?'

'Molt,' the woman said, and added, reluctant to give so much away, 'Molt Magna.'

'And how do I get out?'

'Out?'

Janet raised her arms, embracing the field and its gallimaufry. 'Of this?'

The woman pointed and Janet saw the fairground organ, the gate near by. 'Where did you want to go?' The woman was looking at her intently now.

'I know the way, thank you.'

Even had that been true, there was the matter of how. But the new spirit moved daringly up the lane. 'A clown *and* a witch!' she cried, 'for here is my broomstick!' There were other cars parked behind hers now and she had some difficulty in getting out. When eventually she reached the road across the heath she turned to the left. She seemed to remember that at some stage she had had a loss of concentration and had told herself that it would all come right once she got into the supermarket car park.

It was the shadow and not the new spirit who travelled with her in the car. She pleaded with it, 'How can I *not* care about lads like him? How *could* I reject them?' The shadow pointed out that she had been unaware of them for the greater part of her life and had managed very nicely. If that was so, then it was a blow in the area where she had most pride. She, who was so loving, so caring . . . It was like failing at O level in the subject in which one was particularly gifted. Pride apart, it was unforgivable.

She parked the car and went into the supermarket. People were looking at her strangely. One woman who had been lifting down a bag of sugar almost dropped it. She said to the woman who was with her. 'Gave me quite a turn! I thought it was blood all over her face.'

Janet walked towards the fruit counter and people eased away, allowing her passage. A woman said to a child. 'It's all right, lovey. She won't hurt you.' Janet looked at a vast mound of grapefruit and had a mental picture of Sherpa Tenzing holding a flag aloft. Behind her a voice which was familiar but not identifiable said, 'That's Murdoch Saunders' wife. What a thing!'

Janet did not know which way to move or what to do. 'God,' she prayed, 'help me! Please, please help me!' She put out a hand and stirred among the grapefruit for some clue which might indicate her next move. One grapefruit toppled, then another, then the whole pile avalanched onto the floor. Janet sat among them, talking to the shadow. 'I should have taken him home with me. Why, oh why, didn't I take him home with me?' She clenched one hand round a grapefruit and drummed it on the ground.

An elderly assistant hurried up. 'And they came from Israel only yesterday!' he said, as though the grapefruit were visiting dignitaries upset. When at last he had gathered them up, he looked at Janet. 'What am I to do?' he asked.

Janet, still bashing the grapefruit, cried out, 'I was afraid. You made me afraid of what my children would say.'

He appealed to the onlookers. 'What am I to do?'

The woman who had previously identified Janet said, 'You could try getting her husband. But I don't suppose he will answer the telephone in the morning. That's when he works. He wouldn't expect to be disturbed by anything in the morning.' Nevertheless, she gave the name and address to the assistant. 'He'll be lucky!' she said grimly to her companion as the assistant departed to the manager's office. 'I know all about that house. My sister does for them.'

In a few minutes the manager arrived. 'Now, wouldn't you be more comfortable sitting down in my office,' he said to Janet who had by now reduced the grapefruit to a pulp.

'I don't suppose you got an answer?' the informant said with satisfaction.

'He is coming,' the manager said. 'He didn't even seem surprised. It was as if he was waiting for the call.'

Janet only spoke to Murdoch once on the way home. 'Somewhere out there,' she said, looking across the heath, 'there is a house.'

Malcolm arrived on the twelve-forty bus. His mother often met him at the bus stop and he was disappointed to see that on this occasion she had not done so. Usually, when she did not come, he enjoyed the gentle downhill walk, seeing the stream glinting between the trees, waiting eagerly for his first glimpse of the village, stringing together images of childhood more idyllic than real. But today he was particularly concerned to reach the house by one-thirty when Mrs Thatcher was giving a television interview. Malcolm revelled in Mrs Thatcher. He saw her as one of the great bad performances of all time and considered it a privilege to watch her on every possible occasion. On one of his rare trips to London, which happened to coincide with the Falklands War, he had endeavoured to meet her. He had stationed himself outside Number 10 Downing Street and shouted 'Long live Argentina!' He had imagined the door flung open and himself in personal combat with his idol; but Malcolm's dreams were seldom realised outside the theatre and on this occasion he had been confronted by a drearily unimaginative policeman.

'I shall go to the East End and start a riot,' he had threatened as he was pointed in the direction of St James's Park.

'If you say that kind of thing in the East End you'll get yourself lynched, my lad,' the policeman had told him, insufferably worldy-wise. 'You'd best go and tell it to the ducks.'

It was twenty past one when Malcolm reached his home. The french windows were open and he hurried through the sitting room into the small television-room, announcing his presence by singing 'I'll see you again, whenever spring breaks through again', a song which he considered appropriate to Mrs Thatcher's style if not her period. He had switched on the television and was listening to the interviewer making the most of his introduction – presumably in the knowledge that he was unlikely to have many lines hereafter – when it occurred to him that no one had acknowledged his arrival. He backed towards the door, keeping his eyes on the screen, and shouted, 'I have spent my substance on riotous living and am returned. Did no one see me afar off?' He stopped, not because the golden image on screen was now speaking, but because of the silence in the house. He went into the hall. ' "Tell them I came and no one answered, That I kept my word, he said",' he said. The silence was disturbed by scratching and whining at the kitchen door. Malcolm opened the door and Humphrey reared up, placing his paws on Malcolm's shoulders, licking his face. Matilda was sitting on the kitchen table. She twitched her tail defiantly. The room smelt of fresh air and nothing else.

Malcolm whirled out of the room and went up the stairs two at a time. He flung open the door of his parents' bedroom. The bed had not been made. He said to Humphrey, who had by this time toiled up the stairs, 'What's happened? Where are they?' Humphrey wagged his tail.

Malcolm ran down the stairs to his father's study. Curtains stirred in the breeze from the open window and pages of the manuscript on the desk fluttered. In the television-room Mrs Thatcher was saying, '*Of course* I care; but, you know, Gordon . . .' Malcolm switched off the picture. He went through the sitting room, out of the french windows, to the garage. The doors were open, the car gone. Malcolm ran across the grass and out of the gate pursued by Humphrey.

It was five to two when they arrived in the village, both in rather poor condition. Deutzia was standing at her front door. Malcolm ran up to her. 'My mother isn't there,' he said. Humphrey lifted a leg and sprayed Deutzia's shrub roses.

Deutzia looked at her watch and gazed down the village street. 'Your mother went into town this morning, Malcolm.'

'But she wouldn't go when I was coming.'

'She had probably forgotten to get food or something.'

'But my father isn't there, either.'

'Your father not there?' Deutzia was surprised into attention.

By the time the doctor's wife arrived Deutzia was as disturbed as Malcolm. 'We must see the vicar,' she said, this being the only figure of authority known to be in the village at this hour.

'He'll be having his lunch,' Ann Bellamy protested. 'He only came back ten minutes ago. I saw him drive past.'

'He doesn't have all that many calls on his time,' Deutzia said, enjoying a rare moment of importance. She set off up the street followed by Malcolm, Ann Bellamy and Humphrey.

Mrs Beaney had developed a migraine and the vicar, an austere, troubled man, was left unprotected. 'Your father caught a bus,' he told Malcolm. 'I saw him waiting just before I turned off the main road.' He had thought there was something odd about this, but had not stopped to enquire in case anything were demanded of him. It seemed that, as was His wont, God had been swift to punish this lack of charity.

'Something dreadful has happened,' Malcolm exclaimed.

Mr Beaney said, 'Oh, I do hope not!'

'A car accident,' Deutzia said firmly. 'Janet must be in hospital. That is where he was going.'

Surely an unjust way of making me repent of my dereliction of duty, Mr Beaney thought despairingly.

Ann Bellamy protested, 'But surely in that case he would have asked one of us to give him a lift.'

Mr Beaney bowed his head, aware that the very one who could have given the lift had passed by on the other side of the carriageway. Deutzia said, 'Murdoch always does everything on his own. We must go to the hospital and you must come with us, Mr Beaney. You may be needed.'

Mr Beaney, acknowledging that this indeed was just recompense for putting the pangs of hunger before pastoral duty, agreed that Deutzia was right and furthermore that as his was the larger car he should drive. Deutzia sat in the front and Malcolm and Ann Bellamy sat in the back with Humphrey between them.

'Might it have been wiser to telephone?' Mr Beaney

wondered, his mind refusing quite to relinquish all thought of food.

'When Elsie Marshall telephoned to find out about her mother they told her the old lady was on her way home in an ambulance when in actual fact she was in intensive care.' Deutzia fanned herself, flushed with excitement.

Even in her younger years, however, Deutzia had been unable to sustain any degree of emotional intensity. By the time they reached the hospital she was displeased with the entire expedition. One look at the bored damsel at the information desk convinced her that it was going to be difficult to create the sympathetic atmosphere necessary to the recounting of the few facts at their disposal. She therefore passed all responsibility to Mr Beaney. 'You had better explain.'

'But surely you would like . . . I mean, *you* know the family so well . . .'

'*I* didn't see Murdoch at the bus stop. I have just been drawn into all this.'

'It was at your suggestion, dear lady . . .'

'I may have said something or other, I don't recall. I certainly didn't expect to be swept along like this. We came to you, Mr Beaney, for a mature judgement and you have led us here.' She turned to Ann Bellamy. 'I must find somewhere to sit. All this rushing about has made me feel quite faint.'

Ann led her away while Mr Beaney and Malcolm endeavoured to engage the interest of the young woman at the desk.

'We should have gone to the police,' Deutzia said. 'After all, they could have been kidnapped.'

'But who would want to kidnap them?'

'Who would want to kidnap that nice Mrs Guinness, but someone did.'

'Murdoch isn't connected to any dynasty.'

'He is a very important writer,' Deutzia said huffily.

'But he's not a bestseller, is he? I mean, I don't think people get kidnapped for . . . well, aesthetic reasons.'

'You probably know more about that than I do. I have never laid claim to aesthetic judgement. I'm afraid I can't say any more. I have tried to be helpful and the result is that my whole afternoon has been ruined.'

Mr Beaney came across to them. 'She has made enquiries at Casualty and it seems that Mrs Saunders is not there. Malcolm is trying to persuade her to telephone Out Patients. I thought he might do better on his own.' His eye followed the passage of a trolley bearing hot drinks and a selection of sweets and biscuits. 'I suppose if all else fails, we might . . .'

Ann Bellamy stood up. 'This is preposterous!' She flushed with surprise at her own temerity. 'I am going to telephone my husband's surgery. We should have done that in the first place.'

Deutzia said, 'I quite agree.'

Ann walked away in search of a call box and returned a few minutes later, looking grave. 'Your mother is at home,' she said to Malcolm who had now joined Deutzia and Mr Beaney. 'Murdoch telephoned the surgery half an hour ago. My husband is with your parents now, I imagine.'

Malcolm's face went grey and Deutzia said, 'Malcolm, sit down and put your head between your legs or whatever it is one is supposed to do.' She whispered to Ann, 'He has always been far too attached to his mother.'

'I must 'phone my father. I *must* find out . . .'

'I asked the surgery to 'phone your father and tell him you are on your way back,' Ann said firmly.

'Yes.' Mr Beaney was immensely relieved. 'We must get you back immediately.'

In the car Deutzia said, 'I am afraid this has all been rather a strain for me. Perhaps you would drop me in the square. If I have a little sit down and a cup of tea I shall soon recover.'

Mr Beaney said, 'Oh dear . . .' and Ann Bellamy, sensing irresolution, said, 'If you come back on the ten to five bus I will meet you.'

Deutzia fanned herself. 'One does so hate to be a nuisance.' Humphrey leaned forward and sniffed her cheek.

After she had departed they travelled in silence until they reached the heath where Humphrey became agitated, sniffing the air and whining. Malcolm exclaimed, pointing, 'A fire!' As they came nearer they could see pieces of burning straw blowing in the wind.

'It's the fair at Molt Magna,' Mr Beaney said. 'They do this each year. Some pagan custom or other.' He had wondered whether he might work it into his sermon on Pentecost but had so far failed to make a connection. Great orange tongues leaped from the heart of the fire and even at this distance they could hear the snap, splutter, crackle and, beneath the fizzling ferment, a sound like a swelling drum roll celebrating this inexorable consummation. 'Quite dangerous unless you know what you are doing,' Mr Beaney said.

7

'Leave her,' Dr Potter said omnisciently.

'Her daughter is very concerned,' Dr Bellamy protested.

Dr Potter found this amusing. 'She needs protecting from that daughter — and seems to have arranged it quite well.'

Dr Bellamy looked around his consulting room, seeking protection which he failed to find. 'I feel I should be doing *something.*'

'She is sleeping a lot and she is therefore resting.' Dr Potter stabbed the air with a cigar which she had been threatening to light for some time. 'Your worry is that *you* didn't induce this condition. You are uneasy because you feel it is she, and not you, who is in charge of this breakdown. You will have to learn humility in such matters.'

'I am uneasy about just leaving it to run its course like a bad cold,' he said with some spirit.

'So what do you want to do? Pick at her, prod her, stimulate her? And then, when you have worked her into a fine old state, put her on tranquillisers?'

Dr Bellamy said unhappily, 'It seems so unorthodox . . .'

'Orthodoxy got her where she is now.' She put the cigar away and closed her handbag. 'I don't know about you, but I need refreshment.'

'I have sandwiches,' he said primly.

'And your patients would not like to smell drink on your breath,' she said sympathetically.

'I don't know what I am going to say to the daughter,' he said as Dr Potter prepared to take her leave.

'You don't think it is the husband you should be addressing yourself to? After all, whatever the daughter may say, you will need his permission for any treatment you propose.'

'His attitude is rather hard to understand, don't you think? It strikes me that he doesn't want to come to terms with his wife's illness.'

'The impression he gave me was that it was the medical profession he didn't want to come to terms with.'

'One might almost think they were in collusion, he and his wife.'

'Without a peradventure!'

'And Dr Potter is little better,' Andrew Bellamy said to Ann that evening.

'Is it such a bad idea to leave her alone for a little while?'

'Women have this tremendous feeling about being left alone.' He was shaken to find a hint of it in his own wife. 'I had no idea . . .'

'Anyway,' she said evasively, 'she couldn't come to much harm, could she?'

'Yes, she could!' He was vehement. 'You remember that boy who fell down the mine shaft last month? He lodged on a shelf. If people had just walked away and left him, there would have been no way he could have climbed out on his own. And the real danger was that the shelf would give way and he would fall right down to the bottom.'

'Exactly!' She was equally vehement. 'So they had to go about the rescue very warily – in case they dislodged his one support and sent him spinning down.'

'But they did *do* something! For one thing, they located where he was. *I* don't even know where Janet Saunders is.'

'But they took their time. Give Janet *time*.'

'It's dangerous, though. You don't understand how dangerous it is. I was up there at that mine shaft. I looked down.'

Janet had felt very frightened when Doctors Bellamy and Potter came to see her. Murdoch had been in the room, too. Three was too many.

This fear of being in a room with a number of people had

been growing for some time. She had first been acutely aware of it at Christmas. It was not the pressure of offering hospitality to so many people. She was good at that and enjoyed it as all artists must enjoy the exercise of their gift, while accepting its burden. The difficulty had come when the last meal of the day had been consumed and the washing-up done by the children. 'Now you can rest,' they had told her, meaning, 'Now you can be happy,' seeing nothing but drudgery in her contribution to the celebration of Christmas Day. They had settled down companionably in the sitting room and there it had started – the statements winging from all corners, fast, like arrows. Her brain could not sort out the many thrusts of conversation. By the time she was in bed her mind was in a tangle and she had spent much of the night trying to get the knots untied. She had attempted to replay the scene, taking it slowly, breaking it down into manageable portions. First Hugh had said, then Katrina, then Hugh again, Malcolm ... And Stephanie, who was not usually so silent? There must be a part of the conversation which she had forgotten or wanted to forget. As the hours passed she had become more and more confused and distressed.

After Christmas it had been better with just herself and Murdoch, occasional visits from Patsy, who did not expect structured conversation, and Deutzia who did all the talking. The light had begun to dim, the world to assume a bloodless aspect, but she had managed. Then, at Easter, when the children came again, the fear had developed a new dimension. Up till then she had simply felt excluded by her inability to knit conversations together. But by Easter she was aware that although she did not understand, she was nevertheless at the centre of something. Her children had turned against her. Her gifts, which had meant so much to them when they were young, had fallen out of favour. But the gifts were a part of her and could not be taken away and replaced by more appropriate 'skills'. A remodelling of the person was required. And so they must set about refashioning her in their own image.

The children had some excuse. She and Murdoch had, after all, created, without their consent, the setting in which they had passed their childhood and perhaps this was their revenge. But how had it come about that she had fallen foul of Doctors Bellamy and Potter? They were more powerful than the children. People laughed at Patsy and her friends and called them witches. But the doctors, *they* were the modern descendants of Hecate. If they did not think her personality acceptable they could give her potions which would change it beyond reversal; if her brain did not function as they decreed, they could unleash the power of electricity against it. The minerals of the earth yielded to them, the elements obeyed their command. She cowered among the sheets while they stood on either side of the bed shooting their poisoned darts across her body.

Murdoch sat on the edge of the bed. He held her hand and fear ran down her arm to the tips of her fingers into his palm. He confronted Dr Potter like an uncouth farm-labourer. 'I don't want her messed about, you do understand me?'

'Perfectly. But tell me how you think she got in this condition.'

'That's my problem.'

'So long as you see it as a problem, I wouldn't quarrel with that statement.'

Dr Bellamy had remained silent during this exchange, looking down into Janet's eyes as though he saw himself drowning in their depths.

I *can* drown him, she had realised and a sense of her own power had come to her. But now that they had gone and there was no means of exercising the power, she was more frightened than ever. She had repulsed those who had menaced her, but what was the significance of this success? What would become of her if she refused to let them interfere with her? If she were to be left alone, unaided, this event towards which she had seemed to be moving for so long would happen. The darkness would close around her. People had gone through operations without pain-killers, but operations took place within a limited time scale. How long does darkness last?

Inevitably, Stephanie came. She approached the house prepared to turf out the helpers who must be holding the fort – Patsy, Deutzia, perhaps the vicar's wife. She did not think they would have organised nursing help and she had not much confidence in the doctor's ability to attend to such matters. Humphrey bounded across the grass to greet her. Over his golden head she saw washing strung out on a line hoisted from drainpipe to lilac tree, neither of which supports was doing the washing any good. Patsy, she thought – Deutzia would certainly have used the washing machine. At least we must be thankful she didn't string it along the hedge!

But the only person in the kitchen was her father. He was wearing an apron and there was blood on it. The dyke so carefully constructed to hold back the ominous seas was breached in a single instant. The very house seemed afloat and hurling itself upon her as she stood in the kitchen doorway. She cried, 'What is it? What has happened to her?'

Murdoch held something up in his hand. 'I don't seem able to shred beans with this thing.' She came and stood beside him, looking down into a bowl in which mangled runner beans floated in bloody water. It was too much; the worry of the last few days, the mounting tension of her journey – she had nearly run over a child in Farnham, the fear which had haunted her as she approached the house now justified by blood. There was cold sweat on her forehead, the room lurched.

Murdoch removed Matilda from the chair by the kitchen table and pushed Stephanie into it. 'You never could stand the sight of blood as a child,' he reminded her when he returned with a glass of brandy.

'That's why I never became a nurse,' she said, all authority gone. 'Goodness knows what I think I can do here.'

'The beans, perhaps?'

'All right. But take that awful thing off and put it in a bucket of cold water out of my sight.' She gave a weak laugh as Murdoch did as he was bidden. 'I suppose if Malcolm were here he would say "Who would have thought the old man to have so much blood in him?"'

'That is the last thing Malcolm would say. He finds it hard

enough to bear a name taken from the Scottish play.'

Matilda jumped onto Stephanie's lap and butted her head between the ample breasts, purring and dribbling ecstatically. 'You *are* feeding these creatures?' Stephanie asked.

'On demand.'

Stephanie thought that she would like to remain here, talking about nothing in particular, for the rest of the day. She analysed her extreme reluctance to move as she sipped her brandy: she resented her mother's illness; she resented having to look after her mother because her mother was the person who should be looking after Stephanie. There, it was not so bad once it had been articulated!

'I thought the house would be full of helpers,' she said to Murdoch.

'Half an hour ago it was full of Patsy and the children.'

'You mustn't let Patsy do the washing. Leave that to Deutzia.'

'Deutzia hasn't been near here. She telephoned to ask after Janet and to assure me that she would not dream of intruding at such a time. And *I* did the washing and strung it up. You wouldn't catch Patsy making those bowline knots.'

He was actually enjoying himself, like a little boy who has been left in charge for the first time! Stephanie told herself that she must not damp down his enthusiasm; she must take over gradually. This justified her remaining at the kitchen table, sipping the brandy slowly, kneading Matilda's head, while Murdoch poured fresh water over the beans and put a plaster on his finger. 'I'll get your case,' he said. 'Is it in the boot?'

She handed him the car keys. 'I bought a ham. That's there, too.'

When he came back, she said, 'I feel quite squiffy. I'd better sober up before I see Mummy. She is in bed, I assume?'

'She gets up in the afternoons sometimes.'

Stephanie felt a tightening of her stomach muscles. There was no order here; it would be left to her to devise a sensible routine.

'Well, we'll see about her lunch first. What does she have?'

'Boiled egg, mostly.'

'She mustn't have too many eggs.'

93

He said meekly, 'No, I suppose not. What would you suggest?'

He was feeding Humphrey who had been making strenuous demands ever since Stephanie's arrival. A few weeks of this and even the animals would be out of condition. She went to the refrigerator which seemed to be stacked with offerings from Patsy which Stephanie did not distress herself by trying to identify. On the bottom shelf were three trout.

'How did you come by these?' she asked her father. 'And when?'

'This morning. At the trout farm.'

'Oh!' Her heart lifted. She had been running her own home for nine years, so why was she so overwhelmed by the prospect of preparing one lunch for her mother and father? 'You've done enough beans,' she said. 'Now you can do a few potatoes while I see to the trout.'

'They don't need doing, not new potatoes.'

'But you wash them! You don't eat them, earth and all.'

She stood by the grill, watching her father out of the corner of her eye. 'I should scrub them, if I were you, not just maul them.' It was a wonder they were not all dead.

The heat from the grill was intense and she felt faint again and rather sick. 'I'll get some mint from the garden. The trout doesn't need to go on for a minute or two.'

She walked slowly across the lawn, fighting a desire to get in the car and drive away. It was hot in the garden. It was going to be a hot summer. Hot summers did not suit either her temperament or her Nordic beauty. She picked the mint and went back to the kitchen where she dropped it in the saucepan.

Murdoch said, 'Shouldn't you have washed it first?'

His teasing broke her last resistance. 'I'm frightened. Isn't it silly?'

He put an arm round her shoulders. 'I'm frightened, too.'

She felt better and went to attend to the trout. 'One should be able to cope without props, of course,' she said, standing further back from the grill. 'But apparently I can't.' It was not an admission she would have made to anyone else.

'Wish me luck,' she said conspiratorially as she left the kitchen bearing Janet's tray.

She found her mother sitting up in bed looking clean and tidy, but rather blurred as people do when they have woken from a heavy sleep or when their eyes are not focusing properly.

'I've come,' Stephanie said, setting down the tray and kissing her mother.

'I heard.'

It was surprising that the words, spoken in a monotone, could convey to Stephanie such complexity of meaning – awareness of the time which had elapsed between the daughter's arrival in the house and her presence at her mother's bedside, indifference to that belated presence, and a deliberate intention to hurt and provoke.

Stephanie responded by making her own contribution to provocation, adopting a resolutely cheerful manner which did not quite say, 'Now let's have an end to all this nonsense, shall we?' but came perilously close to it.

'And I've brought your lunch.'

Janet looked at the tray. 'I can't eat all that.'

'It's only trout.'

'Trout is very filling.'

'Eat as much as you can, then.'

Janet studied the trout for further inspiration. 'What's this you've poured over it?'

'Caper sauce.'

'It smells of vinegar. You know I don't like vinegar. I never have mint sauce.'

'I had forgotten. I'll change it. I haven't put any sauce on mine yet.'

'I shan't eat it, anyway. Matilda can have it.'

Stephanie said, 'Then perhaps you can manage the potatoes and beans?' She sounded tolerant, and added, 'And anyway, Matilda doesn't like vinegar either.'

Janet prodded the potatoes with a fork. Stephanie had set the tray carefully so that it looked elegant and had arranged the food artistically on the plate because presentation was important in stimulating appetite. She watched her mother making a laborious mess of it. 'I'll leave you to that,' she said, allowing her mother to see that she was not taken in by this performance, but was amused rather than irritated. 'Would you like some fruit afterwards?'

Janet looked at her reproachfully and then turned her head away. Stephanie went downstairs clenching her fists.

'You know why she is behaving like this?' she said to her father who was standing by the sink. 'It is important that you should understand. The breakdown is the only thing she can believe in. So she must insist that this is the way the world is – she could not bear to have another, parallel world, from which she was excluded, which ran on oiled wheels. The broken down world serves another purpose – it is her justification. I am as I am because this is the way the world is. And so, every attempt to introduce order and hope must be defeated, repulsed, shown up for the sham it is. Otherwise the failure is in her.'

Murdoch said, his voice anxious, 'Darling, do you think . . .'

'I didn't want to upset you, I just wanted you to understand . . .'

He turned to her, his face folded in concern. 'This mark, was it always here? I can't seem to get it off.' He held a saucepan out for her inspection.

'What are you thinking of?' she shouted, staring into the pan. 'It's been there for ever by the look of it.' She took the pan from him and placed it roughly on the draining board. 'For goodness sake, I can't have you going dotty, too!'

After lunch, which was not a meal which Stephanie enjoyed, she tried to talk to her father. But she was so used to talking to clients that she found difficulty in deciding on the right mode of speech for a parent. She experienced a similar difficulty with her husband. The trouble with being so aware was that one ceased to react naturally. Awareness was the very devil! The only time she ever found herself being remotely natural was when she lost her temper. One did not like to think of oneself as the kind of person whose only natural outlet was a display of temper.

'Darling, you have obviously been doing wonders here,' she

said in a tone which she immediately recognised as the one in which she 'rewarded' Marcus when he had cleared his own toys away.

Murdoch said, 'So what have I done wrong?'

'You shouldn't be *doing* at all. We must get you some help.'

'Janet doesn't want help.'

'She is not her usual self, so I don't think perhaps we should take too much notice of that.'

'But this is her home. She has always had the running of it.'

'At the moment, she isn't running it, is she?'

'Mrs Pringle comes twice a week.'

'You need someone far more capable than Mrs Pringle.'

'Janet wouldn't like that.'

Stephanie felt her mouth going dry. 'I don't think she is in a state to tell what is best.'

'If she can't, I don't see how anyone else can.'

'When we are ill,' Stephanie said, speaking quietly and spacing the words, 'other people have to make decisions for us.'

'I don't give a fuck about other people.'

'You are like most men,' Stephanie felt anger quivering in her veins. 'You don't believe in mental illness. You think that if you turn your head away it will all be gone by the time you look round.'

Murdoch said, 'Janet is not mentally ill. And if she doesn't want anyone here, we are not having anyone.'

He strolled across to the kitchen door and whistled Humphrey for his walk. As far as he was concerned this was an end to the conversation; had she not been his daughter, he would have told her so in no uncertain terms. Not entirely a gentleman, my father, Stephanie thought – at the moment he had the look of an old breed of Englishman, by no means the noblest strain, rather one of Falstaff's drinking companions, perhaps, and she a silly woman who had thought to check him.

When she had cleared up in the kitchen, Stephanie called to her mother, 'I think I'll go down and see Patsy.'

She walked slowly down to the village. She did not like to admit that she needed to talk to Patsy, but she certainly needed to talk to someone and Patsy, after all, appeared to have been the only regular visitor.

The children were playing in the garden, Sam in a torn shirt and no trunks, Francesca quite nude, her limbs plentifully stained with purple juice. Patsy was sitting outside the kitchen door renovating a cane chair. Other examples of cottage industry in an unfinished state littered the garden.

'How is your mother today?' Patsy asked.

'In bed and not very gracious. How has she been on other days?'

'Oh, so-so.'

Stephanie sat at her feet because she was tired and there was nowhere else to sit. 'What are we to do, Patsy? Or rather, what can we find for Mother to do? Because that, I am sure, is the root of the trouble.'

Patsy tugged hard on a length of cane. She had strong brown hands which looked capable – in her case it must be the spirit and not the flesh which was weak. She said, 'Janet shouldn't have to *do* anything. It has already been done.'

'And what is that supposed to mean?'

'In another culture, your mother would be honoured in her tribe. She would grow old in dignity, just sitting under a tree smoking a pipe, if that was her choice – just *being*. She has made her contribution. And it was enough. No more should be required of her.'

'She requires more of herself,' Stephanie pointed out.

'Only because you have all denied her her place of honour.'

'Oh, I really don't think I can accept that, Patsy! She is only fifty. She can't spend the rest of her life sitting around being honoured!'

'If she had honour she would continue to contribute. People would come for miles to see her because she was a wise woman, as they came to anchoresses and their like in the past.'

'That awful woman Margery Kempe!'

'Or Dame Julian. *They* were the people with the real healing power. The true psychologists.'

*

98

'So, as you can see, in their different ways, Murdoch and Patsy are prepared to let my mother rot!' Stephanie said later over the telephone to Piers. 'You really must come down here this weekend. Angela will just have to have the children again.'

Piers came by train because Stephanie had taken the car. He was disposed to believe his journey had not been necessary. After supper on the evening of his arrival, he said to Stephanie, 'Your father seems to be managing very well, he's quite a cook.'

'This little spell of housework is the equivalent of one of his gypsy journeys. An interesting novelty. When the novelty wears off he will be back where he has always belonged – in his study.'

'That isn't kind.'

'I don't mean it unkindly, Piers. That *is* where he belongs. It grieves me to see him cluttering up his mind with pots and pans.'

'To some effect, you must admit.'

'You know what it was that you ate, don't you? One of Patsy's herbal brews to which my father in his unwisdom had added chunks of stewing steak. And when I asked him where he had taken the steak from, it was clear that he didn't know the difference between the refrigerator and the freezer! He assured me I didn't need to worry – the meat had been "a bit stiff" but he had poured hot water over it and left it for a while. I didn't find *that* out until after we had eaten it.'

'Well, I don't feel any ill effects.'

'You wouldn't yet.'

'And I am most impressed by his resourcefulness.'

'Anyone can be resourceful with an adequately stocked freezer at his disposal.'

'You seem to be proceeding on the assumption that your mother and father are unable to cope with their problems. If you carry on like this you'll be persuading them to move into sheltered accommodation next.'

'My father is not working, Piers! It worries me almost more than anything else. I've never known my mother to be ill before – that's bad enough. But to find my father is not working ter-rifies me. You wouldn't understand that. But he was always *there*, in his study, all through my childhood. It's as though I had lost him.'

'He is only revising now, so is it so important?'

'Revising doesn't mean just dotting an i and crossing a t – not with him. His publisher once told me that rereading one of the novels was like looking at an old master which has been cleaned and realising that one of its most marvellous effects – the shaft of light falling across a table in the background which seems to illuminate the whole work – had been added at the last moment.' Her face screwed up in misery. 'I can't forgive my mother for doing this to him. She has created the atmosphere in which he can work – *enabled* him – and now, quite suddenly, she has lost interest and gone away.'

The next morning, to Stephanie's relief, Murdoch worked in his study. In the afternoon he and Piers took Humphrey for a walk. It was a fine day and hot. There were full heads of elder flower along the banks of the road and briar roses bloomed in the hedgerows. The woods were dense with the heavy foliage of oak and chestnut and a dainty feathering of silver birch – a many-leaved tapestry with, here and there, spangles of blue sky no bigger than a peacock's eye. Light slanted on twisted branches, making shining green discs of the leaves, liming the trunk of a roadside hawthorn.

It was almost too much for Piers, this lime-green loveliness. He was glad when at last they came to the gorse-clad heath. The expanse was not vast but, uncluttered by hedges, bare of trees, it seemed to roll into infinity. There was no sound of traffic, only the song of larks and the occasional haunting cry of the pewit. Usually even his breathing was hurried and shallow, but here he took long, deep breaths like a man who has escaped from prison and imagines that from now on life will never be the same again. Not true, of course; yet as he and Murdoch walked, the illusion persisted.

'I feel all my problems falling away.' He had never spoken of this need before. 'It's so childish. I suppose one is a child at heart. Always seeking some kind of cure from Nature which she won't give.'

'She gives miles of space and good, clean air,' Murdoch said. 'That's enough to be grateful for.'

'You don't seem to me ever to have been in need of space – you have it around you in your own home.'

'It's the writing,' Murdoch said. 'I have to walk and walk and walk before it lets go of my brain. That is why I usually walk on my own in the afternoons.'

'You mean you can't put it to one side?'

'No, not that. How can I explain?' Usually he did not try. Today was different for both men. 'Can you imagine your head as a balloon into which too much air is being forced, bringing on a bad attack of pins and needles? Something like that.'

'Frightening, surely?'

'It's gone on for a long time without anything blowing up. But you never know. By the time I reach this spot it has usually worn off.'

'It hasn't today?'

'It wore off some time ago. But then it wasn't so bad to start with. Perhaps because I am only revising.' He was puzzled.

They sat on a grass tussock when Piers became tired. 'You never thought of doing anything else?' Piers was envious of so given a life.

'I considered the priesthood.'

The casual revelation came like a blow in the breast to Piers. 'I never knew that.'

'It was a long time ago, before the children were born. Janet and I had begun to attend the Anglo-Catholic church and I was very taken with it.'

Piers remembered the agonies he had gone through when he lost his faith. All that time, Murdoch had said nothing, offered no sympathy, given no hint of understanding. Admittedly he had not been critical, either – he had not involved himself in the affair. Piers said bitterly, 'I don't think you would have made a very good priest.'

'That was the general conclusion.' Murdoch was amused.

'You offered yourself?'

'I did.'

'And you were rejected. Perhaps they did not think you would be very good at communicating with people.'

'On the contrary, it was *what* I would communicate which troubled them.'

'A matter of belief?'

'I have always found this word belief difficult,' Murdoch answered easily, just as though Piers had had no problem in this area. 'I tried to explain to them that I had a profound respect – awe might have been a better word – for the Mysteries, that it was my understanding that one should ponder them in one's heart – like Mary – throughout one's life. I would never have said that I *dis*believed. I don't have any problems about saying the Creed, which I think of as repeating the great beliefs of the Church in the hope that I may grow in understanding. That seems to me all that is asked of one in the Creed. A commendably humble attitude, wouldn't you say? And one surely acceptable to God. But my interlocutors demanded something rather more. And I was unable to say, in the manner in which they wanted it said, that I believed in the Virgin Birth, the Divinity of Christ, the Resurrection – or, for that matter, the Transfiguration. For some reason I didn't have any difficulty with the coming of the Holy Spirit. But comparative orthodoxy in so far as one member of the Trinity was concerned was not enough to satisfy them.'

'I can see it wouldn't have been,' Piers said drily.

'And yet now, many years later, I find that I am able to accept things which at that time were veiled in impenetrable mist. It is still a bit misty, of course – it always will be.'

'And what would you have said to parishioners who had problems of belief?'

'Told them not to worry. That worry was the worst thing. A sin. That one should just look upon one's difficulties, whatever they might be – the Virgin Birth, the Divinity of Christ – as a rock which one was unable to climb so one just found a way round it. Later, one might look back and see that it had become a part of the landscape.'

'That doesn't seem a very solid foundation for belief of any kind. If there is so little you can hold to, one would have thought you might as well be a Humanist.'

Murdoch threw a stone for Humphrey. 'Humanism I find altogether too fanciful. And it ducks so many questions, doesn't it?'

'You would have little difficulty in becoming a priest now,' Piers said angrily. 'In fact, I should think you would be quite acceptable. There is only one position which wouldn't be open to you after the Durham experience. But no one would care much what you believed if you were tucked away in a cathedral close or a Cambridge college.' He hated men who had relinquished their beliefs while managing to hang on to the material rewards – hated them and envied them. He had enjoyed everything about the life of a clergyman except God. But he must have certainty, had demanded a sign and none had been given. Now he was left with nothing but a feeling of rejection. He hated the Church because it laid down beliefs which he could not accept and even more he hated it for allowing heresies to flourish within it. Most of all, at this moment, he hated his father-in-law.

'Did it ever occur to you that you might have been able to help me?' he asked savagely. Then, meticulous in all things, he must qualify this statement – even anger could not be allowed a clear run. 'Not that you *could* have done. But did it occur to you that you should try?'

'I can't say that it did.'

'You were quite unaware of what I was going through?'

'The intellectual process, yes. I was unaware of that.' He sounded as though he thought this unimportant.

'There wasn't any other process. It was purely a matter of the intellect.'

Murdoch said, 'Well, you are out of it now. So what are you so angry about?'

'At the moment, I am angry with you.' Piers turned his head away.

Murdoch said, 'Go on. There are things which need to be said.'

'You are the kind of person who makes me believe in the need for war, earthquake . . .'

'Pestilence, famine,' Murdoch nodded.

'Something in which all men have to share, whether they like it or not. We don't share our comforts, our joys, we keep them to ourselves.'

'Not entirely true. The great violinist, doesn't he share? But I see your point.'

'We all live separate lives in the Western world, we value privacy, individuality . . .'

'You don't think you could scale this down a little? Become less apocalyptic?'

'I am not very good at hand-to-hand fighting.'

'You're not very good at personal abuse, either.'

'I don't want to abuse you.'

'For God's sake, man! There is nothing you want to do more at this moment. You are just afraid I might be better equipped than you.'

'You undoubtedly are!' Piers' anger flamed up. 'But even so, you are safe. You won't need to use your weapons, no one will expect it of you. You are a non-combatant – the artist, the person too valuable to be put at risk. You have been exempted from the human condition. And don't tell me, don't tell me!' He held up a hand although Murdoch had not threatened to interrupt. 'That is exactly what *I* would have liked for myself. But I have no gift.'

'Not for teaching?'

'Least of all for that! I hate the little perishers.'

'Do they know that?'

'I hope not.'

'Mightn't it be better if they did know?'

'It wouldn't be better if the Governors knew. At our school there is an undeclared war between staff and pupils; the Governors pick their way between the belligerents talking about dedication and caring. Not education, mind you. That was accepted as a lost cause a long time ago.'

Murdoch sat, arms hunched around his knees, smelling warm

ferns, feeling the heat of the sun between his shoulder blades.

Piers said, 'We are breaking up. Society is breaking up!' He got to his feet. 'Well, that's the news from the Front today.'

Stephanie wrote to Hugh, 'I think we left things in rather better order. Mother got up on Sunday and actually managed to cook supper. It took *for ever* and she almost gave up when she discovered that I had moved the position of the table (we ate in the sitting room so that it was all more intimate and she had left the little table against the wall where we should have been terribly cramped). I realised how very fragile she still is, unable to adapt to any variation in her plans, however reasonable. But the meal was good. She seemed exhausted afterwards and went to bed. But I am hoping it is a beginning.'

[8]

'Don't you love me any more?' Murdoch asked. Over the last months he had been very patient, accepting that sex – that great cure of headaches, nervous debility, rashes, depression, all woman's little ills – could not reach her malady. But even so, he was wounded in his manhood and needed occasional words of reassurance. Janet was sorry for him in a sick, irritated fashion. She said, 'I shall always love you,' in the manner in which she might have repeated the Lord's Prayer, unaware of a single word she was saying. Had he asked, 'Don't you feel anything for me?' the answer must have been a simple 'no'. He went away, looking dejected as a child who cannot understand that favour may momentarily be withdrawn without a change having taken place in the state of loving.

'I let go of my children,' she had told Dr Potter, who had visited her the day before. 'They walked away and I let them go. It was in the nature of things, their going. I may have been diminished – Stephanie's word – but I did *not* allow grievance to take root within me – Stephanie's words.'

'Yet you sound aggrieved.'

'Why won't *they* let go of *me*? Why do they talk about me, criticising, analysing and yet still demanding the old comforts be available whenever they need them?'

'Most people are inconsistent because they live in two worlds – at least two, some have more than two. Your husband is in his study now, trying to throw off his pain by immersing himself in *his* other world which is always there waiting for him. Your daughter, Stephanie, is probably interviewing a client at this moment and her husband will be playing his role in school.'

'Edward,' Janet said. 'He calls himself Edward at school. And Malcolm is probably one of those dear friends setting themselves to the breach. He had hoped to play King Hal, poor Malcolm!'

'Your older son will be lost in litigation and your younger daughter in her studies. Each one of them has an alternative world in which they can shelter until the emotional storms die down. But your work and your emotional life were inextricably linked. Take away the value from the one and you strike at the other.'

Janet lay back visualising a series of alternative worlds all equally grey and toneless.

Dr Potter said, 'But I would hesitate to suggest that *you* should fragment your life.'

'Then what is the answer?' Janet asked listlessly.

'Oh, answers, answers, answers! I know nothing about answers. If you want an answer, it will have to come from you.'

When Dr Potter was leaving Janet had asked, 'Will you be coming again?'

'I don't see why not. I come out this way to see my egg man. Not that I like eggs myself, but my young women seem to want them.'

'Your young women?'

'I run a hostel, a halfway house, or whatever misnomer you like to give it.'

'Please come again.'

So long as Dr Potter was seeing her they would leave her alone, imagining that at least something was happening – happenings of whatever kind being preferable to inactivity in their view. She did not in fact think that Dr Potter was doing her any good, but she no longer felt threatened by her. Dr Potter said she would come again and Janet had the sense of some kind of wickedness in which they both shared.

Of course, she had not taken too seriously all this business about the departure of the children and its effect on her emotional life. That, no doubt, was a contributory factor, but such had been woman's lot over the centuries and woman had survived. Woman was very tough. No, something else had happened.

She now had a recurring dream. She was in a city in the late afternoon. It was already dark and there were lights in the tall buildings which rose on all sides. But she was on the outside and as she walked she looked in at lighted windows where people moved to and fro performing an incomprehensible shadow play. She was filled with yearning but could make no sense of what she saw. The buildings did not appear to have any entrances, only windows. A few days after she saw Dr Potter she woke from a dream which had been more frightening. She had not known, as she hurried along the street, whether she was seeking a way out of the city, or a way into one of its buildings; she only knew that there was an increased urgency. Not much time left for you, she had told herself.

She woke shivering. It was just after seven and she switched on the radio, wanting to hear a human voice. As she listened, she realised she knew what it was she had to do.

Soon after eight Murdoch came in with her breakfast. She ate it and waited until he came and took the tray away. Then she got out of bed and went to the window, looking out over the garden. When the children had gone the figures in the foreground had moved away and the eyes had been drawn beyond the space which they had occupied. It was out there, beyond the hedgerow that the trouble lay.

She dressed quickly, feeling energy building up explosively in her veins, sending the blood racing in her head. She went down the stairs and Murdoch, whose hearing seemed to have become very acute as his concentration lessened, opened the study door.

'I must get out,' she said to him. 'If I'm not allowed out on my own I shall get worse and worse. I *have* to get out.'

'It's raining,' he said.

'I won't melt,' she said.

His reason told him it was a mistake to let someone so sick go wandering off on her own. But reason can cripple and he let her go. He followed at a distance. Humphrey padded beside him and then catching Janet's scent loped forward. Murdoch called him to heel and Humphrey came back at once, his tail wagging uncertainly, perhaps under the impression that this was a new kind of game.

There was no sound but the steady drumming of rain and the squeak of oilskin as Janet walked.

Raindrops glistened on briar roses and she thought how as a child she had loved everything that glistened! And then, when she got older, looking at the Christmas tree, she had said, having learned in her wisdom to discriminate and reject, 'It's only tinsel.' Oh to be attracted once more by the shining, the glittering and the gaudy! To be thankful for all things bright and beautiful whether roses in hedgerows or azaleas in suburban gardens where every plant knows its place, for moorland purple with heather smelling of honey and vivid, red cataract of rhododendron over stately wall, for lichen, moss, velvet, satin, damask curtains, burnished copper, lustres, rubies, cherries, for all the fripperies, gewgaws, spangles, for all that glitters whether gold or brass, impure or incorruptible!

She was shaking with excitement, words tumbled through her mind and half-finished sentences came staccato from her lips. This would not do. She had some way to go yet and the power within her must be conserved until she reached her destination. She walked more soberly for a time.

The rain had cleared when she came towards the heath. Over the hedgerow loomed a birch, a leaning gossip nodding to a neighbour across the lane. Light shone brightly through the lifting clouds and she saw all the colours – swathes of green turf bisecting rough brown of gorse, still yellow-flowered at the tips; the reddish brown of last year's bracken beneath the brilliant green of young ferns and seedling trees; and in the distance land rising in a patchwork of terracotta, dark chocolate, saffron, and beyond yet another ridge with bobbled trees sown into scrub and gorse.

There was a warm breeze and on either side as she walked the branches of the little larches bobbed up and down like swimmers treading water. Birds fluted. Her face was flushed, her breath came light and eager as a child's. Hope buoyed her up, her feet barely seemed to touch earth.

She came to the main road and found it empty. A caravan of

hippies had invaded the county and, miles from this spot, the police had blocked the road. She had heard this on the news in the morning when she switched on the radio in the hope that some comfort might be provided by the thought for the day. 'Will they go to join in this battle?' she had wondered, 'My tramp and the lad at the fairground?' And then, quite suddenly, she could see the house from which they would set out. Of course! It was the old inn at which she and Murdoch had been for drinks on many a summer evening. Murdoch had told her, months ago, that the owners were selling it. It was, he had said, reading from the local paper, too far from the main road to attract the travelling public and there was practically no local trade. The owners had said, optimistically, that it would make a very pleasant family home if people did not mind being 'a bit isolated'; alternatively, it might appeal to a community of some kind. Janet was sure that it had now found a community of some kind.

On the far side of the road a worn signpost pointed to a track few would follow today, or any day. The narrow road had long been replaced by the main road across the heath and the grassy banks had spread, the tarmac had broken up and it was now little different from the old cart tracks. Above her as she walked the larks were singing and she was up there, too, up, up, up high in the sky, every nerve in her body tingling.

She had forgotten how far the inn was from the main road. By the time she came in sight of it her legs were shaking and the little sobs of ecstasy began to sound more like distress signals — only there was no one at home to receive them. She was right outside her body, floating.

The inn was a wide-fronted, two-storey building, plain, with good sash windows and a small, unpretentious porch. Once it had had a kindly aspect, but now, empty and uncared for, there was a certain grimness about it. There was no sound from within as Janet walked towards it. They had gone, then, to join the hippies, or on purposes of their own. As she stood looking at the building she felt a fluttering in her breast as though a bird had landed there and now folded its wings. Feather by feather she felt the folding of the wings. Perhaps she had been wrong and this was not the place of which the boy had spoken? It no longer seemed to matter. She could not remember why she had been so exhilarated by this discovery or what she had thought could be made of it. Although the bird was still now, the dizzying spiral into darkness which had previously followed the folding of the wings had not begun. She had come so far and must go on. Life is an act of faith, each step a venture into uncharted territory, she thought, stepping across the threshold.

A long, narrow room ran the width of the building, broken into small enclosures by the wooden beams. It contained, by way of furniture, two packing cases, an upright chair with a cane seat through which some large object, probably a foot, had been forced, and an old bench which had once stood outside the porch. There were piles of sacking, old newspapers and torn strips of tarpaulin on the floor, cigarette butts and empty beer cans brushed into a corner, the yard broom standing guard over them. There was a dank, sour smell, mingled with something more exotic which could be joss-sticks – or pot, about which she was completely ignorant. The plaster was yellowed with pale patches where pictures had once hung and soot-blackened above empty fireplaces. There were many hooks but no gleam of horse brass or copper pan. The shelves beyond the bar counter were empty save for three faded postcards and a corn dolly – 'to bring plenty to the house' the proprietor would joke, sounding wry because, even were it so, he was not a man to admit he was doing well. His customers had outstayed him, their names scored on the oak beams.

In the corner to the right of the fireplace a flight of stairs receded into what had been the private part of the house. The stairs were dark. Janet stood, balanced between light and dark. The light was fitful and something drew her to the dark stairs. In the emptiness the treads groaned like the straining of a ship's timbers in a gale. At the top of the stairs there was a low-ceilinged corridor with windows looking to the north on one side and several doors on the other. Beneath one window there was an old ottoman and sitting on it a large black cat which watched Janet with unwinking yellow eyes. 'I am just going to look in these rooms,' she told him, feeling some need to propitiate.

Everywhere ceilings sloped, their different angles giving individuality to each room and an air of unpredictability. In the first room she found a broken carriage clock and scrawled on the dusty window a strange symbol composed of a triangle lofted above a circle; in the next, on a piece of rush matting, there was a candle stump and a paperback copy of *The Prophet*. A putrid smell hung about the third room and her feet disturbed a pile of ashes on the floor. A besom rested against the chimney. The next two rooms were empty, the windows broken and the floorboards splashed with bird-droppings. In the rafters and behind the skirting boards she heard tapping, scratching, scurrying evidence that the house was generous host to many small creatures. The last room had a speckled mirror nailed to the wall and looking into it she saw a face that was not her face, a face planed down to the bone from which eyes looked darkly out, accepting without complaint an undisclosed fate. For a few moments she remained motionless, afraid to break the spell. In the mirror she saw herself gathered into the shadowy room, the sloping ceilings falling about her shoulders like a cloak.

When at last she moved away to the window, she saw that, although the sun was shining, purple clouds were boiling over the distant ridge and casting shadows across the heath. It would not last, this interval of lucidity. The cat spat at her as she hurried past him, down the stairs.

At the back of the building french windows opened on to a narrow terrace. To the left was an old shed from which came the stench of human ordure. To the right, brick steps led down to a tangle of long grass and weeds. A rusty hoe rested against a wall and a broken wheelbarrow was loaded with empty bottles. She took off her oilskins and laid them on top of the bottles, then she went slowly down the crumbling steps. Her balance was bad again and she stumbled and fell in the grass. And there, close to her own cheek, something pale and delicate glimmered like a submerged face. There was no one to whom she could call; the only person who could act was herself. She knew that she would not be effective, yet she was here and so must try her hand. But it was not the task which she dreaded, it was the thing itself, the pale, delicate, petalled thing which might have fellows hidden in the undergrowth, it was this which frightened her. She knelt beside it and parted the grass and weeds; there was little to see but she felt pain and saw blood bubbling across the back of her hand. She closed her eyes, grasped fistsful of grass and tore and tugged until, eventually daring to look, she saw that she had uncovered a shrub rose and knew that hidden under the wilderness there was a garden.

Here the enemy declared itself. Not squatters, birds, rats, but Time. Time was responsible for the breakdown of the house and garden. And yet the house had not stood empty for longer than seven or eight months. How soon Time made chaos of order! She pulled out thin, white stalks which had once supported unknown flowers; now brittle and long-dead, they came away easily, but the grass resisted. All she could hope to do was to create a little space, let in some air.

And then, when she had made a clearing? Then?

All the while that I work to create order, she thought, winding the grass round her wrists to gain greater purchase, Time will be working against me, undoing, breaking apart. She had always believed that order was the rule of life – one ordered one's own home, one's garden, one's kitchen, to say nothing of one's mind and body. Order was the norm, disorder a kind of deviance to be resisted at all costs. Yet here, all around her, was evidence that Time – so often represented as the great sorter out of problems, healer of ills, righter of wrongs, reconciler and arbitrator – was the agent of disorder. Time unravelled, broke down, sent the weeds shooting up between the cracks in the carefully-laid brick steps, wreaked havoc in the lovingly tended garden.

Some of the weeds were tacky and laid hold on her clothes as she worked, others were thorny and drew blood. She broke her nails on sharp little stones. Before there was a Garden there was Chaos on the face of the earth, she thought. That is the way the world goes. It is chaos and not order which is the norm. Time has time on its side, order is impermanent. The weeds yielded, the grass resisted; the grass had been there before the garden and had rights. She cried out, 'Help me!' The battleground is here, does no one understand? Here is where the boundary of civilisation runs. To hold this frontier man must work and work, constantly be on the lookout, never relax vigilance, and when he grows too old and tired, or ceases to care, chaos will choke his every small endeavour.

'Murdoch!' she called. He came round the side of the building. She looked at him without surprise. 'You are in your study,' she said.

'No, I am here.'

'In your study! You must understand me.' In his study, he started with chaos in his mind, slowly imposing order on it as the sculptor imposes order on the rough mass of material, both working against the grain of life. 'But I am not artistic . . . Let go! Let go!' He was trying to stop her tearing at the grass. '*I* need to create order, too.' She must take the scattered bits and pieces which life presented to her and try to extract meaning from them, make sense of experience as she grew older and her body wore out. 'We are mad,' she said to him. 'You know that, don't you? We are mad. All this obsession with order when we ourselves are already decaying.'

'Rest a little,' he pleaded.

'And God?' She sat back on her heels, looking up at the sky above their heads, blue, lucid still, void of cloud . . . lucid and void . . . God, profligate one moment, the next destructive; a random giver, bestowing grace where it had not been earned, withdrawing the gift of life before the entrusted tasks are half-completed. 'God,' she said to Murdoch, 'is fundamentally amoral.'

'Come home now, Janet.'

'But this I can do, this at least! You have words, I have my hands.'

She renewed her attack upon the grass and weeds. She must not stop. The need to cut down, to pare away had become desperate, the making of the clearing a matter of more importance than the survival of the few plants she was uncovering.

Murdoch said, 'Take the weeds up first. The ground is wet now and they will come away easily.' He demonstrated.

'It is the grass,' she said. The choking, stubborn grass overlaid the hidden, obscure things to which she must somehow reach down, which the woman in the mirror already knew.

At last, together, they made a small clearing. Janet stared down at it and then folded over, her head on her knees, weeping. 'There is nothing, nothing . . . I can't go any deeper . . . I am not strong enough.'

He took off his jacket and laid it around her shoulders. She said, 'Don't leave me!' as the darkness closed over her.

Indeed, he could not leave her, so what was he to do? Humphrey, who had not liked what was going on very much, had withdrawn to the terrace, but now, seeing an end to the mystifying activity which had failed to rouse anything to be worried or retrieved, he came slowly down the steps, approaching Janet like a ponderous detective intent on a cautious investigation which he hopes will not uncover anything very unpleasant.

'We shall have to rely on you, old friend,' Murdoch said to him. He tore a page from his pocket book and wrote a note on it which he attached to Humphrey's collar. Then he led the dog round the side of the building and pointed him in the direction of the village. 'Go fetch Patsy,' he commanded. Humphrey put his ears back and his body quivered as it did when he was watching a partridge. Murdoch was both glad and apprehensive that he had always insisted on training his dogs himself. A part of the training was a belief that a dog should be allowed to develop his particular talent. Humphrey's talent was fetching. He said, in case the instruction needed fleshing out, 'Patsy, Sam, Francesca . . . Fetch!' Humphrey departed at speed and in the right direction. He had never been expected to fetch anything at such a distance, but he was a dog with a strong homing instinct. Murdoch hoped he would not simply turn in at his own gate.

Why didn't I go and leave Humphrey here? Murdoch

wondered. I could have fetched the car and he would have been as effective a guardian as I and less complaining. But then, if it rained, he couldn't carry Janet indoors – as I must now, because it *is* beginning to rain.

He sat on a window seat, holding Janet close, knowing that she was not there in his arms but had gone into some dark place where he could not follow her. He could not follow her, but the damnable thing was that he had got as far as the threshold! His experience as a writer was that thresholds, however dark, are for crossing. As a man, he believed his neighbours' thresholds were inviolable and gave them a wide berth. But his wife? As he felt Janet's body, heavy, unyielding as a conscientious protestor in the arms of a policeman, he was aware of a numb misery which was nothing to do with the raw feel of another's pain which he sometimes experienced, but was rather the kind of inarticulate, uncomprehending misery which he imagined Humphrey to feel when something went badly wrong in the routine of attention, exercise, feeding on which his wellbeing depended.

The rain, half-hearted at first, coming in intermittent bursts, had now settled dourly to its task, bubbling the windows, streaming from blocked gutters. Through the open door he could see it at work filling the deep cracks in the terrace, washing away the dust and grit. The wind buffeted the side of the house and drove the long grasses eastward like so many pointing arrows. Usually he did not begrudge the earth this gentle benediction, but today he felt as though all this effort on the part of the elements was directed solely at him. The whole purpose was to liquidate Murdoch Saunders, but slowly, first cutting off the source of power and potential, then withdrawing from him little by little all the favours so freely given, until only a small hard nub of misery remained. Hunched against the wall, the heavy, woollen cardigan sagging like the folds in his face, he listened to the glub, glub, gluck, burp and plerp of the earth drinking its fill and he hated every sodden thing out there, animal, vegetable and mineral. And its Creator, in whom he believed never more than at this moment, Him he hated most of all, because this was no benediction, this was valediction.

Not Janet, of course; he did not hate Janet. But he did feel cheated when he thought of all the years during which she had allowed him to imagine her to be happy and content. How could she have been so deceitful? When her illness first forced itself on his attention, he had felt very strongly that she had a right to her breakdown. Seen from a distance, which was the way he saw most things, it was a sort of clearing and cleansing operation which might well be necessary for the renewal of her spirit. It was not for him to stand in the way.

Inexorably, he had been drawn into it, not to the centre, but certainly well beyond the periphery. This he had accepted. They were man and wife, one flesh. He was confident that she would nurse him faithfully through any illness he might have, and he must do the same for her. He had not been prepared for how disturbing would be the watching, listening, anticipating, how the continual uncertainty would affect him, so that gradually the illness became uppermost in his mind. But this, too, he had accepted, telling himself that it must be allowed to run its course.

He had not foreseen that the course could run downhill, that there might be no cure; or that he would one day come to this place, to sit here in the rain, knowing that something was being taken from him. This, he told himself grimly, looking out at the sheeting rain, *this* is Hell – not all bright flame and parched tongues, but this all-pervasive wetness. This is how the world will end, not in nuclear explosion, but the slow attrition of earth by the one element which preceded all others.

He eased away from Janet and went to the window to see whether help was on the way. He caught his foot on the brush of the yard broom and the handle came up smartly and hit him on the side of the head. 'And the sooner the end the better!' he shouted.

Whatever happened to the world, he could see that this particular episode would end like a fairy story. When they came to fetch Janet they would find nothing beside her but the pool of self-pity in which he had drowned.

But no, they had come sooner than he had anticipated, if he had really anticipated that anyone would come. The footsteps, however, were approaching the rear of the building; which was not the direction from which he would have expected rescuers to arrive. He heard a woman's voice say, 'There's been someone here, planting roses . . .'

There was a silence while the ominous fact of the roses was assimilated. And in the pause he felt their fear, not sharp and glancing and soon to be gone, but the constant, debilitating harrowing of those without the resources to survive in an immutably hostile environment. A last gift! he thought; and as the self-conscious words formed in his mind he knew that his awareness was now of a different order.

Another woman spoke, her voice deeper but no less intimidated, 'I think the roses were there. They've uncovered them . . . sort of . . .'

Shadows fell across the french windows and there they stood, two women and a man. One of the women was small, floatingly robed like a fairground fortune-teller with huge rings hung from her ears and a crimson bandeau covering her forehead. But alas for the brave accessories, the eyes were too scared to look squarely at the present let alone the future. Her companion was a large woman bursting from sweatshirt and old denim trousers cut short at the knees; her face had the look of a fat child used to being tormented. As for the man, hair had taken over his face as the grass had covered the garden and it was difficult to discern any individual features. The three stood close, huddled together as people will for whom all strangers are bad news.

'My wife has been taken ill,' Murdoch said to allay their evident fear of eviction, a design they seemed pathetically willing to believe might be accomplished even by so ill-equipped a pair as himself and Janet.

The man said, 'That's all right, then.'

Murdoch said, 'It isn't really. I need someone to go for help.'

The crimson bandeau said, 'To the police, like?'

'I don't want the police here any more than you do.'

This did little to lessen their apprehension. They edged closer, looking down at Janet suspiciously. 'An overdose?' the man asked.

'Nothing of the kind.' Murdoch was beginning to lose his temper. 'She is exhausted, that is all. I need to get a message to my doctor.'

The crimson bandeau consulted her companions. 'Do you think we ought?'

'I don't know. What do you think?' The big woman looked at the man who tugged at his beard.

'We've got the others coming soon,' the crimson bandeau said. 'Perhaps one of them . . .?' She looked at her companions. 'I think we ought to wait for them. Don't you think we ought to wait for them?'

The big woman said to the man, 'What do you think? Did we ought to wait for them?'

The man said, 'Perhaps one of us . . .?'

The gravity of this suggestion weighed heavily on them. The crimson bandeau said, 'Or we could go, us two, and you could wait here and tell the others.'

Murdoch said, 'Or you could all three go and I could tell the others.'

This brisk intervention tore a hole through the tentative process of their decision making. The man said hastily, 'No, I don't think we could do that. Not all three of us.'

The big woman said, 'Perhaps when they come, one of them . . . ?'

The crimson bandeau said, 'I think we ought to talk it over with them, anyway. It's got to be something we all agree on. That's what we're all about, isn't it?' Thus relieved of responsibility she laid down one of the carrier bags she had been holding; a tin of Heinz beans rolled across the floor. They turned away from Murdoch and Janet, unwilling for further involvement.

The man said, 'Perhaps we should get the fire going?'

'Except we don't know how long they are going to be.'

'How many are there of you?' Murdoch was determined to have their attention.

They did not like direct questions. The big woman said, 'Hundreds.'

'But not here, in this house?'

'We shan't stay here long. We'll be on our way soon,' the crimson bandeau said defiantly.

'What makes you live like this?'

'We're travelling people, see.'

Murdoch wanted to shout that they resembled the Romanies about as much as a tatterdemalion youth with a line over a gravel pit resembles a deep-sea fisherman. Instead he controlled his temper and succeeded in sounding like one of the magistrates with whom they were no doubt familiar. 'This country is too small and overcrowded to support a nomadic people.'

'No one supports us,' the man said. 'We only take what's our due, same as everyone else. We don't beg.'

This momentary flash of pride warmed his companions. The crimson bandeau said, 'All we want is to be left alone,' and the big woman said, 'So piss off!'

'Just as soon as I can,' Murdoch snapped. He would very much have liked to administer his own version of a short, sharp shock; to have left them here, abject and humiliated. The force of his anger communicated itself without words. They turned their backs on him and went to the window, looking south, huddled like besieged prisoners wondering whether help will arrive in time, fearing to see the feathered head-dress parting the long grass.

'Look there!' The big woman pointed.

Murdoch joined them and saw a feathered tail parting the long grass. Relief washed away his anger. 'It's all right,' he assured them. 'It's not the police.'

It was, in fact, Patsy, looking businesslike in slacks and carrying an efficiently contrived stretcher in the guise of a well-roped deck chair. She greeted the squatters with cheerful good-humour and by the time Janet had been made as comfortable as possible relationships were sufficiently cordial for the man to say, 'We'd have given her a hot drink — if we'd got the fire going.'

When they had gone some way from the house Murdoch looked back. The squatters were still standing at the door and he thought they were like characters in a ghost story, forlorn and insubstantial, unlikely to survive long in the full light of day. He felt ashamed of having been so angry with them.

Janet lay on the improvised stretcher, her eyes closed, her face peaceful. Murdoch and Patsy walked slowly and carefully and she was not jolted about unnecessarily. She had not been unconscious during the exchanges with the squatters, but had given way to the longing to let someone else take charge. Now she enjoyed the experience of being carried. Not since she was a child had she let go like this. Always in adult life she had remained in charge, even during brief minor indispositions there had been footsteps on the stairs, the anxious voice at the bedroom door, 'Mum, where do we find ... ?' 'It *looks* done but how do we tell for certain?' and she had roused herself to give instructions, 'You must warm it through thoroughly ...' 'Make sure it is *quite* cold before ...'

Now responsibility slipped like a garment from her shoulders, arms, belly, thighs and she lay naked and heavy-limbed, a vacancy between the eyes which no questions or demands could penetrate. She had drifted beyond them on a raft which was carrying her down a dark river.

By the time they reached the road the rain had stopped and as they left the heath the clouds were breaking apart. There was a glimpse of sun running with the wind across a green field. Murdoch said, 'Oh God, oh God!'

Patsy said, 'Poor old chap! Not much further.'

They passed a paddock enclosed by wooden palings, green as though the sap still rose in them. Murdoch groaned and Patsy said, 'I'll come up this evening and make you a good supper, if you like.'

He looked at her mass of hair and the sweat-soaked shirt clinging to her shoulders. 'I don't think that would be a very good idea.'

Janet lay in the single bedroom where she now slept. Occasionally she heard noises about the house which she made no attempt to identify. A blackbird sang like a ghost in the tree outside the window.

She felt peaceful on that raft which was still carrying her down the dark river. But at night she dreamed she was in the city. It was a cold, bitter night and she and Patsy were standing by a trolley serving soup. She could see that there was very little soup left, but still people came out of the shadows, holding out mugs which she must fill. She dipped deeper and deeper into the cauldron. She was frightened because she knew she would reach the bottom soon and Patsy and the other helpers had gone. She would have to face the people in the shadows on her own when the time came that nothing was left.

[9]

'Deutzia feels that I should be doing more for Janet Saunders now that she is so ill,' Hector Beaney said to his wife over breakfast. Breakfast in the Beaney household usually had something of the confessional about it, the hour when Mr Beaney unloaded upon his wife those cares which the night had failed to dispel.

'It has all been too much for poor Deutzia. She has always put her own interests before those of other people and she can't be expected to change at her age.' Mrs Beaney made this pronouncement without malice in much the same way that a forecaster might speak of the weather in an uncongenial climate. 'But because she is unable to assume this burden, it does not mean that we must take it up.'

Mr Beaney looked hopefully at his wife, waiting for her to develop a cogent argument which would relieve him of a responsibility which they both knew he was unfitted to bear.

Priscilla Beaney said, 'They live too much to themselves as a family. She has hardly had an existence beyond the walls of that house. But that was their choice. It is necessary, and surely good, that we should have to face up to the results of our choices.'

Her husband crumbled toast and wondered how many more times he was to be reminded that he had made a choice. Mrs Beaney, who herself had made a choice when she married this melancholic man, briskly disposed of the last portion of poached egg and said, ' "No man is an island." Perhaps you might refer the Saunders family to John Donne?'

'Murdoch has been about quite a bit. I seem to remember that when he was young he went off with a travelling circus . . .'

'That I can believe, circus people and gypsies! But he never seems at home with his own kind. He doesn't know how pro-

123

fessional people converse. Do you remember when we went to dinner with the Hardings and he and Tim Harding had the most frightful argument about whaling, of all things! What does either of them know about whaling?'

'Most men argue over things about which they know very little.'

'And he used *language*!'

'Ah, yes . . .'

'I really think you have enough to do without becoming involved with people who only call on your services when they are in trouble.'

'That is rather an unfortunate way of putting it, my dear. When people are in trouble is the very time when I should be there.'

He was such a good man and yet unable to do much good, Mrs Beaney reflected as she poured another cup of tea for herself. The ways of God were mysterious indeed! She applied her mind to buoying up his spirit. 'What nonsense, Hector! If you only sat down to think about it you would realise that almost everyone in the village is in trouble of one kind or another. You cannot be involved in everyone's pain. Even our Lord had doubts about whether his mission extended to the woman of Samaria. It is necessary to discriminate.'

'Janet Saunders is very disturbed about this anti-nuclear meeting which Patsy Saunders is so insistent we should all attend. And if my parishioners are to be disturbed I feel that the least I can do is to be confused with them.'

'Janet Saunders is hardly typical of your parishioners.'

'She says she doesn't understand what is going on in the world today – I would have thought that was fairly typical. Then she goes on to say that she is beginning to realise she never *has* known, that life is not as she had imagined it.'

'Well, I think it all a waste of your time, but you would probably have to waste even more time justifying a decision *not* to go to this wretched meeting; so you will have to read all their literature, just to satisfy yourself that you could not possibly espouse their cause.'

'That won't take long. It is very repetitive – a series of questions with answers. I don't see why they need a meeting if they already know all the answers.'

'How naive you are! Most meetings are held to reinforce opinion. I suppose, when you come to think of it, that is why we go to church.'

'My dear, I do hope not.'

'I certainly don't go in order to have my opinions changed. And Patsy will not be going to this meeting to have her opinions changed, either. She actually said to me that the Chernobyl disaster proved everything that the anti-nuclear lobby has been saying! The West had over-reacted; the press had behaved disgracefully, saying that thousands were dead, when it was the Russians who had been telling the truth all the time; and, in addition to that, the Russians had proved far more efficient in dealing with the aftermath of the disaster than most people in the West had believed possible. Whereas I would have said exactly the opposite – it had proved that the Russians are completely untrustworthy and hopelessly inefficient. At a time when even the Poles were warning against eating fresh fruit and vegetables and drinking milk, the Russians were still saying there was no danger. Moscow didn't know what was happening and their leader had gone to earth somewhere. Imagine what Patsy would have said if that had been Mrs Thatcher!'

'I am not entirely happy myself . . .'

'Oh, the woman has no social sense at all, I grant you that. But at least she would have spoken to the nation.'

'But would she have told the truth? One has to ask oneself these questions . . .'

'Not unless one can provide a sensible answer.'

'Janet Saunders sees the answer as some kind of participation . . .'

'Janet Saunders, don't forget, has always fancied herself on the stage – particularly as St Joan. Because she wishes to take an acting role, there is no need for you to contemplate it, Hector. We have to learn to live with nuclear power, just as we learned to live with the bow and arrow. Or, if you would prefer it in theological terms, man has eaten of the fruit of the tree of knowledge and he cannot unlearn what he has learned. It is just another example of living with the consequences of your choice.'

'There are people with first-class brains in the anti-nuclear lobby. They put forward very telling arguments . . .'

'The great majority don't have arguments – they have emotions.'

'People's emotions are sometimes their surest guide.'

'And have frequently led them into war. You must not get yourself involved in this, Hector. It is all much too *close*, with these antinuclear groups all around us. You have always become confused when issues get on top of you. Remember how disturbed you became about Suez. And who thinks of that now?'

'There are usually two sides of an issue, Priscilla.'

'That kind of thinking leaves people unable to make decisions and it destroys their peace of mind.'

'Well, my dear, I have never had peace of mind, so you must be right. But I have made two decisions this morning. I shall go to this meeting with as open a mind as possible, and I must continue to talk to Janet Saunders about this. Not that I expect anything to come of either.'

As he sat in his study he wondered what he was to say to Janet Saunders. He had no idea how one set about counselling others on their problems, least of all a woman in her fifties who, he could not help but feel, had no business to have problems. Not for the first time he asked himself whether he should have become a monk. The contemplative life, seen from the outside, seemed so comfortable. But at his retreat house he had often been assured that the most trying thing in the monastic life was the other monks. Certainly Priscilla was not the most trying thing in his life. 'I have been very blessed,' he said humbly.

'Why did you marry Patsy?' Deutzia asked, proffering cucumber sandwiches. Tea was a meal at which she excelled, the only meal which she took any pleasure in preparing.

'She seemed different from the other young women I knew,

who were all rather ambitious. Career women frighten me. I thought Patsy was . . .'

'Like your mother.' Deutzia nodded her head, a satisfied smile brightening her eyes. 'When you are my age you notice things.'

'Be that as it may, I *didn't* notice the disorder.' He himself was immaculate in pale silver-grey slacks with a darker grey shirt, an outfit which, with his pale colouring, made him seem quite spectral in a cool, unemphatic way. Even as a ghost he would not create undue excitement.

'Your mother isn't very orderly,' Deutzia said. 'She does produce meals on time – or used to – but I wouldn't call her orderly about the house.' She gazed round her sitting room in which every ornament and chair had its proper place. 'Mrs Pringle, our daily help, once said to me – not that I encourage her to gossip, of course – that your mother's house was always in a mess. Not dirty, but with books and papers and sewing everywhere. She said that if she made a space your mother always filled it.'

Hugh said, wanting to change the conversation, 'All I ask of a woman is that she produces meals on time.' In fact, he asked for love and comfort, strength, security and stability. Patsy had not done so badly with the comforting, but had failed notably to provide stability. Being married to Patsy had been like living on a ship whose ballast has shifted.

'Shall you marry again?'

'I couldn't afford to.'

'Now you are not speaking just about money, are you? You are afraid of being hurt again, poor boy. But it's bad for you to live alone. When you are my age, of course, there is no choice. But you have your life ahead of you.'

'It is what is behind me that worries me.'

'You mustn't think like that. It is the present which is important. One must enjoy the present. That is one thing I am always thankful for – I got so much enjoyment out of life when I was young. Mind you, our pleasures were much more simple in those days. We only went abroad once a year and I never went sailing. But there was the theatre in the winter and tennis in the summer. Oh, those long summer evenings! After we had finished playing, we would go off, a whole crowd of us, to a country pub. I remember the Royal Standard of England was a particular favourite. Or was that later? I seem to remember men in uniform there ... I forget the details, I just remember this sense of everything being very special. If your boyfriend was rich – and I confess without shame that many of mine were – you would be taken down to the river for dinner. Bray. There was a good place at Bray – I can't recall the name, but the food was delicious and there would be a table overlooking the river ... You should be doing that sort of thing, Hugh. Girls don't change all that much, in spite of all this talk about being liberated, whatever that means. Find a pretty girl and take her to a hotel by the river.' For her, that had been an end in itself. She barely remembered the men. But the little breeze stealing up from the river, the table with its single rose in a vase, the crisp cloth, the misted glass from which she drank her wine, the memory of these things gave her a little thrill of pleasure even now.

Hugh said abruptly, 'We hardly see you now. Not even for Sunday lunch.'

For years Deutzia had come for Sunday lunch. It was nice, she had maintained, for Janet to have the company of another woman; and then Janet loved cooking while she hated it, so it was a very congenial arrangement for both of them. Now she said fretfully, in a tone of one tried beyond reason, 'My dear, I have come for years on a Sunday, but I have other friends of whom I must think and they are becoming very insistent that I shouldn't neglect them any longer. Such a dear couple who live just outside town. Rodney drives over to fetch me.'

'But Deutzia, we are in trouble, and you are the only person outside our family on whom we have any claim.'

'Really, Hugh!' Deutzia plucked at the wide, flowered skirt, arranging and rearranging its ample folds with trembling hands, as though quelling some subterranean insurrection. 'One does not speak about *claims* to friends. Claims, indeed! Have you been keeping an account? All those years when I gave your mother my friendship, *toiling* up that awful hill to your house, so bad for my poor old heart, were you *counting* the number of visits in the expectation of some sort of repayment?'

'I'm sorry, Deutzia; I am terribly sorry. It's just that I don't know which way to turn, I'm so worried.'

'I think you must ask yourself *why* you don't know which way to turn. *Why* am I the only person outside the family to whom you can turn? And why, indeed, do you make this distinction – one of which, I must tell you, I have always been conscious – between the family and myself?'

'It's only a manner of speaking, Deutzia. The relationship is a bit distant, that's all.'

'It is not a blood relationship, you mean. Oh, I have always been very aware of *that*, Hugh. Why, the last time I came to visit you all on a Sunday – though I missed seeing you to my great disappointment – I was not invited to lunch because Janet said that now you were so seldom together as a family.'

'I don't know anything about that.'

'I am sorry for you all. But you have always kept yourselves apart and now you will have to manage as a family.' She made a final adjustment of the folds in the skirt. 'We sow as we reap.'

'If you were ill, my mother would come to you.'

'Your mother is fifty, Hugh, and I am eighty-three next January.' She took a handkerchief from her sleeve and patted her face. 'Oh, there's nothing for it – I shall have to move away. I simply cannot withstand the pressures which are put upon one in this place.'

'What pressures, Deutzia? I have only asked . . .'

'It is not just this illness of your mother's – though that is bad enough! There are other things. *You* should know, none better. Your wife, Hugh, is now agitating for people to attend some meeting which is to be held next month about nuclear power. You will find a leaflet about it over there under the Radio Times. It is headed "After Chernobyl . . ." '

'I shouldn't let that worry you. It's no use arguing with Patsy – just say you will go and then cry off at the last minute.'

'And be subject to constant rebuke afterwards? I tell you, Hugh, I have nightmares about the nuclear winter, sitting holed up with Patsy in her gas cape telling me it has all come to pass just as she prophesied.'

'There is something very uncomfortable about absolute moral rightness, I know that. And I think it probably does more harm than good to any cause. But Patsy doesn't mean to hurt anyone. It's just that she suffers from the simple solution syndrome.'

Dr Potter had suggested that Patsy was a prisoner locked in a pattern of behaviour from which she could not escape. But what is that to me? he thought. She didn't love me. If she had loved me, at my touch she would have been freed from her prison. That was all that was expected of knights errant, simply to touch the woman. That, and the killing of a few dragons on the way . . . He experienced the faintness of extreme weariness as he thought of these things. Instinctively, he looked out of the window, seeking, beyond this room in which the faded green velvet chairs, the silk-tasselled lampshade, the china figures on the mantelpiece and the photographs in their silver frames, all contributed to an atmosphere of languid regret, something to record in his diary which would redeem the day from failure. Deutzia's gardener had laboured lovingly on the long flower border. In the early evening light, huge orange poppies, bold purple lupins, yellow iris and soft umber pansies all shimmered with that radiance – perhaps an effect of the angle of light – which makes each brilliant petal and every green leaf seem stencilled on the blue of the sky. He recalled how this morning, walking down the lane, he had seen buttercups on a green verge, their stalks barely visible, so that the bright flowers seemed to leap in the air. He was conscious of the great energy which had been loosed in life and sitting in this decorous room, he felt that both he and Deutzia were observers of a feast to which they had not been invited – or had refused to participate.

Deutzia was saying, 'They are sharp enough when it comes to their own interest. When the council was thinking of developing that meadow just beyond the stream, Patsy and her friends all protested as loudly as their Conservative neighbours – in the name of the environment, of course.'

'Didn't you protest?'

'Yes, because I like my view. But then, I am spoiled and selfish.'

She not infrequently made this sort of statement, needing a robust denial. He, however, was silent, angered not so much by her refusal to help his mother as by the old resentments and feelings of inadequacy which her talk of Patsy had stirred up within him.

She said, 'This is a very small place, Hugh, and I cannot stand, I have never been able to stand, other people's displeasure. It is weak of me, I know, but I am very sensitive.'

He saw, looking at her flushed, crumpled face, that she was genuinely unhappy. Earlier on, she had referred to a couple whom she could not neglect, but no reference had been made to the needs of her own children. It would seem that she had accepted that to them she was merely a nuisance. Hugh recalled that she had not been a loving mother, but it seemed hard that accounts should be rendered so late in life, long past the possibility of redeeming the debts. He said gently, 'I am truly sorry, Deutzia. It was wrong of me to have spoken of claims.'

Deutzia folded her handkerchief and tucked it carefully in her sleeve. 'Has your mother asked for me?'

'She doesn't ask for anyone – not even us.'

'Has your father asked for me?'

'My father seems to be trying to manage on his own.'

Deutzia said, 'If they had asked, I might have come.' There was a hint of sadness in her voice. One might almost have thought that, for a moment, she regretted that this effort was not to be demanded of her.

When he left one of Deutzia's neighbours was cutting the grass and its dusty smell sweetened the air. He felt again that sense of the energy to which every common weed attested – the Church taught that this energy was love, but if it was frustrated or refused, what then became of it?

Murdoch watched a woman turn over a pile of avocado pears, then walk away looking angry. He stared down at the pears, wondering what had made her so angry. Tentatively, he prodded one. It was hard. He prodded a number of them. All hard. But there were so many – surely supermarkets would not waste this amount of space with a display of unripe fruit? He passed on to the pineapples where he found himself standing beside the angry woman who was tearing at a leaf at the base of one of the pineapples. He deduced from the contemptuous way in which she threw it down that the leaf should have come away more readily. He wondered why she had not simply squeezed the pineapple. Perhaps constant pummelling, while acceptable for avocados, was not good for pineapples? He picked one up and pulled at a leaf which came away at once. He could smell the juice. The woman gave him a furious look. Pineapple was not on his list, tinned or otherwise, but he had no mind to give up his prize and he put the pineapple in the trolley and moved on.

He consulted his list. Only a few items remained to track down. Capers was one of them. Janet did not like capers but Stephanie did and as Stephanie was coming to stay Janet had said that he should buy capers. He could not see why, but as it was the longest conversation they had had in a week it seemed important that he should do as she asked. An exhaustive search revealed capers in vinegar. Did they always come in vinegar? Nothing had been said about bottled capers. A young man was advancing towards him pushing a huge trolley loaded with reinforcements for the shelves, his manner conveying much of the contempt for human life displayed by the railway porter, but his vehicle, having no warning buzzer, giving the quarry even less chance to escape before impact. Murdoch pushed his trolley sideways across the aisle and stepped away smartly. The collision had more effect on the store's overloaded trolley than on Murdoch's more modest one and a cascade of tins, packets of tea and sugar, and cartons of milk fell on the floor. One of the milk cartons broke open. The young man came round the side of the trolley spoiling for battle. He was an angry young man but not a brave one and something about Murdoch's waiting stance reminded him of a wrestler he had seen at a fair. The man had taken on all comers with small damage to himself. The most intimidating thing about him had been the way his feet were planted on the ground as though only an earthquake could shift them. The young man's face crimsoned with the effort of controlling his temper.

Murdoch, well aware that apology would lose him his advantage, said unconcernedly, 'I wanted to ask you – have you any dried capers?'

The young man said through closed teeth, 'The dried goods are in the next bay.'

'Thank you. Now if you could move your trolley a little to the right I could extricate mine.'

'Anything to oblige.' The young man jerked the rail of the trolley viciously and it turned on its side, tumbling the remainder of its ill-balanced load onto the floor.

Murdoch pushed his trolley to the next bay. The dried goods consisted of apricots, prunes, figs, dates and a miscellany which even he realised would be unlikely to include capers. However, he saw that he was near the pasta section and made a selection of macaroni and spaghetti before returning to the scene of the collision. Here the manager greeted him with upraised hand like a policeman on point duty. 'If you don't mind, sir. The floor is rather slippery.' An elderly woman coated in milk was being helped away. Murdoch said, 'Perhaps you could hand me a bottle of capers.'

The manager picked his way daintily to the shelf. When he returned with a bottle of capers he was looking thoughtful. 'Aren't you the gentleman whose wife was taken ill here a few weeks ago?'

Murdoch said, 'More importantly, I am the gentleman who was rammed by one of your assistants who was in charge of a vehicle over which he had inadequate control.'

The manager turned on his heel, not a wise manoeuvre in the circumstances. He slipped and sought to steady himself on the now empty trolley which took off at speed down the length of the bay, the manager skidding behind it. Murdoch watched as they approached the T junction where, perhaps in an effort to avoid collision with the oncoming poultry stall, the manager flung out an arm and grabbed the egg rack with foreseeable consequences. Murdoch walked away.

'Oh, that manager!' a woman exclaimed. 'He's not up to it. I've said that all along. They appoint them too young and now he's gone off his head.'

The tone of sorrowful pleasure was unmistakable. Murdoch turned to her. 'Mrs Pringle!'

She gave a start and gathered her shopping bag to her breast like a shield.

'You haven't been to us for the last couple of weeks.'

'It's my sister,' she said. 'She's not well.'

'You've never failed us before,' Murdoch said, ignoring what he had no difficulty in recognising as a red herring.

'She has these upsets.'

'Don't you *want* to come any more? If not, say so.'

'And it's a large house. She can't manage all on her own.'

'Can we expect you next week?'

'I said to her, "You ought to find somewhere smaller".'

'And *why*, if you couldn't come, didn't you let us know?'

'It's all very well, putting everything on me.' There were tears in Mrs Pringle's eyes. 'I told her, "I'm getting older," I said, "I can't do as much as I once did".' She backed, weeping, into one of the check-out stalls.

Murdoch was aware of the girls in the check-out stalls averting their eyes, he could almost hear them praying, 'Please don't let him come to me!'

He walked down to the far end of the stalls where a middle-aged cashier was intent on helping an old man put his purchases in his shopping bag.

'No, that's *yours*, Mr Perry,' she said in a jolly voice. 'You've just paid for it, dear, so you don't want to give it back to me, do you?'

Murdoch unloaded his trolley and she began to ring up the purchases while keeping one eye on the old man who was furtively trying to unload his shopping bag. She paused to beckon a young assistant. 'Take him outside, will you, Robin. He's all right once he gets outside.'

She turned back to Murdoch. 'Sorry, dear. Oh! This is a Nine Items Only queue. Didn't you see the notice?'

Murdoch said meekly that he had not seen the notice and the woman behind him sighed.

'Well, I've started, so I'll have to take them now.' She dealt briskly with the purchases and said, clearly and slowly, 'Twenty-one pounds and fifty-three pence.'

Murdoch took out his chequebook. The woman behind him sighed again. The cashier said, 'No cheques at this counter, dear. Not at the Nine Items Only counter.'

Murdoch took out his wallet. His fingers were trembling and the woman had to separate the five pound notes for him: there were only three. 'Is that all you have, dear? Nothing in your trouser pocket? Oh well, we'll have to have a cheque then, won't we, as I've rung it all up. You do have a banker's card, do you, dear?'

As he fumbled for his card, watched contemptuously by the woman behind, Murdoch thought that he knew how Janet had felt when she sat on the floor among the grapefruit. On the whole, he thought it had been quite a sensible thing for her to do. He found the card and when his cheque had been accepted, he managed to load up the trolley and wheel it out to the car without the cashier having to summon Robin to his assistance.

As he drove out of the car park he saw the old man standing looking around him vacantly. The old man might well have found a place in one of Murdoch's books had he felt him, but on this occasion he saw him. He braked and, ignoring impatient hooting from the car behind, called to the old man. 'Can I give you a lift?' The old man came obediently forward. It occurred to Murdoch afterwards, but not at that moment, that the old man was probably taken to the town's House of Friendship during the week and imagined himself to be on the way there. For whatever reason, he allowed himself to be installed in the back seat – Murdoch did not think the business of negotiating a seat belt in the front was within his compass. 'Where?' he asked, as he drove forward, 'do you live?'

The old man looked cunning. This, of course, Murdoch should have foreseen.

Back in the supermarket he managed to attract the attention of Robin. 'He only lives a few blocks away.' He gave the address.

The old man had got out of the car, leaving his purchases behind, by the time Murdoch returned. It took some time to find him.

A few blocks away it might be on foot, but not, thanks to the town's intricate one-way system, by car.

'Are we going to have a sing-song?' the old man asked as the car crawled down the crowded high street. 'I like it when we have a sing-song.'

'Perhaps you would like to sing now?' Murdoch suggested, hoping thereby to alleviate any regret the old man might feel on finding himself in his own home with no musical diversion in prospect.

'I can sing "White Wings",' and the old man began to sing in a quavering but surprisingly sweet voice, ' "White wings, they never grow weary . . ." '

Twenty mintues later Murdoch stopped the car in front of a small terraced house facing immediately onto the pavement. He stood waiting patiently while the old man fumbled for his key. After a time the old man lost interest and stood looking vacantly down the street. 'Where be the chapel, then?' he asked.

'They have pulled it down to build that block of flats,' Murdoch said. 'Did you go there?'

'No, I went to The Black Bull.'

The front door had a handle. Murdoch tried it and the door opened. The old man went in.

Ten minutes later, driving out of the town, a disturbing thought occurred to Murdoch. He stopped in a lay-by and examined the back seat. Then he turned the car and drove back to the town. The front door had been secured and he could not summon the old man, but the woman next door took the purchases from him.

'Been at it again, has he, the naughty old thing?' she said kindly.

'Does he have any family?'

'Not that you'd notice.'

Whereas, Murdoch thought, as he drove away, I seem to be noticing rather too much. He was upset and when he reached the lay-by he stopped the car again. He sat hunched over the wheel, his head resting on his folded arms. After quite a long time a helmeted head appeared at the window.

'In trouble, sir?'

'To everything there is a season. Now is the time for the burning of the leaves.'

There were no fumes of drink and the constable was shortly going off duty. He decided to treat this as a piece of harmless eccentricity. 'Then I'll leave you to get on with it, sir, so long as it's in your own back garden that you're thinking of having a bonfire.'

'You are constantly answering unseen challengers. How did you get yourself in this state?' Dr Potter asked.

In any contest, the person who plays on the home ground has the advantage and this holds true not only of sport but of social engagements. The hostess is mistress of her domain, the guest who does not conform to her will is more likely to undermine her own confidence than that of the lady of the house. It had been a mistake, Stephanie acknowledged grimly, to insist that there was no need for her to come to Dr Potter's consulting room since what she had in mind was an informal talk between fellow professionals. That 'fellow professionals' had been another mistake – psychiatrists being so morbidly jealous of psychologists that they could not acknowledge that their work was in any way comparable. The unfortunate result of these mistakes was that Stephanie was now seated in Dr Potter's living room.

Dr Potter lived in an old farmhouse situated at the end of a long, narrow, unmade-up lane with no turning places. Anyone would have thought that tradesmen and postal services would have refused delivery but, judging by the number of times which Stephanie had had to reverse down the lane, this was not the case. She had arrived in sight of the farmhouse late and in a state of nervous and physical tension. On seeing yet another vehicle about to come through the farm gate she had hooted vigorously thus causing violent disturbance within a horsebox. The driver of the vehicle had descended and addressed Stephanie in language wholly unacceptable in a woman – and Stephanie had no little experience of the grey areas of acceptability. She was aware that Dr Potter housed several ex-convicts in her home, but this woman, a small, coppery vixen, had laid about her with that air of complete confidence which one imagined to have characterised landowners in the days of serfdom. Stephanie could only conclude that this was the woman with whom Dr Potter lived.

When the occupant of the horsebox had been appeased and towed away at funereal speed, Stephanie had got out of the car, only to be threatened by two sheepdogs who came hurtling out of a barn followed by a scrawny young woman who seemed to have come to watch the fun rather than with any intention of rendering aid. Stephanie, who was a magistrate, could not remember having heard that Dr Potter had come up before the bench charged with owning a dangerous dog. She had pursued her way, not exactly undaunted, but with some determination and had reached the front door with no greater misfortune than having trodden in a cow pat.

'You should look where you are walking on a farm,' Dr Potter had greeted her.

'I was too busy keeping an eye on your dogs, since your "farm hand" did not seem disposed to call them off.'

'A lot of resentment to be worked through there, I am afraid. But I don't need to explain that to you.'

Dr Potter had led the way into a big room with lattice windows which would catch the western light. At this hour of the morning it was dark. The floor was stone-flagged with rugs cast about here and there to trip the unwary. Stephanie and Dr Potter had seated themselves on either side of a large brick fireplace with a pile of logs to one side of the empty hearth. It was too warm to need a fire. Even so, Stephanie, who had grown up in a house where the lighting of fires was an essential to winter warmth and comfort and therefore a symbol of love and care, had experienced a feeling of desolation as though the hour and the season had conspired against her.

'Now,' Dr Potter had said, 'we are to talk informally. You no doubt have a subject in mind.'

The misshapen face was in shadow, but a chance – or was anything chance here? – glimmer of reflected light illuminated the one good eye. A woman slowly trundled a wheelbarrow past the window, closely followed by another woman defiantly bearing a pitchfork aslant one shoulder in the manner of one about to lead a peasants' revolt. It was at this point that, although her business was urgent, Stephanie had given way to an imperative urge to demonstrate that she was not impressed by Dr Potter's brand of philanthropy. There were, of course, people who gave their whole lives to others, but they mostly lived in distant places – like India – and one was not called upon to measure up to them.

'Of course,' she had said, '*I* worked in a London borough clinic at one time, dealing with what, in a franker age than ours, would have been termed the dregs of society. But it wasn't that which bothered me. It was the hypocrisy of my colleagues, who were quite incapable of thinking honestly. In fact, it was very difficult to understand how they felt about anything because they had been lying to themselves for so long. Take the Miller family. The plain fact of the matter was that the Miller family did not go straight because they got on much better the way they were. But we were all supposed to see them as victims of the capitalist system ...' What *was* she doing pouring out all this resentment of the Miller family whom she had not seen for at least five years? The thought was like a piece of paper glimpsed floating in the air from a fast moving train. The train powered on. 'Crime pays. It's their way of life. And it has nothing to do with lack of opportunity – the Millers of this world never let anything get past them in the way of opportunity! They size up the situation according to their lights and they play the game their way. All this rubbish about middle-class affluence! There was more money coming in to that house than I shall ever see.' She came to a grinding halt and said breathlessly, 'I can't imagine why I should tell you this, except to illustrate . . .' What had she intended to illustrate, other than her contempt for Dr Potter's pitiful attempt to rehabilitate ex-prisoners? She could hardly say this in so many words and must hope that she had made her position sufficiently clear.

It was then that Dr Potter had said, 'You are constantly answering unseen challengers. How did you get yourself into this state?'

Stephanie thought of the long narrow lane down which she had passed to reach this dark room. Oh dear, oh dear, the psychological implications were inescapable! And she, by refusing to go to the consulting room, had brought about this imprisonment in the womb of Dr Potter's house. Well, she must make the best of it and proceed coolly and calmly, not allowing her good judgement to be disturbed by any antics Dr Potter might indulge in.

She said good-humouredly, 'I am not in a state at all. I was merely making a few observations on the criminal fraternity.'

'All your conversation seems to be addressed to someone against whom you have to defend yourself.'

Dr Potter had moved in her chair and Stephanie could see her more clearly now. She had a dreadful thicket of hair. Stephanie could not make up her mind whether it was naturally curly and at some stage in her life Dr Potter had given up trying to get a comb through it, or whether she actually paid money to achieve this bizarre effect. Stephanie was aware of the weight of her own heavy plait between her shoulder blades. Usually she liked the feel of it, reminding her how thick and rich was her flaxen mane; but for some reason it was now making her feel obscurely uncomfortable.

She said, wriggling her shoulders very slightly, 'Yes, I suppose one does have to defend oneself from time to time. Or simply conform. I don't conform.'

'Yet you strike me as someone who has spent the early part of her life conforming to one kind of authority and is now contemplating spending the remainder submitting to another kind.'

Stephanie gave a laugh that was a shade too boisterous, an echo of the schoolgirl Stephanie. 'I am not at all submissive, believe me!'

'But from what you have been telling me about your work in the London borough, you would very much like to have thought as your colleagues did. You would like to see yourself as a front-line worker – teaching in an inner-city comprehensive, running a canteen for striking print workers in your spare time and camping at Greenham Common at weekends. You feel quite terrified at finding yourself on the outside when all your childhood you were so acceptable.'

She was formidable. Questions, answers, images flashed fast, seemingly irrelevant, yet always on target – had she *known* that Piers taught in an inner-city comprehensive? She reminded Stephanie of one of those ruthless women tennis-players who always knows where the ball will go before her opponent strikes it. Now, raising her hands above her head to adjust one of the wilder coils of hair, she seemed poised to launch an overhead smash across the hearth. Stephanie could see herself standing at the net, very vulnerable, her pigtail swinging about helplessly while she hit all the balls on to Dr Potter's racquet.

She said, trying to slow down the pace, 'One is only human. It would be stupid to pretend that I did not mind being told by my erstwhile colleagues that I had "sold out", accused of no longer caring about the future of the world, the starving millions, apartheid . . . Even my husband . . .' She faltered, this was a shot she should not have attempted. 'I sometimes feel that even he thinks . . .' The ball trickled miserably down the side of the net.

'So why *did* you leave the London borough clinic and go to work in this privately funded establishment in Surrey?'

'Because we see people there whom it is possible for me to help.' Stephanie conceded the game to Dr Potter. 'Working-class people don't respond – not to me, at least. They don't like being counselled by someone who has no idea about their way of life.'

'Whereas at this private clinic you see people whom you do understand and whom you feel you have a chance of helping? If this is where your particular talent lies, I see nothing wrong in that.'

Absolution from this quarter was so unexpected that Stephanie felt an overwhelming need to make further confessions. 'Understanding, perhaps. I think I do understand ... quite often, at any rate. But help? I *do* help. I have often been told so. But I am never sure of my motives. The truth is, I don't like people very much. I find them quite interesting, but I don't really like them.'

'And you are ashamed of this?'

'This is a caring society, isn't it?'

'*Why* are you ashamed?'

'I have been ashamed most of my life of one thing or another.' Stephanie eased her pigtail forward so that it hung comfortingly between her breasts. 'I have never much liked the grown-up world. I had to get into it too quickly; with three younger children, I was always the one who was put in charge. It's the old story, of course, I am aware of that. Nudged off my mother's knee to make way for the new baby.'

'And you were grudging about it, no doubt?'

'Everyone thought I managed very well. In that sense, I was, as you say, acceptable. But inside, I wasn't at all nice. I grudged my brothers and sister every bit of my mother's love. It seemed to me there wasn't enough to go round and I lost out. It has been like that ever since. The world is full of people ... all trees.'

'Trees?'

'Something happened when I was quite young ... I got lost. All the people were so tall, like trees.' She burst out suddenly, 'I don't know why we are talking about me. I came here to talk about my father. It's my father who really worries me. Only yesterday, I told him he had got short-grain rice instead of long – and *tears*, real tears, came into his eyes.' Tears came into Stephanie's eyes.

Dr Potter said, 'Ah, your father.'

'He *must* have time to finish his revise and he never will while my mother is at home. So, either she comes to me and I will take time off to look after her.' Which she would refuse to do, or so

Stephanie profoundly hoped. 'Or she must go somewhere . . . a nursing home or some such place . . . just for a few weeks to give my father a break.'

'It would have to be with her consent. Your mother is not certifiable.'

'But persuadable, one hopes.'

Dr Potter shrugged her shoulders. 'That depends on your powers of persuasion – and your relationship with your mother.'

Stephanie saw that it had been a mistake to let her case rest on the needs of her father. Dr Potter was nutty as a fruit cake and by no means as wholesome. Also, she was undoubtedly a lesbian. She would think nothing of sacrificing Murdoch to what she saw as Janet's good. And that is how I shall refer to her in future, Janet, Janet, Janet . . .

When she left, the dogs who had been slumbering in the yard awoke and came circling and snarling around her. All her own sleeping dogs were awakened and continued with her as she drove away.

Katrina was seated by the window, facing the engine; a canvas bag was dumped beside her and one trousered leg was cocked over it, boot resting on the next seat. Although from her vacant expression one might imagine she had blocked out the other passengers, she was not unaware of the irritation she was causing. In spite of the fact that she wore headphones, the music was just loud enough to make a faint scratching on the air, distracting but not sufficiently so to warrant complaint. One would, in any case, think twice about attempting to remonstrate with her. Her clothes were unexceptional and clean. The spiky red hair was neat in its own fashon, her skin clear, the colour pleasing. But there was a wilfulness about the full mouth and the narrowed eyes suggested a spiteful mood. Of late she had frequently played this game of keeping people at a distance while making it extremely difficult for them to distance her. She was aware that a time would come when she would be forced to make some kind of accommodation with life, step out of her fastness and accept that others existed in no less urgent a way than herself. Sometime, and she sensed it would be soon, it would be necessary to switch off the transistor and listen to what was going on outside her own head. But not yet. For the present, she had business to attend to. While the music played hoarsely she took pen and paper and began to write to that loving, understanding friend, that constant companion, the more ideal for being as yet unfound, with whom for years she had shared her most private and deepest experiences.

'My great discovery has nothing to do with all the stuff they get you to cram into yourself here (they call it leaving the students to educate themselves, but really they make you do the work because they are too busy getting their books ready for publication). It's to do with Ewett. I expect you guessed that. I thought it was going to be such a big thing, his wife pleading with me, and the children there in the background. *She* was the one it meant most to. She was the one who made it so *significant*. With a build-up like that I was sure he would take his time, work out a campaign, plan a careful assault, or whatever the modern equivalent is of being wooed. He must have known how awful and torn I felt, that he must break down the barriers without harming the prisoner. I thought he would turn it into a game that I could learn to play so that when the time came I'd be good . . . I *needed* that. Breaking up hearts and homes is new to me. Besides, there is something inside me I don't want to part with. But that was all right because Ewett didn't want it anyway. He got all he wanted (which didn't amount to much, let's be honest) and I was welcome to keep the rest. It was all pretty perfunctory. His wife screwed by far the most out of it. And my discovery? Well, of course, it's not the old tag about men losing interest once they've got what they wanted. But, before you breathe a sigh of relief, I have to warn you there is worse to come. I'm making so much of the preliminaries because I don't know that I'm going to be able to write this down. But I must, because I have a feeling it is very important that now, at this moment, I actually make myself say this. It is *you* I want.'

Katrina stared at what she had written, then, scarlet-faced, she tore the pages across and across and scattered them on the floor.

A woman said, 'She ought to be made to pick up every single scrap.'

Katrina, sensing outrage, turned up the volume.

Stephanie was waiting at the ticket barrier. Katrina looked at her in dismay. As they walked towards the car, she said, 'What have you done to yourself?'

'Done?'

'Wearing your hair on top of your head like a bread basket. You don't look like my big sister any more.'

'I am Piers' wife and mother of two children. We all have to grow up sometime. I thought I might set you a good example. There is still time for you to look fresh and youthful – not much time, but a little.'

Katrina ignored this and said, 'I hope no one else is going to change. There have been enough changes around here!'

'Then you had better prepare yourself for the fact that your father has taken to domesticity.'

'You mean he helps with the washing-up now?'

'If only that were all!'

In the car Katrina switched on the transistor. Stephanie said, 'Cigarettes, smoking, drinking, drug-taking, constant input of beat music ... I'm sure my crowd wasn't so obsessional.' Katrina stared vacantly out of the window.

Stephanie stopped the car in a lay-by. Katrina came out of her trance to ask, 'What's this in aid of?'

'Switch that thing off. I have to talk to you.'

'I don't want to talk.'

'Suit yourself.' Stephanie opened the window and gazed out at the passing heavy lorries, her eyes half-closed, as though breathing in wafts of balmy air in a summer meadow. Katrina sighed. 'Oh, all right. But while you're driving. I'm starving.'

As she drove, Stephanie said, 'We have to get Janet away for a little while. This is all too much for Murdoch. He isn't writing.'

'What's all this Murdoch and Janet business? That's never been our style.'

'We have to get your mother away.'

'She's your mother, too.'

'Katrina! Can't you concentrate on essentials?'

'I'm not sure which is essential. Something odd seems to be going on here.'

'I propose to suggest that our mother goes to a nursing home, or rest home, or some suitable place, for a little while. Just to give our father a break.'

'Why? When we were ill as kids she didn't pack us off somewhere else. If you don't think Daddy can cope, I'll quit college and come and look after her. I'd be only too glad to.'

'Which? Quit college or look after our mother?'

'Both.'

'You couldn't anyway. You've never done a hand's turn about the house.'

'It would be good for me, then. It's time I learned. There are all sorts of things I haven't learned that I'm certainly never going to learn if I stay at university.'

'You are learning things which will see you through life at university.'

'No, I'm learning things which will prevent me having a good life.'

'Well, I can see it is no use talking to you in this mood. Let's hope that after a few days at home you will be cured of any notion of moving in and shouldering all our burdens.'

'Do you realise, Stephanie, that whenever I try to tell you things about myself you always listen with a sweet, sorrowful smile fixed on your face? Is that how you maintain superiority over your clients?' Katrina's voice had become shrill. 'I'm sorry for them. They must feel so diminished.'

As they drove up to the house Stephanie's smile was positively seraphic. She switched off the engine and said, 'I have to warn you that Patsy is here "helping". I wanted to see her off, but Murdoch . . . our . . .'

'Just say Murdoch. Anything rather than Our Father '

'Well, Murdoch insists that Patsy has tried to help and that we shouldn't send her away now that we are here. So she is in the kitchen, making a nuisance of herself and upsetting Hugh. The children, as you can see, are creating mayhem in the garden.'

Katrina remained in the car while Stephanie got out to open the garage door. When Stephanie returned, she was still sitting there, gazing at Patsy's youngest who was energetically beating the dustbin lid with a soup ladle.

'What's wrong with us all, Stephanie? Don't you wonder? Mummy is ill and we make this awful balls-up of looking after her. And now you want to put her away somewhere. How are you going to manage that? Rent a crowd to come and chant "Janet out!" on the lawn beneath her window?'

'I'll leave you to put the car away.' Stephanie turned and marched into the house.

Katrina followed, leaving the car outside. She dumped her gear in the hall and ran up to what was now her mother's room.

Janet was sitting in a chair by the window, a rug across her knees. As Katrina came towards her, a book slid off her lap. She paid no attention to it, nor did she turn her head towards her daughter.

'I feel so ashamed,' Katrina said.

'Ashamed, ashamed, ashamed . . .' Janet repeated. 'Oh dear, oh dear.'

'How could we do this to you?' Katrina persisted.

Janet made fussy adjustments to the rug, frowning intently.

'Let me help. What is it you want to do?'

As soon as Katrina touched the rug, Janet lost interest. In the garden the children were fighting over the dustbin lid. Hugh shouted at them from the kitchen. Katrina said, 'How do you put up with all this racket?'

Janet repeated 'all this?' as though she was unaware of the presence of other people in the house or garden. It occurred to Katrina that her mother had found her own way of distancing herself without the aid of headphones or transistor. As she knelt beside her, she wondered whether they would ever come really close again.

Stephanie called from the stairs, 'You do realise you left the car out and that the children might have got in it and played with the brake and . . .' She went on and on, building up a series of disasters to relieve some need in herself. From the window Katrina could see her father walking towards the car while Patsy knelt beside her children like a mother hen gathering its brood under its wing.

Supper was a silent meal. Patsy had taken the children home and Hugh was depressed. After they had all got in each other's way doing the washing-up, Murdoch went for a walk with Humphrey.

Katrina settled down in the television-room to watch *A Very Peculiar Practice*. To her annoyance she was soon joined by Stephanie. Katrina had spent some time before supper trying to come to terms with her relationship with Stephanie. She had acknowledged that Stephanie would always be the elder sister in whose presence she herself would become immature, gauche, and, worst of all, shrill. It would be sensible to accept this and never, never get into an argument. She had not wanted her new-found wisdom to be put to the test so soon.

Stephanie, who was never able to watch television without instructing other people as to what was happening, said, 'I find the reversal of the roles particularly amusing, don't you?'

Katrina grunted.

Stephanie watched in silence for a moment or two and then said, 'And rather more interesting than all this business with the lesbian woman doctor which I find rather obvious.' Katrina began to file her nails. 'It's the old Hollywood story of the Thirties. In fact, I suppose one might say that it is the eternal love story in reverse. The man it is who nearly drowns and has to be rescued by the big, strong policegirl. Who then discovers that he is wounded and vulnerable, poor chap, having been ill-used by a brute of a wife. So she must teach him the gentle art of loving. But, note, warning him that she is not to be tied to any one man, which he meekly accepts, just grateful for her attentions while he is in receipt of them. One can see Clark Gable and

Janet Gaynor playing the Thirties version.'

Katrina said, 'And that appeals?'

'I find it amusing.'

'But the idea of playing the Clark Gable role appeals to you?'

'There are times when I feel the urge to mount my horse and ride off into the sunset.'

'That was Gary Cooper – *The Plainsman* and all that – not Clark Gable. Anyone can tell you're not a cinema buff.'

'Oh well, whichever . . .'

Katrina said, keeping her voice at its lower register, 'Well, it doesn't appeal to me.'

'You have led a rather sheltered life, Katrina. I can see that the ideas of the Women's Movement would come hard to you.'

'I liked the way women were before they started moving.'

'You could hardly remember, I should think.'

'Well, I've had a few opportunities to see what happens to men. And if being liberated means having all the things a man has, I don't rate it that highly. The more I see of them sweating themselves to an early death to make it to the top, all the freshness and vigour gone by their forties, thick round the waist and puce in the face with drink, the more I pity them. As far as I am concerned they can have all the room at the top.'

'Are we by any chance talking about a particular man?'

'Fuck off!'

'We *are* talking about a particular man.' After a pause she put an arm round Katrina's shoulders and gave her a little hug. 'Oh, lovey, I *am* sorry. But whatever you do, don't let it ruin your time at university. No man is worth that.'

Katrina, now puce in the face herself, began to talk rapidly, her voice rising in pitch. 'It's funny, there is all this stuff written about school, and how they try to mould you and how bad it is for you. And then you go to university and there's this myth that they *aren't* trying to mould you. It's all free and liberating. And people really believe it. They go through life congratulating themselves on their independence of mind as though people couldn't even guess whether they were at Oxbridge or LSE. And they never cotton on to what has happened to them.'

Stephanie smiled her sorrowful smile. 'One of the faculty, is he? And married, no doubt. A pity.'

'Oh, you're so clever, Stephanie!'

'There must be things you can get involved in – theatricals, debating societies . . .'

Katrina took a deep breath and said, quite calmly, 'I go for long walks, up in the hills. There's a farm . . . I've learned quite a lot about animals.'

'Yes, well, that will do no harm. In fact, I expect it helps to distance this wretched affair.'

It was Katrina who smiled now. 'Quite a bit of distance, in fact, on the Cheviots.'

Since there seemed little to be gained from further conversation with Katrina, and she did not anticipate much in the way of support from Hugh, who had, after all, been unable to handle Patsy and was unlikely to prove more effective with his own mother, Stephanie decided to have a word with Murdoch before tackling Janet.

As she stood outside his study door, aware of noises from within, the occasional squeaking of his old chair and the thud of something, probably a book, on the floor, all notion of treating him on equal terms deserted her. She opened the door softly and peeped inside. He was sitting hunched over his desk; papers were spread about the room, on the floor, the armchair, even the window sill.

'I don't want to interrupt you if you are working on the book,' she said. He was usually much more orderly than this.

'I'm doing my accounts,' he said shortly. 'And you *are* interrupting.'

'I thought your accountant took care of all that?'

He ran his fingers through his hair. 'God give me patience!'

'And anyway, it's a bit late, isn't it? Aren't you supposed to send details off to him in April?'

'Since you are here . . .' He looked round, his face wrinkled in rueful misery. 'How much is a large packet of Daz?'

'What?' She came and stood beside him and saw the long strip of figures, some ticked.

150

'Your mother was so careful always,' he said rather desperately.

She folded her arms around his shoulders and rested her head against his. 'Oh Daddy, darling, you *mustn't*, not you!'

'But who am I?' He cupped her face in his hands. 'Tell me that. I used to think I was the provider. But now I see how very little I earned and what miracles your mother wrought with it.'

I have never felt so close to him, Stephanie thought; but it's not right, not for him, this closeness.

'What are we to do about Mother?' she said softly.

'That is for Mother to decide.'

'Has she made any suggestions?' Not that she would have done, but it was important to keep talking now that the subject had been broached.

'Nothing serious . . . She did say one evening she thought of becoming a parish worker.'

'A parish worker!' The very idea roused so much anger in Stephanie that she scarcely knew on what to concentrate her scorn. '*Now*, when women are being denied the priesthood? She would be satisfied with *that*!'

'I don't think she meant it. She was annoyed with the vicar who had been to see her. She said she could have been more helpful to someone in her condition than he was.'

'Oh well, even if she were serious, they would never have her. Not after this breakdown.'

'I suppose some people would say that a breakdown is almost a prerequisite to entry into any form of deeper spiritual life.' He was only half-mocking. 'A broken and a contrite heart is something that must never be despised.'

'*I* have no difficulty in despising it! Male language.'

'To describe a condition also applicable to men,' he said, making one of his wry, clown's faces.

'You aren't serious about this?' she said hopefully. 'You wouldn't countenance it?' She was shocked to think that he might even consider putting his own future to one side to assist her mother in this, or any other whim.

'Countenance sounds rather grand.' He patted his stomach

which was no longer so paunchy. 'I don't think I have ever visualised myself "countenancing".'

'I have always thought you were so good at defending yourself. But now I wonder if it wasn't Mother who did all the defending.'

'That is a thought, certainly; one of many to have been presented to me of late.'

She thought he sounded altogether too good-humoured. 'Your book is never going to get finished if you don't learn to defend yourself.'

'Oh that? I've sent it off to my agent, didn't I tell you?'

'But you had only just started revising it.'

He shrugged his shoulders. 'There wasn't any more I could do to it.'

'You mean you didn't bother?'

'I bothered quite a lot, in fact. But it was no good.' He looked at her quizzically, not a fatherly look, more that of a social scientist trying to evaluate the worth of a potential observer. 'I suppose it has to be said ... probably it will have to be said rather often. So why not now? It is over, Stephanie.' He said the words slowly and clearly and then waited with that alert interest with which he had sometimes confronted her when she was young and had tried to be too clever; she had known at such times that he would give no quarter.

She felt a slimy coldness at the pit of her stomach as she repeated foolishly, 'Over?'

'Once, when I shut that door, I was in a world over which I seemed to have complete control.'

'We never interrupted,' she said tremulously, not really wanting to know any more about this.

'You have done plenty of interrupting lately, so you had better listen. Now I come in here and shut the door and I wait. And deep inside me where once strange things stirred, nothing happens. But I can *feel* the space and I know I am standing on the edge of a precipice. And I know also that whether the door is shut or not, visitors are getting in over whom I have no control.'

'I didn't think you worked at night, I . . .'

'I don't mean you, you silly girl! It is not external, an invasion from the outside world. It is happening within me. My mind – or my receiving apparatus or whatever it is – is working differently.'

'Then you will write a different kind of book. Think how exciting that will be!' In her nervousness she spoke in the terms in which she encouraged her sons when some new encounter with life alarmed them.

He shook his head. 'The ideas and insights which begin to fill my head now do not cry out to be *written*.'

'You're not going soft, are you?' Dismay made her bold. 'You are not trying to tell me that it is more important to do than to write?'

'No, no, no! A change is taking place somewhere inside me which it is beyond my power to reverse.'

'But you mustn't simply give in.' It wasn't just *his* gift he was renouncing; that life beyond the closed door belonged to all who had held it sacred throughout their childhood. 'You must *fight*, not assent!'

'Assent!' He drove his fist against the desk. 'I have assented a hundred times and then withdrawn from the abyss, unable to stand on its giddy edge. I have walked around it, prospecting for hope and alternative explanations. Believe me, I have done that times without number in the last months. But eventually it must be approached cold, with clear head and prepared heart.'

'I don't understand. I don't understand what you are saying. You are tired. This business of Mother's has upset your balance as well as your routine. You are suffering from writer's block, you . . .'

But he shook his head and would not speak of it any more.

The next morning, after breakfast, Stephanie went to see Janet. She was surprised to find her looking composed, if remote, propped against the pillows, hands still on the turned-back sheets.

There were flowers in a bowl on the bedside table and

Stephanie bent to see if they needed more water – and to give herself time for composure. In doing this she knocked over one of a little pile of books placed beside the flowers. Stephanie recognised the products of the Women's Press and Virago. She was disturbed to find, on picking up the fallen book, that several passages had been marked with comments in Janet's handwriting. Was it possible that, while they had imagined her lying here day in and day out doing nothing, Janet had, in fact, been reading all this subversive literature, searching through it perhaps for something to hold on to? How maddening and how pathetic! Stephanie said gently, replacing the book, 'Did Patsy provide you with this? I do hope you haven't taken it seriously, or let it upset you?'

'I think I knew most of it already.' Janet, as so often lately, seemed to be addressing someone beyond the window. 'I was born knowing it.'

'Mother!'

'It's all very one-sided, of course, don't you think?' Janet consulted that outside observer and waited for a moment to see whether he – or perhaps it was she? – consented. 'All about how men have used women. No mention of women using men. Women do. I suppose you could say I used Murdoch because I wanted children. One has to be fair.'

'But you *loved* him!' Stephanie tried urgently to draw attention to herself. Usually, with her majestic physique this did not present any difficulty; but at the moment she felt like Alice suffering one of her diminutive transformations. Janet pondered the question, seemingly unaware of its source.

'*Did* I love him? He excited me physically and stimulated me intellectually. The loving came later, much later. What I most remember of those early years is the moment that I saw my first baby.' She turned her head slightly, gazing wonderingly down as though the infant lay beside her. She was not telling Stephanie something, it was doubtful if she connected the baby with the woman beside her; she was reliving the moment which had given her the most joy in the whole of her life.

After a little while she went on, no longer looking out of the window but into the far corner of the room, 'To me, it was a miracle. Now people talk about it as if it is just a function. And while all these books are being written, men are plotting a takeover; wresting the power and the mystery from the woman, transferring it to their own laboratories, engineering it, reestablishing themselves as God. It's all jealousy. Men have always been jealous that it is the woman who bears the child. She is the fruitful one – they call it passivity. That is why I never envied Murdoch his gift. Why I always wanted him to have every opportunity to exercise his creativity. Nothing compared to mine, but some recompense. I was so sorry for him, shut up all day over dry old bits of paper.'

Stephanie said shakily, 'I think you are a little mad.'

'Am I?' She registered Stephanie now. 'I brought *you* into the world. Don't you think you are of more value than one of your father's books? Now what have I said?' For Stephanie was crying. 'What is so terrible about that?'

'Well?' Katrina asked a few minutes later when she came into Stephanie's bedroom. 'Did you make her agree to go into a rest home? Is she crying, too?'

Stephanie blew her nose vigorously. 'I didn't mention it. I decided . . . after a little preparatory exploration . . . that this is something she and Daddy will have to work out between them. I don't know about you, but I propose to go home tomorrow. I . . . I have quite a few matters to attend to.'

[10]

One winter evening, many years ago, when she had been sitting looking at the fire sinking in the hearth, Janet had said, 'Women are the true explorers.' Although she had spoken quietly, this had startled Murdoch. Even then, so long ago, he had been aware of a feeling too deep for him to reach. Why had she said it? Had some lack in him occasioned the remark, or had he said (recently or distantly, women can brood long before speaking) something hurtful, committed one or many an unconscious cruelty? For whatever else had been in doubt, there had been no mistaking the fact that the statement related not only to woman's potential but to man's estate. He had pressed her in a manner which suggested he had rights over her mind as well as her body. It was not usual for him to behave like that, but he had encountered a door closed against him and like a child in a dark place had tried to batter his way to the light. She, of course, had refused to say any more. The words had stayed in his mind and had seemed to grow in importance. He had told himself, 'There is a book here; it will come to me one day.'

It was only now, when there were no more books in him, that his greatest revelation came upon him. And came, as great moments so often do, unheralded by significant signs, as he stood at the kitchen window. He could see Janet propped in the cane garden seat, a flimsy dress billowing about her thin body, indifferent to her surroundings as a scarecrow hoisted to frighten the birds away. He said involuntarily, 'Women *are* the true explorers!'

Malcolm, who did not find this a surprising discovery, continued to whisk vigorously some concoction which, since if Malcolm was to cook it would not be sufficient to do it adequately, he had promised would be a gastronomic miracle.

Murdoch's mind, accustomed to making great leaps in time and place, now presented him with a fleeting but perilously authentic image of a girl in a garden at whose edges the sea curled. From her island home he had uprooted this girl carelessly, without thought. It is, after all, the lot of most women to be uprooted, borne far away from their homes to the strange, barren places which men make for themselves; and there to be left stranded, with no resources than those which she brings with her, no corn in this alien territory. While the man pushes forward towards his intellectual goal, the woman mines the hard, crusty soil of their lives. It is she, not man, who must push beyond the barriers of the possible, expand the known limits of feeling, create love and comfort in emotional atmospheres one would not imagine capable of sustaining human life. Triumphantly she makes the desert flower, water to flow in parched soil, the grudging earth to yield its hidden riches. What engineer can match the miracles quiet women have wrought in humble homes, unknown, but surely not unrewarded? Did Janet think she was unrewarded? As she sat out there had she come to the end of his exploring and found that he had led her into a polar wilderness which even her gifts could not redeem? There was a bleakness about her which frightened him.

'What would you say was your mother's greatest gift?' he asked Malcolm.

'Being my mother,' Malcolm said, piping a froth of cream about a nest of raspberries.

'Take yourself out of the picture. Then what do you see?'

'A homemaker.' Malcolm put the pipe down on the table. 'I've spoiled it. You shouldn't have talked to me.' His face was pale.

Murdoch said, 'I'm sorry.'

'What has happened to her? Why is she like this? What does *she* say about it?'

'She can't talk to me about it. I've tried.'

'But she was always so easy to talk to. I could talk to her about *anything*.'

'Anything to do with *you*, you mean.'

Malcolm looked vaguely at his father; his mind had a habit of switching off when things were said or done which might threaten him.

'I'm not criticising you,' Murdoch said. 'Believe me, I am far beyond criticising anyone other than myself.'

Malcolm turned away to the sink. He found his father's behaviour almost as strange as his mother's.

The sun was warm now. Janet could feel it on her hand. But she was aware of the warmth only distantly as if it was happening to another person. The members of her body seemed separate entities going about business unconnected with her. But at some time there had been a resolve. She had woken early, responding to that alarm in her brain which had once alerted her to the slightest stirring from the cot in the night. How strange that it still operated even now when all the children had left home. But this one child, the most vulnerable, had returned. Malcolm was here. And it was for Malcolm that heart and hands had made the strenuous effort of washing and dressing, that legs had carried her out here into the garden and deposited her in this chair; for Malcolm that she had exposed herself to the dangers lurking beyond this garden with its high hedges over which birds flew so unconcernedly. And more would be required, much more. It had been such a long, hard business, his separation from home and parents; she could not undo the process now, let the threads slip between her fingers, unravel, come apart . . .

He was coming towards her wearing an immaculately starched butcher's apron. 'What are you doing in that?' she asked.

'I am cooking. A talent too long unrecognised.' He held up a hand as though a silver dish was balanced on it. 'From now on you will have superb meals.'

She shaded her eyes with one hand as she looked up at him. 'What do you mean – "from now on"? You are only here for the weekend.'

He sat on the grass in front of her, legs entwined in the lotus position which he was able to adopt effortlessly. Speech on this occasion was not quite so easy, but he contrived an airy nervousness as he said, 'I think I might stay a little longer. I need a rest from the theatre.'

Usually he needed a response and was quick to notice its absence, but he hoped to get this matter over with as little fuss as possible and so was grateful for the pause during which she probed to see what resources were still available within her.

'But this is your first year in rep. You can't talk about needing a rest! Resting is something you don't do voluntarily.'

'A period of meditation, then. We are due to start rehearsing *Time and the Conways*. I am cast as Ernest. Can you imagine? I'm not in the least like Ernest.'

I am waiting in the wings, she told herself; I am sick with nerves but as soon as I get on the stage it will be all right and I shall be in control. She said, 'Ernest is a good part. The *only* good part.'

'The play is so dated. It's pathetic!'

'But it does give a splendid opportunity to age.'

'I'm not sure about this acting business, anyway.'

Janet sat up straight in her chair, stretching her spine and moving her head slowly from side to side to exercise the shoulder muscles. She swayed as the blood came rushing to her head and put a hand on the arm of the chair to steady herself.

'What is it?' Concern tricked him into looking at her carefully. She seemed to have shrunk, but she did not look exactly frail, more like a wooden image long neglected from which sun and rain have peeled away the inessential gloss of colour, leaving the woodcutter's work unadorned. The eyes, looking out with a message too direct to bear understanding, seemed to say, 'It is you who equivocate, not I.' This was one of those images which, if asked the right question, will answer truthfully. But sons and daughters are the last to wish for that. Malcolm said in a rush, 'You're not eating enough. I am going to build you up. You won't know yourself in a few weeks.'

Janet said, 'Where is your script? Get it and we'll have a run through.' As he hesitated, she said irritably, 'Please, Malcolm! It will do me much more good than your superb cooking.'

It was a long time since she had initiated conversation, even longer since she had had any sense of purpose, and she found herself shaking and breathless as if there was not enough oxygen in the air. She took several deep breaths, but this made her even more dizzy. Malcolm returned; gliding across the lawn he came behind her to produce the script from his shirt in the manner of a conjuror, laying it before her with a flourish. 'Now, if it was Puck I was to play . . .'

Janet said, 'Get me a drink, would you? Anything will do. I'm dehydrated – or something . . .'

'I don't want to tire you.'

'Oh, Malcolm! Don't make me say everything twice! Just get me a drink.'

He stalked off, shoulders ungracefully hunched, head thrust down.

The little flash of temper drained all Janet's energy. Malcolm returned with a glucose drink and a piece of fruit cake. She drank and felt slightly better. 'Now.' She took up the script. 'We'll do the bit between you and Hazel in the last act when you finally get her to yourself for a few minutes.' Malcolm sat on the grass, clasping his knees and looking cross and awkward, much as Ernest might have done if forced to join a picnic party. 'Let's score each speech – one to ten according to how strong you feel yourself to be in relation to other characters. Now, you are just about to say goodnight to this girl you are so fascinated by . . .' She drank a little more.

Malcolm began, ' "It's been a great pleasure to me to come here and meet you all." '

'But how do you score when you say that?'

Malcolm rested his forehead on his knees and addressed the grass. 'Five, I think. Because he *is* here, in the Conways' house, where he has wanted to be; but they are a cut above him socially and he's in awe of them. While she hadn't wanted to be left alone with him. So I think they are evenly balanced.'

Janet thought, without satisfaction, that at this moment she was scoring higher than her son. She said, 'Start again, then.'

' "It's been a great pleasure to me to come here and meet you all." '

Janet read, ' "Oh – well –." '

Malcolm said, ' "Especially you." Four – he's not sure he's going to get away with that. "I'm new around here, y'know. I've only been in the place about three months. I bought a share in that paper mill – Eckersley's – out at West Newlingham – you know it?" '

Janet held up her hand. 'Wait a minute, not so fast! What happens to your score when you tell her you have bought a share in the mill?'

'My score goes up to eight.'

Janet took a bite of the fruit cake and they went on. After a few lines she said, 'Do you mind that she's not impressed?'

'I don't think I would let it worry me,' Malcolm pulled up a clover leaf. 'He's the archetypal male chauvinist pig. He *knows* the mill is important and if she doesn't understand that it's because she's only a woman.'

'But it is the one thing you can boast about, isn't it? And she doesn't respond.'

'Maybe I would be a bit crestfallen. Four, perhaps?'

She began to cough and he rolled to one side and knelt beside her. 'I think we should stop now.'

'No, no! It's only that I haven't talked so much for a long time.'

He looked at her doubtfully. Her face had become flushed and the words seemed to be coming too fast for breath, outrunning thought. But she had always been a bit like that when she was excited, so he sat back on his heels and continued to play Ernest.

After the entrance of Robin, Janet said, 'How do you react to him, do you think? To *him*, not what he is saying about stoking a train to break the strike. What is your score?'

'I don't *say* anything to him at first.'

'No, but you are observing him.'

'I think I rate higher than him. Seven.'

'That's high! After all, he is in his own home, where he belongs and you don't; and he is surrounded by members of his family. So doesn't he have the advantage of ownership and collective power?'

'Ernest has a share in a paper mill.'

'*And* Robin is in uniform. An air-force officer.'

'Which is probably a disadvantage. Because the war is over and he will have to put his uniform away. And he doesn't know what he is without it.'

After a pause during which Janet remained silent, looking down at the script, he went on, speaking quietly now, 'And the Conways are always playing dressing-up games. So really, Ernest looks down on them. Because they behave as if life is a charade and they are all trying out parts; while he knows who he is and where he is going . . .'

'But he still wants the things the Conways have got – the family magic . . .'

'Which he also wants to destroy.'

'No. They destroy that themselves.' Janet closed the script.

'Do you admire Ernest, Malcolm?'

'I don't understand him. It's Robin I should be playing. He sees life in terms of costume. When he talks about his future after the war he says "... if I'm going to start selling cars I've got to look like somebody who knows a good suit when he sees one." '

'Ernest wears formal clothes.'

'But underneath you can feel his body protesting. Whereas Robin *is* the clothes he wears.'

'Robin had a devouring mother.' She tossed the script on the ground.

'Unlike you,' he said quickly, taking her hand.

She jerked her hand away, her face twisted with the distaste of an ill person for any display of physical affection. 'I don't want to devour. Neither do I want to be devoured. Please note that.'

The silence seemed to stretch a long way. When she turned to look at him he was kneeling in the posture of a courtier who has incurred the monarch's displeasure and fears for his life. She put out a hand and touched the soft, brown hair. 'I should think your score is about half at this moment, isn't it?'

He made no reply.

She shrugged her shoulders. 'Or perhaps you think that, being hurt, you score rather higher?'

'What has happened to you?' he cried.

'I would have liked time to find that out.'

'You can have all the time you want.' He flung up his head, an angry boy.

She caught his arm as he threatened to move away. 'Let's talk about you. You were always good at finding something to trouble you in whatever you did. What is it in the theatre? Are you afraid you will never be a person, is that it? Just a role player.'

'Something like that.'

'But everyone dresses a part. Not just you. Patsy and Deutzia – their clothes say something about the parts they see themselves playing. People dress up, or dress down.'

'The theatre doesn't exactly encourage one to find a particular identity.'

'Then that is a risk you will have to take.' She tapped her fingers impatiently on the arm of the chair. 'There are risks in every walk of life. If you were a bank clerk you would probably succeed in sinking your precious identity much more effectively.'

He turned away, his mouth working, his whole face dissolving as if a great cascade of water was tumbling over him. 'How *can* I . . . with you like this . . . can't you understand that it's too hard?'

'Yes, I do understand. It was hard enough anyway . . . and then I did this to you.' She patted his cheek. Her fingers were dry as fallen leaves. 'But I can't improve while you are here. So what are we going to do about it? You can't make a success of your life in the theatre while you are worried about what is happening to me; and I can't get better while you are here pestering me.'

'You are not giving anything, are you?' he shouted angrily. 'I am to go back while you – you won't even try!'

'I will try. I promise you that. What would you like me to do? What would convince you?'

'Start going out again.' He was still resentful. 'You haven't been beyond that gate since the time when you went to that old place on the heath. Only don't go *that* way again.'

'After lunch, I will walk down to see Patsy.'

'There you go again! It would be much better to see Deutzia. She has all sorts of ideas about what you should do.'

And all of them more harmless than anything Patsy might have in mind, Janet read his thoughts. She said, 'But Patsy *does* something. No, don't laugh. She does try.'

'To sort out the affairs of the world while neglecting her children and poor old Hugh.'

'She thinks she is saving the future for her children and I expect she thinks Hugh is old enough to look after himself. We shouldn't sneer at Patsy, Malcolm. People who live their lives behind high hedges forfeit the right to criticise what goes on beyond the garden gate.'

Malcolm, who did not have a long attention span, was not listening. He said, 'On second thoughts, I don't think you are ready to go out again, just yet. You could do something here. The garden is a mess.' He encompassed it in a gesture worthy of Oberon. 'Then, in the autumn, the dramatic society will start rehearsing again. You're bound to get a part.'

I am not capable of surviving in the outside world, is that it? she wondered. Or is it – and this is more likely – that he does not want me to be capable because he needs to think of me here, to have an unchanging presence at home, a constant to sustain him in the shadowy, precarious world in which he now moves. She was seized by the fear that he was too sensitive, a little too ready to please, that he would become an easy prey to the more vicious elements in the twilit realm to which those not entirely successful in the theatrical profession are so often consigned. The temptation to say, 'Stay Malcolm' was great, not only for his sake but for her own. 'Stay with me and together we will defy time's slow corrosion.' But she had struggled this far and the gesture would be costly and almost certainly pointless. Until this moment she had not thought of her illness in terms of distance covered, but now it seemed she had come a long way and was not sure she could turn back, or that the person whom Malcolm needed was any longer there. A decision was demanded of her; but her brain, which had become so lively while they were acting, was dull as if a sudden fog had descended, immobilising interest and feeling, blotting out the patterns of thought which had seemed so clear only a few moments ago, leaving only an aching tiredness behind the eyes. As she sat there, spent and helpless, Murdoch came out of the kitchen and walked towards them.

'What train are you catching tomorrow morning?' he said to Malcolm.

'The nine-fifteen,' Malcolm answered promptly. He seemed to feel that something had been settled. And it had, of course, but by Murdoch, not him.

Murdoch helped Janet to her feet and then offered her his arm. How strange, she thought, he seems to have kept abreast of me and I had not noticed. As they paced slowly across the lawn, she thought, we haven't progressed in so stately a fashion since he led me from the altar.

In her dream that night no one kept abreast of her. Once there had been lights in the city, but now it was dark. She was alone and as she walked she knew that soon, very soon, the thing which threatened her was going to happen. When she woke she thought that it wouldn't be so terrifying if she was with people, working with them, sharing in the nightmare . . .

The meadowsweet was in flower. Deutzia said, 'A sign of high summer! It always makes me feel sad.'

It was a windy day with altocumulus mottling the blue sky. The wind blew downy thistle seedlings into the river, worried at a piece of sheep's wool caught in barbed wire; light flickered fast through the leaves of the willow.

'It is too windy to sit in the garden, I'm afraid,' Deutzia said sadly to Rodney and Patience who had come to tea.

'Isn't that your friend Janet?' Patience asked. 'I did not know that she was out and about again.'

Deutzia looked out of the window and saw Janet walking in the jerky fashion she had recently adopted in order to keep her balance. 'She is probably going to see Patsy. She has been out with Patsy once or twice in the last two weeks.'

'That must be a great relief to you,' said Patience who did not really believe that Deutzia was a devoted friend.

'I am afraid she is not fully recovered,' Deutzia said, pouring tea. 'We have a newcomer in the old dower-house and I thought it would be nice to have a tea party to introduce her to one or two people. It is always a good way of getting a look at a new neighbour and then if you don't much care for each other you don't need to bother again. I asked Janet because I thought it would be a little outing for her. And a very trying occasion it was. The dower-house woman is a rather jarring creature – orange hair, orange lipstick, a rather orange sort of woman altogether. She didn't help the conversation along but laughed a lot at things which did not strike me as particularly funny – her lipstick had smeared her front teeth. But we managed quite well. The vicar's wife, Mrs Beaney, told her about the history of the old house and Ann Bellamy described the Warringtons – those eccentric people who used to live there. And this woman just sat looking around as if she was planning to do a sketch of each one of us, which made me feel very uncomfortable. She wasn't a *kind* person. And then Janet suddenly burst out, really quite emotionally, and à propos of nothing, "You look marvellous in that gown, as though you and it were woven all of a piece." "Gown", I may say, was hardly the appropriate word, more like a rag an artist uses to clean the paint brushes! But the woman was highly delighted and said, "Well, I do take it off sometimes. But I am so glad you like it. I printed it myself." Which I could well believe. And she began to tell Janet about some design group which makes up these "creations". It ruined the tea party, of course. I don't think Janet intended to be disruptive. She just didn't seem aware that one doesn't take over the conversation in another person's house. She would never have been so gauche at one time. But I suppose one has to be thankful she is as well as she is.'

She proffered scones and went on, 'I only hope she is not overdoing it. We are all going to this meeting on Thursday. I do wonder whether that is really wise.'

'Which meeting?' Rodney asked irritably. He had reached a stage, Deutzia was sad to see, when he took offence if anything was said which he did not immediately comprehend.

'Why, this nuclear jamboree to which we are all invited.' Deutzia was pleased to sound so *au fait* with current affairs. 'Are you not going?'

'Going?' His face had turned plum colour. 'You will be joining the Communist party next, Deutzia.'

'Hardly that,' Deutzia said, as though this was a possibility she had indeed contemplated and rejected. She was excited by his disapproval. 'One must be tolerant. I always like to hear what other people have to say.'

'I can tell you what they will say without your putting yourself to the trouble of attending their meeting,' he said loudly. 'A lot of bloody rubbish. They haven't an idea between them.'

'Then you don't need to worry about them, dear,' Patience said.

'But I do worry.' He turned to her, shouting even louder. 'I fought a war for them. To keep this country free. And now what do I find?'

'That people are free to disagree with you, dear,' Patience said irritatingly.

As a result of this conversation any doubts which Deutzia might have had about attending the meeting were dispelled. She looked forward with pleasure to recounting her experiences to Rodney and Patience, who had so little to recount other than problems with their gardener and the question as to whether Rodney should have a cataract removed. Moreover, she was encouraged by their reactions to hope that she might even surprise her own children.

But what to wear? Perhaps because of a tendency to grey and black in their posters and publicity she thought sober colours were called for at any meeting involving nuclear protestors. One did not, after all, go to a funeral arrayed for a garden party; and it was the funeral of the world to which these people seemed to look forward with such passionate intensity. Nothing light-hearted would be appropriate, certainly nothing joyful. It was a hot, sultry evening and she chose a navy cotton with a defiant little scarlet scarf at the throat.

Ann Bellamy had gone into town to have dinner with her husband and they would join the contingent from the village at the hall. The vicar and his wife were dining with the incumbent of St Peter and St Paul and they, too, would make their separate way to the meeting. Deutzia was sorry that neither pair had thought to ask her to join them. Other people from the village had assumed she would travel with Janet. She had hoped that Murdoch would be persuaded to attend, or at least to drive them to the meeting, but he had agreed to look after his grandchildren. Janet seemed content to put herself in Patsy's charge. Deutzia sat in the back, not because she felt any safer but because she could see less. Patsy, in fact, was quite a good driver, the fault lay in her car. This was not a distinction which seemed material to Deutzia.

'Now, tell me again,' she said to Patsy once they were on the long, straight section of the main road and she felt able to carry on a conversation. 'This is organised by CND.'

'No,' Patsy corrected her, not for the first time. 'It is not organised by CND.'

'Really?' Deutzia was disappointed, just as she might have been to discover that it was only the touring company's production to which she had been invited at Glyndebourne.

'It was thought very important that this meeting should be broadly based,' Patsy explained. 'We want to bring in all shades of opinion. Some people can't quite take the things which CND stands for.'

'You mean they stand for something more than peace?' Deutzia asked.

'Rather that some of the hangers-on stand for something a little less than peace,' Patsy retorted. 'Also, CND is very well organised and some people don't like that.'

'They have cells,' Deutzia said triumphantly. 'And people who are trees and branches and trunks. At least, if television serials are to be believed. It all sounds rather fantastic – and a bit silly – to me. But I daresay I shall be convinced.'

'This is not a CND meeting,' Patsy said patiently.

'Really! I quite thought . . .'

'Of course, CND members will be there. All the peace organisations will be represented. Including the Christian peace movements – such as they are. No doubt you belong to one of them, Deutzia.'

Deutzia was prevented from pleading her age by the memory of pictures in the local paper of a doughty ninety-year old who had spent a weekend at Greenham Common. She contented herself with saying truthfully, 'I have never been one to belong to movements.'

They arrived early at the school at which the meeting was to be held because Patsy had been mistaken about the time.

'We shall have to sit near the front,' Deutzia said when they entered the assembly hall. 'People do mumble so nowadays. It's the effect of television. We have lost the art of speaking out. I have quite given up going to the theatre.'

'I expect there will be microphones,' Patsy said.

'But do you remember when David Steel came to speak at the Town Hall?' Deutzia asked. 'Not one of the microphones worked.'

Janet had the feeling of being in a theatre and as they seated themselves in the second row she experienced that sense of anticipation which not even bad notices could entirely quell.

Apparently it had been considered undemocratic to set the speakers above the audience, so the stage had not been used and the heavy gold curtains were drawn across it. On floor level, there was a modest table behind which two people could sit in comfort. It was doubtful whether it would be visible from any but the first few rows. A young man trailing yards of flex was testing the microphone which coughed and spluttered spasmodically. To one side of the table a bearded man was leafing through an untidy folder watched by a middle-aged woman with a wiry thatch of hair brushed across her forehead like a well-trimmed hedge from beneath which she regarded his labours with scepticism.

'I *know* I brought them with me,' he said despairingly.

'You will have to manage without them,' she told him. 'There isn't time to go back for them.'

They were joined by a younger man carrying a sheaf of papers. 'I think I'll just make a few announcements before the meeting gets going,' he said cheerfully.

'Not too many,' the woman said.

'It isn't often we have so many groups all together and it will save postage,' he continued as if she had not spoken.

In the event he made a considerable number of announcements while people greeted one another and formed their own groups. The clergy, watching the Chairman's ineffectual protests with sympathy, thought that by contrast the parish notices were commendably brief.

As soon as she arrived Patsy had been surrounded by friends. Deutzia had gone to talk to Mr and Mrs Beaney. Janet stayed with Patsy. This turned out to be a mistake because Patsy introduced her to her friends who greeted her with touching generosity, embracing her in a sisterhood to which, simply by virtue of being with Patsy, she was immediately granted admission. They talked of matters with which they assumed her to be conversant — answers to letters in newspapers, success with a question on a phone-in programme, the wording of a questionnaire, plans for a projected demonstration at the County Library, whose committee had transgressed in some way of which Janet was unaware. As they talked Janet felt an increasing awkwardness accompanied by a desire to please, to ingratiate, to be as caustic, witty, well-informed and strongly motivated as they; in fact to establish an identity other than her own which would justify their acceptance of her. It was not their fault that she reacted in this fashion. They were not manipulative or, individually, dominating women. The impulse to find favour sprang from no pressure on their part, rather from a need in her to identify with these women, to draw on their energy, to find a warm, secure place among them. But she could not manage their language, nor match the spontaneity of their feelings. She was reminded of her attempts to join in a prayer group at which, week after week, her feeling of alienation had increased and all her notes had rung false.

As is so often the way with outsiders, Janet began to look for faults to justify her inability to make significant contact. And, faults never being hard to come by, she soon noted how easily Patsy's friends categorised other people — officials, politicians, security forces, policemen became something less than human, creatures of a lower order to whom the worst motives could be casually ascribed, politicians being accorded the most virulent abuse. There was real hatred here. These women might preach peace but their vocabulary was more likely to promote discord. Several of them had recently attended a demonstration at Molesworth and as she listened to the description of the conflict between the protestors (gallant, high-spirited folk sharing snatches of song as they linked hands) with the forces of order (hard, brutal, grey-faced men) she was left in little doubt that she was now among a new kind of chosen people. She sat back a little relieved thus to have tarnished their bright image and was glad to see that attempts were now being made to call the meeting to order. The bearded man had taken the chair and had been joined by another man who was looking around with lively interest as though he, like Janet, was a stranger to such gatherings.

The Chairman tried to speak into the microphone, abandoned the attempt and rapped on the table. 'If you have any more notices, they must wait until afterwards, Kevin.'

Kevin said rapidly, 'A vigil is to be held as close to the war memorial as we are allowed to get to commemorate Hiroshima and Nagasaki . . .'

A gaunt man who was sitting next to Janet said, 'Will it also be in remembrance of the men who died in Japanese prisoner-of-war camps?'

Several people sighed audibly and Kevin said quietly, 'I don't think we want to make this an occasion for controversy.'

'Why should it be controversial?' The gaunt man was wounded by this response. 'Can anyone tell me what is controversial about remembering our own dead as well as those of the Japanese?'

The Chairman intervened, 'Well, I hope you have all jotted down those dates in your diaries. But if anyone missed anything, Kevin will be glad to answer any queries after the meeting. Incidentally, the microphone doesn't seem to be working, so perhaps those further back would like to move forward. There seem to be plenty of empty seats. I know that the southern contingent couldn't come because they are mounting a demonstration outside the hall where Michael Heseltine is speaking.'

During the ensuing shuffling the gaunt man said to Janet, 'This happens every time. If they don't like what you say they simply do not listen.'

The Chairman said, 'I am afraid I have lost my notes. But as we are running a little behind schedule, I don't suppose you will object if I am brief. I will simply emphasise that this is not a meeting about disarmament. It is about something more fundamental. Do we want nuclear power at all? Do we, in fact, really need it?'

A woman said, 'Yes, we most certainly do!' in an authoritative tone. Patsy whispered to Janet that this was the leader of the Conservative Party on the local council.

The Chairman said, 'You will have your chance to speak to that later, Mrs Dobbs, and I am sure we shall be very interested to hear how you justify that choice.'

Mrs Dobbs evinced a readiness to justify it at once. The Chairman continued, speaking more loudly, 'I have to emphasise that this is not a discussion about weaponry. Of course, we are concerned about weapons, indeed that is our prime concern.' He looked severely into the body of the hall as though seeking to quell unspoken opposition. Janet tried to control her growing impatience by telling herself that this was like a bad rehearsal and it would all come right once the meeting started. The Chairman was saying, 'But it is felt – by some of us, it is felt – that there has been too little positive discussion about nuclear energy generally. The Chernobyl disaster has highlighted the fact that we do not need a war to put us in peril.' He continued for, some minutes to justify the decision not to discuss weaponry, about which he appeared to have some misgivings.

A dark, saturnine man rose from the rear of the audience and said, 'As the meeting started twenty-five minutes late, Mr Chairman, perhaps we could all agree not to talk about weaponry and you can take it from there.'

The Chairman, flustered by this intervention, said rapidly, 'The first part of the meeting will take the form of a talk on alternative forms of energy. This is a matter to which we must give increasing attention . . .' As he was interrupted by further protests from the rear of the audience, he said irritably, 'I *must* make this point. If we are not to be justifiably accused of being purely negative in our outlook and concerned only with gloom and doom . . . I quote, of course . . .'

At this point a ginger-haired young man erupted into the hall and strode down the aisle waving a sheet of paper in his hand. 'Before we start, Dave. This is urgent.' Ignoring protests from the Chair he turned to the body of the hall and said, 'This is the

statement which we agreed to let Cliff have for the *Recorder*.'
He appeared to assume that everyone present was acquainted
with Cliff and began to read, "The Chernobyl disaster is a
preview of what could happen here in Dorset. At Chernobyl
only twenty-three people may have died . . ." I think that's the
latest figure?'

The woman at the information desk called out, 'I don't think
we ought to say "only", Bill. It might sound as if we regretted
that the numbers were so low.'

'I take your point, Kay. "Twenty-three may be the number
who have died so far, but . . ."'

'I don't like "so far", either. There are people – and we all
know who they are – who would be only too ready to read into
that that we are hoping for more deaths.'

'Then how *do* you think it should be worded?'

'I don't think we ought to mention numbers at all.'

The Chairman said loudly, 'I am now going to call on Dr . . .'

'This statement has to go to press tonight.'

'Later, Bill, we'll stay on after the meeting.' The Chairman
said with some desperation, 'I am now going to call on . . . '

'Later isn't any good if we are going to get this in the paper.'

The man at the rear of the audience was on his feet shouting,
'Do you realise, Mr Chairman, that eleven of us have travelled
over twenty miles by bus to this meeting, that the last bus leaves
in forty minutes, that you propose to have a talk from the
platform before any of us has a chance to speak, and this meeting has not yet started?'

Janet shouted, 'Here, here!' and then clapped her hands to her
face. Patsy looked at her reproachfully and Deutzia fanned herself with a glove.

The Chairman said unhappily, 'Yes, yes, yes. We really
must . . .'

'Perhaps we can rustle up some transport to get you back.'
The ginger-haired man looked round hopefully.

'How? How do you propose to rustle up transport for eleven
people at short notice when you can't even begin to think about
"rustling up" a statement for the paper until the presses are

rolling? If this is a sample of what is in store for us this evening I might as well have stayed at home and watched *Crimewatch*.'

'Yes, well . . .' The Chairman braced himself. 'I think we must make a start now. I call upon Dr Harrison.'

Dr Harrison leaped to his feet, almost knocking over his chair, which he steadied with one hand while rapidly introducing himself to the audience as a scientist engaged in research into environmental health hazards. Janet saw one of those lean, long-faced men with the look of the visionary who crop up from time to time on the English scene, the T. E. Lawrence of the laboratory. He compelled her immediate attention as he embarked at a spanking pace on a survey of the development of various types of energy, beginning with coal and describing in graphic detail the devastation of the Welsh valleys. He spoke very fast and it was not until he said, 'We are told coal is safe and underground, a hazard only to those who mine it and increasingly benign even for them — don't you believe it!' and proceeded to ask his audience to consider various matters unpalatable to Mr Scargill, including the fact that many of the old coal tips still gave off poisonous gas — it was not until then that it became apparent he was not speaking to his brief. A man of undoubted integrity and, as befitting his occupation, formidable energy, it was almost impossible to stop him once in motion. Regardless of protests, whose nature he genuinely appeared to misconstrue — 'later, later, any questions you like to ask, later' — he passed on to attack the oil industry. 'The worst health hazard with which we are faced today is created by the motorcar. The cancer rate, the number of respiratory complaints in big cities, can be linked with lead in petrol. You may have heard this before, but I guarantee you have yet to organise sit-downs outside petrol stations and that you will, in fact, continue to queue outside them! Yet people are in greater risk than those who live in the shadow of a nuclear reactor. And why is this not better known, why does it so singularly fail to disturb our sleep?' His voice soared above those seeking to provide him with comments, if not answers, as serene as a great tenor effortlessly dominating the chorus line. 'Because unlike the nuclear reactor, the motorcar is loved by us all. The problem is not even given a serious airing, so effective is the combined power of the manufacturer and the car user. We are a car-owning civilisation.'

This time the interruptions were so forceful, and accompanied by such a degree of physical protest, that he was able to recognise hostility. 'You care?' he asked, pointing a finger at the most gesticulatory of the objectors. 'You say you care about the environment, but I guarantee that you own a car and would not consider exchanging it for a bicycle. Yes, yes! The very idea is laughable. How would you get to your demonstrations without the aid of the motor vehicle? But what is needed is not Friends of the Earth but Friends of the Air.'

Patsy, who had been very distressed by what was being said, and who believed that challenges should be taken up without delay – or even a pause for thought – stood up and cried out, 'We *do* care! And if what you say is true, I should be willing to give up my car tomorrow!'

Janet shouted 'Bravo!'

There was little support from Patsy's friends, one of whom said, amid general laughter, 'More likely your car will give you up, Patsy.'

Patsy rounded on the speaker. 'I should be quite prepared to walk.'

'Or go by pony and trap,' Janet suggested.

A man in the front row said acidly, 'Have you any idea of the cost of a trap?' and another said, 'To say nothing of the cost of the pony and the matter of training and stabling it.'

Voices were raised on all sides.

'Do you realise what the running costs would be?'

'The pony would have a longer life expectancy than a car.' Patsy gallantly adopted Janet's alternative means of transport. 'And the maintenance costs wouldn't be so high.'

'What about parking? Can you imagine the parking areas that would be required if we all had ponies and traps?'

Janet said, 'There would be side benefits, like manure, instead of side effects . . .'

'We are a travelling people now, like it or not.'

This turn of the debate delighted Dr Harrison. 'Yes, yes. You are right, of course. We *can't* go back. People adapt. They have to travel because jobs are centralised, mainly in towns, and so are food and other commodity stores. Even if this were not so, they would not give up mobility. And people love their ruined Welsh valley towns and fight to save them and the coal industry which crippled their menfolk, and refuse to leave the houses encircled by the great tips. People don't care about the environment. It is not pollution which worries them, it is other people's pollution, the pollution which doesn't threaten their interests. And in time nuclear power will take its place along with the coal and oil industries and man will accept the risk and live with it sooner than sacrifice what he has come to see as his need. Man is quite incapable of sustained altruism, which, I suspect, is why the anti-nuclear lobby needs to be boosted with regular injections of fear.'

In the silence which followed this statement an elderly man rose from the body of the hall, a dry, attenuated, fastidious man, he said quietly but in a voice that carried, 'I have no high hopes for the future. In fact, as I grow older I have come to subscribe to the pessimistic view that "the light at the end of the tunnel is an oncoming train".' Sadly he allowed a pause for laughter, which was forthcoming and in which Dr Harrison joined. 'But I will take my stand – in what I suppose might be called, even in someone as totally free of religious belief as myself, an act of faith – I will take my stand against the idea that man is unredeemably base.'

'I hope you are right, sir,' Dr Harrison said pleasantly.

'And this is what happens when we try to be positive!' Patsy cried. 'You should be ashamed. You should all be ashamed!'

The man at the rear of the audience, more saturnine than ever now, said, 'While I have little else in common with the two ladies at the front, that sentiment has my complete support.' There was much muttering and scraping of chairs as he and his ten companions made their way out of the hall to catch their bus.

'I declare the meeting open for discussion,' the Chairman said, dispiritedly.

Voices rose on all sides. Deutzia fidgeted and fanned herself, Patsy argued with passionate inconsistency, Janet sat in silence, her hands slack in her lap. It all matters so much to them, she thought, and yet really they are quite helpless. They can't even order their own meeting so how do they think they can get the world back on course? As she listened to the confused noises her mind persisted in universalising its own sickness and interpreting the disorder accordingly. This is the sort of thing the bomb will do, she thought; it will take everything apart, just as time does. Time is a bomb with a very slow fuse. But she wished she could be one of those who were standing up and shouting defiance.

For her this had been a crucial occasion, her chance to break out of the nightmare isolation, to participate however humbly in great issues, to join hands around the camp fire lit by a new generation of pioneers. However muddled they might have seemed on this occasion, their fervour, stamped on furrowed brows and flashing from angry eyes, was undoubted and fervour meant considerably more to her and to most people than organisational ability. Fervour could sweep a country, a continent, while the organisers were still studying their computer programmes. Somewhere, in this vast movement which crossed barriers of birth, race and creed, there should have been a place for her, a role, however modest, which she could play, if it was only to spend chilly nights monitoring the passage of army trucks down country lanes.

She had wanted desperately to become part of this community and it hadn't worked. She was like the outsider drawn into chapel seeking a revelation and coming away repelled by the ugliness of the architecture and the banality of the hymns.

The Chairman was on his feet waving his arms about like a conductor summoning an orchestra to make music after a prolonged tuning-up process.

Janet experienced a feeling of total rejection, as if this farce had been laid on simply to discourage, or worse, to debar her from going forward.

As they made their way out of the hall, after the meeting had been brought to an abrupt end by the caretaker, they were joined by the Beaneys and the Bellamys. They walked together to the car park.

'I don't know how Dr Harrison expects me to do my rounds without a car,' Dr Bellamy said.

'You did threaten to take to horseback last year when it was so snowy,' Ann Bellamy pointed out. 'Perhaps we should learn to think of the disadvantages of the car, rather than its advantages? More and more roads to enable people to travel about solo . . .'

Deutzia thought that Ann Bellamy was rather a silly young woman. She turned to Mrs Beaney for a more considered judgement. 'What did you make of it?'

'Most interesting. And profitable.'

'Profitable!' Deutzia wondered whether there could have been a conversion. She had heard of a BBC man who had been converted by one of those sandwich boards which, no doubt owing to lack of space, usually asked questions too direct to be taken seriously.

'Yes, indeed.' Mrs Beaney was briskly unrepentant. 'Now we know that their ideas are not worthy of consideration. There was hardly a person capable of sustaining a sentence, let alone an argument, with clarity. Apart, of course, from the admirable Dr Harrison.'

'I'm not so sure about that,' Mr Beaney said, tapping the curb with his stick. He had poor night-vision. 'Articulacy is the art of expressing thought with ease. Our deepest beliefs are not capable of easy expression.'

Mrs Beaney took his arm. 'Come along, my dear. You are doddering. The church has produced people quite capable of vision and lucidity.'

'Not all that number in two-thousand years.'

'Poor Mr Beaney,' Deutzia said when they had parted company. 'She does bully him so.'

Patsy unlocked the car without speaking.

A few minutes later, seeing the bonnet dimly reflected in a shop window as Patsy drove out of the car park, Deutzia said, 'You have got your lights on?' Patsy switched on the lights without so much as a thank you.

'Now, what are we to make of this meeting?' Deutzia asked as they headed into the darkness beyond the town. As neither Patsy nor Janet replied, she went on, 'I can't say I got much out of the discussion. If only people would realise that if they will insist on all talking at once none of them will be heard.' She grasped the front seat as the car swerved round a corner. When they were once more on the straight, she said, 'And I didn't really like Dr Harrison. He struck me as being rather supercilious.'

'*Like* him!' Patsy spoke for the first time. 'How they got hold of him I can't imagine. He must be the establishment's secret weapon.'

When they arrived at Deutzia's house Patsy refused to come in for a cup of tea.

'But I thought it would be nice to talk about the evening,' Deutzia protested.

'It wasn't a theatrical production.' Patsy sounded unusually sharp.

'Then surely it is even more important to talk about it.' Deutzia who did not sleep well, was always anxious to persuade people to stay with her as long as possible. 'Don't you agree with me?' she appealed to Janet.

Janet said, 'I think we should go back for the children.'

Deutzia went indoors looking hurt.

Patsy drove the car a little way down the street and then stopped. 'I don't suppose you'll be joining us?' she said, staring ahead.

'I'll pay a subscription. But I don't see myself being active.'

'I can hardly blame you after tonight. The hard core, the people who really know what they are about, were picketing the Michael Heseltine meeting.'

'I'm not criticising your friends, Patsy. They are good people. I could see when I looked at them depths of concern I had never suspected. The couple who run the wine shop – easy-going hedonists, as I had thought them – and there they were transformed into the stuff of which the saints of old were made!'

Patsy seemed, if anything, more oppressed than ever by this tribute. Janet tried to breathe renewed life into her. 'I marvel at these people – at their ability to steer a way through muddle and confusion, mismanagement and . . . oh, the human multiplicity of motives! That above all. And they can do this because they have this one clear goal. Even though they may never see the Promised Land they will go on struggling to the end.'

Patsy said bleakly, 'So why won't you join us?'

'It's a matter of size. I am not big enough.' Beside her, she saw Patsy's face, silver and black as a vampire demanding more and more. She struggled to give more.

'Even while I've been so ill, I've managed to drag myself to church once a week for the Eucharist. Usually on a week day because there are only a handful of people then. I find many of the religious intolerably pious and I abhor platitudinous priests. But I go. I know that the Anglican church is weak, vacillating, out of touch, unsure of what – if anything – it believes, has lost sight of its priorities, that it will fail Christ and all His saints again and again and again; but I go. Because of what lies beyond, I go. So why can't I shrug aside the aggressiveness of your peace people? Why can't I tolerate their kind of piousness? And, most important of all, why can't I see beyond their unhealthy fascination with disaster? I don't know. But I *can't* see beyond it. "The light at the end of the tunnel is an oncoming train" doesn't strike me as funny – it is absolutely unacceptable. I need hope. I need hope more than anything else, without it I should dwindle away.' She laid a hand on Patsy's shoulder. 'I think you are very brave.'

There, she thought, that is an end to it. She was hollow, dizzy, held in place only by the body of the cramped, intransigent little car.

Patsy said, 'But not effective. I wouldn't say that to anyone but you. But I would like you to know that I know that I am not effective. Not at anything, not even at being a woman.'

' "Even"!' Janet sighed. 'Oh, Patsy, that, from you!'

'I am so terribly unhappy. Nothing I do ever seems to work out. And I do try. I let people think I live the way I do because its the way I want to live, but the truth is I work just as hard not getting things done as other people do getting them done.' She began to cry. 'I spend all my time trying to bring things about that won't be brought . . .' She put her head down on her clenched fist and wept. Janet reflected, as though viewing a strange phenomena taking place in a capsule, that whatever Patsy did she devoted herself to it with remarkable singleness of purpose. Certainly, she was putting her entire being into the business of crying. The sobs seemed to have their origin somewhere in the region of the bowels and from there they travelled extensively, racking chest, heaving shoulders, tearing throat and agitating limbs. Janet watched, her own bowels of compassion unmoved, until the disturbance ceased and Patsy addressed herself to the more tractable problem of starting her car again.

On their return to the house Patsy went upstairs to the children who were asleep in the room which had once been a nursery.

Murdoch was in the kitchen doing the ironing. He studied Janet's face and said, 'Not a success?'

'I should be useless to them.'

'You're not useless to me.'

She shook her head. 'No. I am useless.'

'Would you like coffee?'

She turned and walked away from him. She had done this so often over the last months that he paid little attention and continued with the ironing. She went into the sitting room and closed the door. Humphrey was in his basket. He sat up and shook himself, looked at her, contemplated a greeting, decided against it and settled himself again.

Patsy cried, Janet thought, and I had nothing to offer. Every cell in her body had become a weight dragging her down. She took a few paces towards the corner of the room, then the pressure was too much. She gave way and curled up on the floor. The dog raised his head and eyed her mournfully.

Patsy left with the children. Murdoch said, 'Janet has gone to bed, I think. Better not disturb her.' He bolted the door and went slowly up the stairs.

For hours Janet lay still, huddled on the floor. From time to time the dog cried to himself. At first, as she lay there she saw quite clearly a picture of houses wrecked in the Blitz on London, all the futile pretence of permanence ripped away leaving here the remnant of an upper floor projecting a few feet from a jagged wall, still supporting an ironing board with a shirt neatly folded on it, and there a mangled bedhead topping a fallen chimney like the antlers of a mythical beast. Then dust rose from the ground and blotted out this surrealist obscenity. There was a wind howling and nothing else. Except a clock. She could hear a clock and knew that it was slowly draining her; drip, drop, hope leaking from the arteries as the dust dribbled from the wrecked building; drip, drop, gradually breaking down the organs of resistance where the will sought refuge. She abandoned herself to this inexorable process, mind, body and spirit. When it was done the clock stopped. She was empty, yet heavy.

She was going down, down, down into the familiar nightmare from which in the past she had always woken just as the sides of the tall buildings closed like a well around her. But now there was no waking; she was really falling into the blackness which had blotted out the bombed landscape. She had come at last to that moment to which the dream had seemed to be leading her. There were no lights in windows now and no people moved in the streets. The curfew had tolled and every other soul had found shelter. She was in a dangerous place, abroad and bolted out. She had nothing with which to bargain for clemency, no case to plead, no papers to prove an identity; she was stripped, bankrupt, the title deeds of her poor estate nullified. Something so incredible was happening that the knowledge of it could not be contained within the body's framework which had never been intended for such enormity; ribs and breastbone must crack, the structure of the skull splinter as she came at last to this forbidden depth from which self-preservation had so long protected her. She had never known such fear. The nightwatchman was upon her; she felt his arm on her shoulder bearing her down amid the misjudgements and evasions, the unanswered needs and flawed affections, all the failed promise and fumbled chances of her life. Then complete cessation of feeling, no heartbeat nor intake of breath as dread struck upon the thing most dreaded. The second between the lightning flash and the thunder's roar was her whole lifetime. She lay in the unnameable void and the arm held her, light as a feather. And there was peace.

The morning light came faintly through the curtains. The dog was sleeping, one paw hanging out of the basket. She got up and went to the window, moving stiffly. Her body was cramped, yet she felt nimble as if she had laid down a burden. She drew the curtains. Outside there was a curtain of gauze stretched across the sky through which colour strained faintly. It must be early. She stood and watched as the sun climbed higher and gradually the veil was lifted, outlines grew sharp, colour strong. The garden glistened and she could smell the dew on the grass.

Humphrey decided that he wanted to go out. She went into the kitchen and opened the back door for him. She stood on the threshold for a little while, remembering the tramp and other things. Then she filled a kettle and made tea. She was drinking it, looking through the window at the blue tit on the nut stocking, when Murdoch came in. He was startled to see her there.

'It's all right,' she said. 'It's all over.'

He came towards her, still looking alarmed. 'I don't understand.'

'Neither do I. But it's over.' She began to massage her eyes.

He walked towards the table, slowly, carefully, like a man skirting a minefield. He sat down beside her and put his head in his hands.

She felt that she understood now about the man who had seven devils cast out. But undoubtedly there were dangers in taking recovery for granted. The end of that parable was that the devils mounted a successful counter offensive. She said, stirring her tea, 'Patsy cried last night and I did nothing.'

*

Later she walked about the house and saw the sheets and pillow

184

cases in the linen cupboard, newly laundered and ironed. The windows had been cleaned, the flagstones in the hall scrubbed, and even the stairboards were polished, which was not very wise. Was it the house which had meant so much to him?

She went downstairs and found him still sitting at the table in the kitchen. Over the past months he had shed probably as much as two stone; this weight loss added years to him – only the young look well for being thin. And the perky cheerfulness, had that been an illusion of the flesh? Now, the feelings which had sometimes surprised her in his novels because they seemed beyond his compass had at last found expression in the eyes and mouth – grief, pain, even horror. What had he looked upon that was so horrid? She had imagined herself to have a monopoly of horror.

'Were you very proud when we came here – to our first home?' she asked, sitting beside him.

'I was too daunted by the responsibility of it,' he said drily. 'The pride came a good deal later when we paid off the mortgage.'

So it wasn't for the house he did all this, she thought. For me, then? A labour of love – or a coming to terms? A combination of the two perhaps, since they are usually inextricable. As yet, she could not bring herself to be grateful. She was not even sorry for him. Her reaction was one of dismay that his wellbeing should have been so dependent on her.

'I'll get on with things in here now,' she said, crossing to the sink. He left her without argument and went into the garden.

We are like a couple who have been away travelling separately, she thought, watching him through the window. Now we have come together again we have things to tell each other. Shall we be able to do that? We are not quite the same people who set out on our journeyings. I want him to accept that I am changed, yet am dismayed by the change in him. There is so much talk about weathering storms, not enough about the reconstruction work that must follow in their wake.

It will take time. Travellers need time to reorientate themselves. The place to which they return has become smaller, or dearer, or less relevant; is found to hold more of memory and less of the future than before, or offers possibilities not seen until distance separated the traveller from it. How will it be for each of us? Shall we find a meeting place, Murdoch, now that I can no longer accommodate to your vision, letting it suffice for me?

'Did you do this for me?' she asked in the evening when they were together in the sitting room. For much of the day they had avoided each other, each needing time alone. Now they sat on the sofa, a little apart, wary of physical contact which might be misunderstood – or too well understood. 'All this work for me?'

'Well now.' Murdoch looked at the convex mirror above the fireplace which encapsulated two miniature figures in a formal pose. He rocked back, locking his fingers behind his head. 'I did it because it needed to be done and you weren't doing it any more. It struck me as a return to childhood – the moment when your mate throws down her spade halfway through the building of the sandcastle and says, "It's your turn now". Either you get on with it, or you lose your temper and knock down the whole edifice.'

The superficial common sense of this response irritated her. 'Time will destroy the sandcastle anyway,' she said.

He shrugged, irritated in his turn. 'I didn't make a theology of it. And anyway, the answer to that is to build another castle when the tide goes out again. Time is cyclical, not linear.'

'I hadn't thought of that.' She would have liked him to develop this theme, but he went on:

'And irrespective of time and tide, there were days when I was minded to knock down the castle.' He stretched his clasped hands above his head and studied them. He found difficulty in knowing what to do with his arms since the physical solution which had in the past proved efficacious in resolving their differences was now denied to him. He compromised by stretching them along the back of the sofa.

She said quietly, 'And then?'

'Then I began to *need* the work. My thinking has been largely of one kind – a kind which required hours spent staring at my desk, or taking long walks. You know all about that. But now there was a new kind of thinking which seemed to be taking over which didn't react at all favourably to quiet hours or solitary walks. I found that this kind of thinking responded remarkably well to the stimulus of cleaning windows and scrubbing and polishing floors. As though inner spring-cleaning demands the outward rites. So I suppose if I am truthful, I started to do it for you and ended, as is the way of so much of my endeavour, in doing it for myself. But there again, where is the truth of it?' He let one hand rest lightly on her shoulder. 'You were my inspiration. At first, I was humbled by the realisation of all that you had done for me without my being aware of it and I felt ashamed and angry with you for putting me in the position of debtor. And then that passed. I became interested in the fact that I was seeing and experiencing things in a different way, noticing more of the detail of living, taking the scenery into account.'

Janet remembered Stephanie saying, 'Daddy goes straight to the guts of the matter, without having any idea how he got there. He never describes the landscape through which he has passed.' She had been speaking of one of the novels.

'Is detail good for your writing?' Janet asked.

'Death to it.'

She turned her head sharply towards him. 'And I am to blame for that?'

'No. Whatever else, we are not going to talk of blame – either of us.' He pressed her shoulder, more to stay her than as a gesture of comfort. 'As for my writing, there was no need to resort to dramatic renunciation, drowning it deeper than did ever plummet sound or making a bonfire of the pages. The gift was gone. I always knew it could happen one day.'

She bowed her head, appalled and angry. She had, after all, lived a long time in the shadow of his gift. 'I don't know what to say.'

His hand moved automatically to the nape of her neck. 'I think that now we have to talk about you – and your gifts.'

She was still as the shrew beneath the hovering hawk. If he should demand too much, or she be prepared to offer too little, all would be over between them. Was that what she wanted?

Once more and so soon she was in a dangerous place where there was no easy comfort and never would be again. Wants were irrelevant, so much excess baggage. There was something here more than love, custom and companionship, the tests of marriage and the ties of children, something quite outside the affections of individual man and woman. Beyond the window the shades of evening had darkened the lawn so that it merged into trees and shrubs and the sheltering hedge was already lost in night. What was at issue here was necessity. She could not go back to what she had been, nor could she reach out to what she might become, without him. Slowly she turned her head until her cheek rubbed against the palm of his hand, a gesture instinct with that particular tenderness which is also a statement of trust, as binding on the recipient as the giver.

'There go Stephanie and Piers,' Deutzia said, looking from her window. 'All the others have already arrived, the poor things.'

Mrs Beaney said, 'I must say I find it hard to understand how she can do this to her children. The whole venture will undoubtedly fail and it will all fall on them.'

'*And* on Murdoch! If they had done this when they were younger, I might have understood. But now, when she is getting old and has been so ill. He is doing it to please her, of course. Whoever would have thought it of him? Sacrificing himself like that! He has quite changed. They came down to tell me and naturally I was upset. Another link with the past gone. I tried to warn them about rushing into things without sufficient thought. "After all," I said to her, "there is so much you could do here – taking people to keep hospital appointments, changing library books, writing letters for the disabled and the blind – or simply taking old people for a run in your car . . ." But I could see she wasn't listening.'

'It would have to be something more dramatic to suit her,' Mrs Beaney said. 'She would never settle for the humdrum.'

'I daresay you are right. But I wouldn't have believed she could be so selfish. I used to give up a lot of my time to her; for years I went up there to lunch every Sunday. *He* was more aware of my feelings than she was. "Of course we shall still see you," he said. "We shan't be so very far away." "But I shall hardly feel able to call on you *there*," I told him. "And you won't have time to come here just to see me." He admitted they were going to be very busy at first. "And what about your books?" I asked him. "You won't have time to write with all that going on around you." "No," he said, "Not another line." ' Deutzia turned away from the window. 'She has ruined his life, of course.'

*

Piers drove in silence up the hill towards the house. His face was white and tense. This has reopened old wounds, Stephanie thought; over the last few days he has been reliving the time of his own testing, perhaps regretting his choice. When they came in sight of the house, he said, 'We have got to stop them! At their age, one cannot start a new life. It is just too difficult.' He is afraid they may succeed, she realised.

'But how to convince them?' he went on. 'The trouble is neither of them has ever really had to make something *work*. They don't know how hard it is.'

They approached the front gate slowly. Stephanie dreaded that the FOR SALE board would be up already, but this was not the case. As they came to the gate she saw that there was a board, but it said SOLD.

'We're too late,' she said.

'Nonsense!' He turned into the drive. 'They can move to the village. Or into town. Even better.'

'But *this* is home.' She looked at him in amazement. He simply did not understand what this meant to her.

He jammed his foot on the brake. 'Your home is with me and the children. You can have no idea how hurtful it has been all these years to have you referring to this place as home.'

'For Heaven's sake, we're not going to start *that* again! The only reason we live in Surrey is because it is a sort of no-man's-land between your job and mine.' She got out of the car and slammed the door.

Katrina and Malcolm were sitting under the apple tree shelling peas. Stephanie could see at a glance that they had accommodated themselves to the situation, whatever it might be. Malcolm was saying, 'There's nothing to it – no bulk, no thrust, no . . . '

Katrina said, 'You really *are* going to be an actor, Malcolm. I had my doubts at one time; but now I can see you when you are old, grumbling on telly about modern playwrights' inability to create great parts and rambling nostalgically among your past glories.'

Stephanie walked across the lawn towards them. 'Is *that* all you can find to do? With all this nonsense going on?' She swept an arm towards the SOLD board.

Katrina said, 'It's no use each of us nibbling at them individually.'

Malcolm said, 'We were waiting for you to lead the chorus of disapproval.'

'And what is Hugh doing about it?'

'The conveyancing.'

'You mean that Hugh is supporting them, actually helping them to buy that . . . that . . . '

Malcolm pointed a dramatic finger eastwards, ' "Something lost behind the ranges, lost and waiting, Go!" For "ranges", read "blasted heath". Hugh thinks they should have a shot at pioneering in the outback.'

'But why? Hugh, of all people the least adventurous!'

'He foresees that Patsy may become involved,' Katrina said, 'and there would be the possibility of a limited reconciliation – periodic comings together without the disadvantage of his having to endure Patsy's housekeeping.'

Stephanie looked at her sister thoughtfully. 'You seem to find this amusing.'

Katrina shrugged. 'There is probably nothing we can do about it, so we might as well go along with it, don't you think?' Her hair was reverting to what, as far as Stephanie could remember, was its natural mid-brown shade. Whether this was the sobering effect of her parents' madness, or whether something rather more significant – such as a quest for identity – had led to this toning down, Stephanie could not be sure. She rather hoped the question of identity was not involved, any amount of tediousness might follow from that. She said to Malcolm, 'I'll help Katrina with these while you carry my case indoors.'

'Piers has done that already.' Malcolm got to his feet. 'Perhaps you would like me to supervise the unpacking.' He strolled across the lawn.

'Malcolm seems in surprisingly good form,' Stephanie said. 'I thought he would be hardest hit by all this.'

'The stage manager has fallen in love with him and taken him to her ample bosom.'

'Is he in love with her?'

'How you do cling to these old-fashioned notions, Stephanie!'

'I don't, but Malcolm does.'

'Wrong again. Being in love isn't of first importance to Malcolm – except for portraying it on stage. The essential thing is that he should be cherished and protected.'

Stephanie sat beside Katrina. 'And what have you been up to?'

'Down used to be the word.'

Stephanie ran a nail along the side of a pod and skimmed out the contents before she said, 'Are you telling me something?'

'Only because you will have to know sooner or later. I'm not going back to university.'

'May one ask why?'

'One would rather you didn't.'

'Because I love you, pet, and I would like to know.' Stephanie had boundless reserves of affection which could always be called into play when needed.

'All right.' Katrina surrendered. 'It's worse than you think, so prepare yourself. I am going to help to run a farm up in the Cheviots.'

'Oh well, so long as it's a nice family.'

'The family will consist of me and one other person.'

Stephanie closed her eyes. After a moment she said quietly, 'Not Heathcliffe, I take it?'

'Her name is Phyllis. I have been helping her for some time now, so we know it's going to work.'

'Oh, dear God! How old is this woman?'

'Nearly forty.'

'Oh God, oh God! It won't last, you know. Twenty years older.'

'If it was a man you would have accepted the twenty years, regretfully perhaps, but reminding yourself of all the cases you have known where it worked very well.'

'But none of that is relevant to this case. You are so young.

Katrina, and very immature. And you had a bad experience with your tutor.'

'Our mistakes are our stepping stones, Mr Beaney would have it.'

'I doubt if he would want to be quoted in this context! Do you . . . is she . . .?'

'Oh, come on Stephanie, spit it out! After all, you deal with matricide and incest without batting an eyelid, so what is a little lesbianism?'

'At least you have the grace to blush!'

'Anyway, it's not like that. She is the most wonderful companion with whom to share a life.'

'Of course, you are very immature. I can see that for a time you probably need a mother substitute to help you to break away from home and . . .'

'It's the sharing, Stephanie, the sharing of a whole way of life. And it's a way of life that isn't competitive, that is slow and patient and . . .'

'And harsh.'

'Hard, anyway. We are up on the hills by six in the morning. I didn't know I could live like that, that I had it in me. I am finding out so much about myself.'

'Grinding poverty for those who have no choice . . .'

'Then I'll be ground down, too. I think wealth is obscene.'

'Crippled by arthritis by the time you are forty . . .'

'I didn't grow up in a home where you just touched a switch to get hot air and water. And, anyway, better arthritis at forty than high blood-pressure and a couple of failed marriages.'

'There is a middle way, Katrina. Take Piers and myself . . .'

'I'd sooner take Phyllis. She shares the cooking and the housework.'

'Darling, I know you are disillusioned and insecure just now. But have you thought that you are living at a time when whole new worlds are opening out for women – and what do you do, but run away from all these wonderful new opportunities!'

'They aren't *my* wonderful opportunities, Stephanie. I don't suppose I can make you understand, but I'll try. Once, on my way home, I stopped off in London and went to the Elizabeth Frink exhibition at the Royal Academy. I felt a bit low so I treated myself to lunch afterwards. At the same table there were a couple of women – in their late thirties, I would guess. They were both business consultants and much of their talk was too specialised for me to understand. But the purpose of their meeting seemed to be to float the possibility of starting up on their own and they were assessing the market. They talked about places in the Third World as though they were on their daily route to work. It was all quite low-keyed, they weren't trying to impress each other, let alone me. They took the travelling and the expertise for granted. One of them said she felt that if she went solo she would need something behind her as security, so she had bought a hotel in Berkshire. The other one approved of that; she herself was toying with buying a gallery in Farnham. They were, you might say, doing pretty well. But not only that. They were – not enjoying life, they were beyond anything as superficial as enjoyment – they had found something that challenged and stimulated them. I realised how much I envied them. And do you know why? It wasn't the money or the little businesses on the side, or six months of the year in India or Africa or wherever; it was because they were planning to set up together. The globe-trotting and the high-powered jobs were right for them, you couldn't doubt it listening to them talk; but that didn't interest me. What I *ached* for was the sharing and companionship, the integration of work and friendship.'

'Dear me!' Stephanie was disturbed by the picture conjured up of Katrina sitting at that table measuring herself against these two women who sounded so admirably in control of their lives and then coming to such a wilfully injudicious conclusion about her own life. She said, 'I can see it's no use arguing with you. Time will take care of it. A few more nuclear mishaps and the glamour will go out of sheep farming.'

'That's sick!'

'However high up the hill you go, you won't get away from the twentieth century.'

'Which is on its way out, anyway. There'll be different patterns of living in the twenty-first century.'

Stephanie, recalled to the reason for this visit, asked, 'What does Mother say about all this?'

'She's not very pleased; but she couldn't say much, could she, considering . . .'

Stephanie looked around her unhappily. 'It seems Piers and I are going to be the only members of this family who are making any sort of attempt to come to terms with the real world.'

'Someone has to shift the centre of the real world.' Katrina stood up, holding the pea shells in her apron. 'Cheer up! Think of all the lovely holidays Marcus and George will have at our farm while you and Piers go off to the Greek islands to recharge your batteries.'

They had lunch in the garden, a cold collation set out on an old trestle-table. It seemed easier than gathering round the dining-room table as though they were still the same family. But there was no escaping the moment when they must come together in the sitting room or the awareness that this was the last time they would gather here. The discussion was inevitable. But it was not this enterprise, foolish or inspired, which troubled them; it was that most delicate of all human operations, the severing of bonds. Although Janet seemed composed, there was in her eyes something of the defiance of the child who knows it must walk away; while the children expressed the pain of letting go. Murdoch's face was aged by a sadness which he now accepted as a permanent part of life to be accommodated without fuss or dwelling on particular hurts. To some, he might seem diminished, but others would recognise in him that ability to give sympathy and understanding which comes of valuing the essential separateness of each other individual. Of all the people present, he was the one who set himself to listen.

'I'm just surprised,' Stephanie began, because she had not the nerve to wait for others to speak, 'that you could do all this without consulting any of us except Hugh.'

'They didn't consult me,' Hugh said. 'They instructed me.

Which, of course, is only proper,' he added in case he might have sounded hurt.

'But you minded.' Stephanie was not prepared that anyone should be miserly with feeling at this time.

'Yes.' He looked at her with distaste. 'I minded.'

There was an uneasy pause. In the past, when they had been parents and children with roles written for them by the archetypes talk had come easily. Now they must speak for themselves and listen to replies from people who had become strangers.

It was Piers, whose problems were of a different nature, who began. 'Suppose we talk about what it is that you intend to do. You are proposing to move into this house on the heath and establish some kind of community there. Is that the idea?' He had had no difficulty in arriving at this conclusion since it was something which he had once envisaged doing himself.

'Not a community, no.' Janet sought words as though this was an exercise in naming. 'A staging post, I suppose you might call it.' Stephanie felt her mother would have liked to be doing something – arranging flowers, perhaps – while she talked, to illustrate her detachment.

'But you have no qualifications,' Piers said.

'We are not going to *treat* anyone. We shall offer food and shelter – or board and lodging, if you prefer it. I have had quite a bit of experience in that.'

Piers said impatiently, 'But why here, in Dorset?'

'Because we are here.'

'I assume you intend to render some kind of service, not simply to set yourselves up in the roadhouse business?'

'Yes.' She seemed reluctant to be tied down to any very specific description of her intention. 'We shall take people for whom there is nowhere else to go.'

'And how many of them are there in Dorset?' he said scornfully.

'You mean you don't think there are people who sleep rough – tramps, drop-outs, disaffected teenagers – in Dorset?' Janet asked.

'Not in comparison.'

'But leaving aside comparisons?'

'Well, I suppose there must be some,' he conceded. 'Yes, of course there must be. A few.'

'We couldn't cope with more than a few,' Janet said. 'I got so depressed talking to Patsy about all the things which are wrong in the world. And then I began to see that anyone is going to be unhappy who spends so much time brooding on things which they can't alter and so little on what it is in their power to change. For me, any venture has to be small.'

Malcolm, silent in his corner, comforted himself with the reflection that this was remarkably like the last act of a Priestley play. Soon, after everyone had had their say, the curtain would come down and all that would be required would be for them to step forward and take a bow. It would all be over. Then, with any luck, they would find themselves playing something more congenial.

'All this upheaval!' Stephanie was intent on prolonging the scene. 'For something that hardly seems worth doing.'

Murdoch said quietly, 'But if it is all that *we* can do, isn't it worth doing?'

She was silent, remembering her own conversation with Dr Potter. The voice came to her now quite clearly – 'Whereas at this private clinic you see people whom you do understand and whom you feel you have a chance of helping? If this is where your particular talent lies, I see nothing wrong in that.' A disturbing thought occurred to her. She said, 'I'm not at all sure you can do this on your own without professional advice. And what will you use for money?'

'We *shall* have professional advice,' Janet said. 'And I think the money may be forthcoming. In fact, we believe we might be funded by some sort of trust . . .'

'I knew it! Dr Potter! That woman is behind this! She has always been able to raise money for unlikely ventures.'

'She thinks there is a need for this kind of place up and down the country,' Janet said. 'And we shall try to be as self-supporting as possible . . .'

'You and who else?' Stephanie demanded. 'Where are your helpers to come from?'

'We have one or two already. Patsy and . . .'

'I should have thought *that* set the seal of doom on this silly undertaking,' Stephanie said bitterly.

Murdoch said, 'We have reached an understanding. Patsy is prepared to make a few small concessions as regards timekeeping while we have agreed to accept that the area in which she can operate successfully is limited and not to press her beyond those limits.'

'And Ann Bellamy is going to do the secretarial work,' Janet said. 'Then, if people stay with us for long, we shall ask them to do some work on the land . . .'

'So you *are* thinking in terms of a community?' Katrina said.

'That might grow out of it. But the really important thing is that they should always be free to stay or to go, to leave and to return.'

Stephanie said, 'They will take advantage,' and Janet replied, 'We hope so.'

There was a pause. Janet, who had found this more difficult than her composed manner might have suggested, got up and went to the window. Malcolm's eyes followed her. The turning of the leaves reminded her of the time of her life; she had been prepared for that, but not for how small the garden seemed.

Malcolm said, 'Why shouldn't we all give you a hand?'

Janet drew in her breath sharply, remembering the fierce joy she had once experienced looking out from this window at her children each separately engaged, yet held together within the border of flowers. She felt again the longing to enfold them in this quiet, safe place.

Stephanie said, 'Make it a family undertaking? I suppose, between us, we can muster a good many of the appropriate skills.' She felt a quite dizzying release from pressure as she thought of the corner she and Piers might occupy.

'You already have a solicitor,' Hugh pointed out.

'Assistant cook?' Malcolm made a supplicating gesture with steepled hands. For a moment he saw them all close together, drawn into that brightly-lit area where the stage hands had laid the furniture on the square of carpet and where all the action takes place; what happened beyond – the dusty floorboards, the wings, dimly-lit by a blue lamp in the stage manager's cubbyhole – a shadowy unknown.

Stephanie summoned psychology to her aid. 'And you wouldn't need to get rid of the house. Because, don't you see, it *must* be this house. If we are to put things right – and I think this is what is troubling you, our almost incestuous concern with family – then it needs to be put right here, where things first began to go wrong. We have to take the things which were good and hold on to them fast. We mustn't run away and think because we are somewhere else we can be *somebody* else, that we can start afresh without a past. It has to be *here*.'

Murdoch, who had been watching Janet, said quietly, 'I think we need to sleep on this.'

He knew his own mind and that night he slept heavily. But Janet drifted between dream and waking, scarcely knowing which was which. She saw Malcolm gliding across the lawn; a tray balanced on one outstretched palm, he approached a figure seated beneath the apple tree, a half-turned figure whose identity was not clear. It was a tranquil scene, bathed in pale-lemon light which gradually turned to gold, yet she woke frightened. Stephanie loomed over her offering comfort and advice. 'She is very bossy,' Piers said. 'But let her be. She is fulfilled now.' Janet turned on her side. Hugh was in the box room, working at a desk, while his children played outside on the lawn. The room was small, cramped. She said agitatedly to Murdoch, 'We must get a bigger room for Hugh.' She went into the hall and stood looking up the stairs. 'Katrina!' She woke murmuring the name. Katrina should be here, she thought, to make the circle complete. With her woman, if need be . . . I have always got on well with other women, so why not? *What* other women? She gazed up at the ceiling. What woman, other that Deutzia, has there been for me to get on with? Trying to find this other woman she drifted into sleep.

It was autumn. She could see excited faces in flickering firelight. There was a huge bonfire in the garden and Murdoch was bending forward, roasting chestnuts. She shouted to him to be careful, frightened again. The sparks glowed in the darkening sky. There were frosty stars.

'It's going to be a cold night,' she said. 'We must go into the house now.' They came close about her into the house and shut the door. The windows were patterned with frost but the faces of her children, red as so many robins, gave warmth to the house; and behind the children she saw the faces of Murdoch and her mother and father, her brothers and sisters . . . I have everyone I have ever loved here, she thought and she clapped her hands and cried out, 'I have never known such happiness.'

Somewhere, the dog was barking. Fear in the sound. Malcolm went out to him, came running back, screaming, 'There's a man on the bonfire.'

She was screaming now. 'It's straw. It's all right, I tell you. It's only a straw figure that they sacrifice.'

She was outside and alone. Gone were the frosty stars; the whole sky was alight and the roar of the flames drowned all other sound. At the heart of the fire it was not the straw figure blazing, but the tramp. She wanted to run but her feet would not move and she watched until the body was totally consumed and all that remained was a huge, disfigured face.

'It won't work, will it?' Katrina said the next morning when they were all together after breakfast.

'It's going to make you ill, you know that?' Stephanie said to her mother.

'I had a bad dream.' The memory of it marked her face; she looked years older.

'Even if you don't want us to help, at least you could keep the house,' Stephanie persisted. 'For our sakes.'

'Or find a place in town where you will be more accessible,' Piers said.

Murdoch intervened. 'It wouldn't work in this house because you would all think of it as your home, which had been temporarily invaded. And I don't think the kind of person we could help would come to town — townspeople wouldn't like it if they did.'

'But this is a very narrow range of people you can hope to do anything for,' Piers protested. 'You're not going to be able to cope with drug addicts or anyone who needs specialist attention. It's going to whittle down to a handful of misfits and tramps. And there are millions of people in need!'

Murdoch shrugged. 'If we start thinking in terms of millions we shall never do anything.'

Janet said, 'I shall feel we are lucky if we have a handful of people in a year.'

'It's all so pathetically unreal!' Stephanie pleaded with her.

Janet turned away. 'Life is real wherever people are living it.'

'But what will it lead to, Mother? Just another commune at the most.'

'And another and another and another.' Katrina had been won over – but then she was up in the clouds somewhere on Cheviot. 'It could be a way forward, the way of living in the future.'

'It won't last,' Piers said sadly.

'Perhaps we set too much store on things lasting?' Murdoch got up and Humphrey padded hopefully to the door. 'It may be that we should accept that the most that can be asked of any venture is that it should serve a good purpose. In time, something else may be required as new problems demand different answers.' He held out a hand to Janet. 'But for now, this is *our* answer.'

Later, Hugh wrote in his diary, "When I was a child I was loved and cherished, but as I grew older I saw that this awareness of being loved came to me when we children had our mother or our father to ourselves. When they were together they unconsciously excluded everyone else. There was one fire which burned in our house at which the children could never warm themselves. Lately, planning this new venture, they had seemed more absorbed in what was going on around them than in each other and I had thought they were drifting apart. But this morning, watching as they left us to set out on their walk, I saw that I was wrong. They walked a little apart and seemingly occupied with their own thoughts, but only people who have great trust in each other can do that. They *are* together but in a different way. And now there is another fire, but this time all that prevents me from sharing its warmth is myself.''

'If they were doing something significant, I could understand it,' Stephanie said to Piers when they went for a last stroll in the evening. 'But it is such a small step they are taking.'

'Small steps may be all they are capable of.' He sounded more envious than disparaging. Perhaps he regretted having set himself aims beyond his capabilities.

They walked slowly down the drive. The gate swung on rusty hinges, the SOLD board shifted in the hedge.

They had come here so often for rest and a brief forgetting of the strain and stress of what they would continue to regard as real life, and had left refreshed and better able to face their coming trials. They had spoken of Janet and Murdoch with affection, agreeing that 'the twentieth century has passed them by' and had thought of the house as a place out of time. They had been grateful that it was there, somewhere to which they could always return. Where would they go now?

The Truth About Lorin Jones

ALISON LURIE

Lorin Jones, an undervalued artist, died of pneumonia contracted from snorkelling in a cold sea. Polly Alter, art historian, feminist and fugitive from emotional chaos, has a mission—to wrest her from her ill-deserved obscurity and reveal for the world's judgement the truth about Lorin Jones . . .

'Alison Lurie's tone is unerring, no word wasted. As slyly cool as Jane Austen, she subjects to pleasantly relentless examination the woman's movement, art and the deep flaws in us all'
Daily Mail

'Miss Lurie's skill and lightness of touch conceal a highly elaborate technique. Her book is funny and shrewd . . . a polished example of the American comedy of manners'
Daily Telegraph

Also by Alison Lurie in Abacus:
REAL PEOPLE
FOREIGN AFFAIRS
IMAGINARY FRIENDS
LOVE AND FRIENDSHIP
THE NOWHERE CITY
THE WAR BETWEEN THE TATES

0 349 10066 7   FICTION   £3.99

0 349 10101 9   FICTION   £4.99

A
CAPOTE
READER

A Capote Reader contains virtually all of the author's published work – including several short pieces that have never before been published in book form. It is divided into six parts: *Short Stories* (twelve of them, all that Capote ever wrote); two *Novellas*, *The Glass Harp* and *Breakfast at Tiffany's*; *Travel Sketches* (thirteen of them, mostly around the Mediterranean); *Reportage*, including the famous Porgy and Bess trip to Russia *The Muses Are Heard*, and the bizarre murders in *Handcarved Coffins*; *Portraits* of the famous, among them Picasso, Mae West, Isak Dinesen, Chaplin, André Gide, Elizabeth Taylor – who radiated 'a hectic allure' – and 'the beautiful child' Marilyn Monroe; and *Essays* (seventeen of them, including *A Day's Work*). Each section is in chronological order of publication, demonstrating the evolution of the author's style and interests.

Also by Truman Capote in Abacus:
ANSWERED PRAYERS
MUSIC FOR CHAMELEONS
IN COLD BLOOD
BREAKFAST AT TIFFANY'S

0 3491 0095 0   FICTION   £6.99

GLASS-HOUSES

Penelope Farmer

Grace is a glassblower. A taciturn farmer's daughter from Somerset, she is able to set up her own glasshouse with the legacy left to her by her old mentor, Reg. Accompanied by her young apprentice, she moves to Derbyshire. But when Jas, once both a glassblower and her husband, and Betsy, Grace's ghostly and goading alter ego, appear, the characters, in their obsession with glass and each other, are slowly brought to explosion point.

Glass itself is the heart of the novel, the focus of its narrative, its symbolism, its elusive, illusory magic. Wrought from the earth by fire, cooled by water, it determines and describes not only the characters, the landscapes they move in, the society they are part of, but also the way the story progresses, hypnotically, through each of its stages, to a terrifying climax.

Also by Penelope Farmer in Abacus:
AWAY FROM HOME
EVE: HER STORY

0 3491 0109 4   FICTION   £3.99

GRACE
Maggie Gee

Grace is eighty-five, was once loved by a major painter, and now deplores the modern evils that rampage across the world. To escape the tyranny of silent phone calls that plague her, she goes to the seaside. To Seabourne where nothing ever happens except quiet deaths and holidays. Paula is her niece. Also a victim of mysterious harassment, she lives near the railway line that carries nuclear waste through the heart of London. She feels curiously, constantly unwell. Bruno is a sexually quirky private detective who attacks daisies with scissors, germs with bleach, and old ladies for fun.

A novel of towering stature, with all the stealth and suspense of a thriller, *Grace* is written in condemnation of violence and secrecy, in praise of courage and the redeeming power of love.

'*Full of poignancy and power*'
JEANETTE WINTERSON

'*Heart-stoppingly exciting*'
TIME OUT

'*Controlled and highly imaginative . . . this exceptional novel should be read everywhere*'
LITERARY REVIEW

'*Magically, I finished this book with the almost cheerful feeling that things are still hopeful as long as people answer back and write as well as this*'

GUARDIAN

0 349 10103 5   FICTION   £3.99